THE MAN WHO . . .

THE
MAN WHO . . .

Stories by

CATHERINE AIRD
ERIC AMBLER
SIMON BRETT
LEN DEIGHTON
ANTONIA FRASER
MICHAEL GILBERT
REGINALD HILL
P. D. JAMES
H. R. F. KEATING
PETER LOVESEY
RUTH RENDELL
GEORGE SIMS
MICHAEL UNDERWOOD

M

MACMILLAN
LONDON

First published 1992 by
MACMILLAN LONDON LIMITED
Cavaye Place London SW10 9PG
and Basingstoke

Associated companies in Auckland, Delhi, Dublin, Gaborone,
Hamburg, Harare, Hong Kong, Johannesburg, Kuala Lumpur,
Lagos, Manzini, Melbourne, Mexico City, Nairobi, New York,
Singapore and Tokyo

ISBN 0-333-57437-0

A CIP catalogue record for this book is available from
the British Library

Phototypeset by Intype, London
Printed by Billings & Sons Ltd., Worcester

CONTENTS

INTRODUCTION

A fiction Festschrift. Nothing else will do to celebrate eighty years of – he has anathematised the phrase – the doyen of British crime writers, Julian Symons, former President of the Detection Club, worthy follower in the weighty footsteps of G. K. Chesterton, E. C. Bentley, Dorothy L. Sayers and Dame Agatha Christie.

It was with this in mind that I invited those among the Club's members who have been perhaps most closely linked with Julian to contribute to this volume. I laid down only a few stipulations. Each story was, in tribute to the author of *The Man Who Killed Himself*, *The Man Whose Dreams Came True* and *The Man Who Lost His Wife*, to have a title beginning 'The Man Who . . .' (but, indulgent as ever, I allowed a little latitude). I added that the stories under these titles should, while being altogether the author's own, refer in some way to Julian's oeuvre. A request my fellow members treated with the circumspection proper to any edict of mine.

But Julian's oeuvre, what an edifice it is. It begins with the spoofy *The Immaterial Murder Case* of 1945, actually written a good deal earlier but left in a drawer during the war years to yellow away (or it would have yellowed, had it not been typed on the green paper Julian favoured in his young poetical days), left until Kathleen Symons pulled it out, found 'parts of it quite funny' and persuaded him to send it to a publisher.

From then onwards the oeuvre grows and grows, right up until this year when we are given *Something Like A Love Affair*. A total of twenty-seven books in all, covering much of the wide field of crime fiction as it is today. It includes the virtuoso ingenuity of *The Plot Against Roger Rider* as well as the psychological probing of *The Players and the Game*, that meditation on the infamous Moors murderers. Or we can go from the dissection of the literary and artistic world of the past half-century in *Death's Darkest Face*, with its brilliant time juggling, to mysteries of the Victorian days in *The Blackheath Poisonings* and *The Detling Secret*.

Or, again, we can savour both that tribute to the master of us all, *A Three-Pipe Problem* (I was there in a train with Ngaio Marsh when Julian asked for a Sherlockian quote for his still-untitled book, and have ever since regretted not being quick enough to beat Dame Ngaio to the answer) and that reconstruction of a great real-life murder mystery in *Sweet Adelaide* ('Now she's acquitted she should tell us, in the interests of science, how she did it.' Mrs Bartlett did not: Julian did).

Yet all this is only his crime fiction, and neither does it take account of a large and varied output of short stories, whether ingenious or corrosive. But we criminous authors, ma'am, owe Julian an even greater debt. For many years he was *The Sunday Times'* crime fiction reviewer and there can scarcely be a practitioner of that time who did not benefit from his analyses of their books, from his praise, which we swarmed to reproduce on the back of our next volume, to his pointing out where we had gone wrong, always preferring illumination to annihilation. Nor is that by long chalks the only debt we owe him. In 1972 with his magisterial *Bloody Murder* (in America *Mortal Consequences*), now in its third edition, he was, I believe, the first to give our works both a reasoned history and a decent status.

But the tally of his achievements is by no means finished here. Poet (with in his output 'The Guilty Party', one of the rare poems devoted to our art), biographer (of, among others, Edgar Allan Poe, godfather of all mystery writing), quietly charming autobiographist, social historian (go with him lecturing in Europe and see the hungry buzzers-round waiting to discuss his *The Thirties*) and thoughtful reviewer of much else besides crime fiction: he is all these things. For them we in the

Detection Club delight now, in our possibly off-beat way, to do him this honour.

H. R. F. KEATING
President

CATHERINE AIRD

THE MAN WHO ROWED FOR THE SHORE

Norman Pace only made one mistake when he murdered his wife. That was to engage Horace Boller of the estuary village of Edsway and his boat *The Nancy* for the final disposal at sea of Millicent Pace's ashes. Norman didn't know, of course, at the time he did it, that hiring Horace Boller's motor-boat would be his only mistake.

By the time he came to do so he thought – and with good reason – that all danger of detection was well and truly past and that he would very soon be able to give the nubile young lady in Personnel – she who saw no distinction, semantic or otherwise, between Personnel and Personal – more of his attention than would have been prudent as a married man.

Besides which he was then considering something which had turned out to be an unexpected problem. If anyone had told him beforehand that the main discussion point with his wife's family attendant upon her murder would be a sartorial one he would have laughed aloud; had he been the sort of man who laughed aloud – which he wasn't.

The right clothes – rather, the correct ones – to wear for the ceremony of casting Millicent's ashes into the sea had considerably exercised the mind of her brother, Graham Burnett, too. In fact the two men even discussed the matter at length – oddly enough it was manifest that the two brothers-in-law were on friendlier terms now than they had been before Millicent's death.

1

This was no accident. Norman had realised very early on that his main danger of detection in the murder would come from Millicent's brother Graham – a chartered accountant with a mind trained to expect cupidity in those with whom he dealt, money bringing out the best in nobody at all. In the little matter of averting his brother-in-law's possible suspicions Norman Pace felt he had been really rather clever . . .

First of all, as all the good books suggested in the matter of winning support from those whom you have reason to suppose do not like you, he had asked Graham a favour. Taking him quietly aside after luncheon on Christmas Day he had said: 'I wonder, old man, if I might put you down as one of my executors? I've got to go over to the States in the spring for the firm and I thought I'd tidy up my affairs first. I've never really enjoyed flying and you never know these days, do you?'

'Of course.' If Graham Burnett was surprised at the request his professionalism was far too ingrained for him to let surprise show in his face. 'Only too happy to help.'

'I know you'd look after Millicent anyway if anything happened to me,' he had said, 'and so it seemed easier to make it all legal.'

'Much better,' said the accountant firmly.

'By the way,' he had murmured as they had rejoined their respective wives, 'will you remember if anything does happen that I want to be cremated – we both do, actually.'

'I shan't forget,' promised Graham Burnett.

And he hadn't.

When Millicent Pace had died while Norman was safely in America, Graham had arranged for his sister to be cremated – as Norman had been sure he would. The fact that Norman was not able to be contacted in the United States of America at the critical moment was also the result of some careful forward planning. After his business was done, Norman had set off for Milwaukee to visit a second cousin there.

Actually the second cousin wasn't there because he had died the year before but Norman had carefully neither mentioned the fact nor acknowledged the letter apprising him of it. Just before the time that he had calculated that Millicent would have died he checked out of his New York hotel without leaving a forwarding address and set off for Milwaukee. That he chose to do the journey by long-distance bus would, he knew, come as no surprise to his wife's family, among whom he had a fairly well-deserved reputation for being 'ower careful with the bawbees'.

His colleagues would not have been unduly surprised by his economy either. Always very attentive to his expenses claims, he was more than inclined to parsimony when it came to sub-scription lists and whip-rounds at work. In fact the only person either at work or among his family and friends who might have been surprised at his frugality was the nubile young lady in Personnel upon whom he had already lavished several gifts – but then she had been brought up by her mother on the well-attested aphorism that it was better to be an old man's darling than a young man's slave . . .

In the United States Norman had been written off very early as a tight-wad, and it was this knowledge of his basic meanness which had led his brother-in-law Graham to turn down the undertaker's offer to keep Millicent Pace's body in a refrigerator until her husband's return. Finding out what it had cost to leave the coffin in the Chapel of Rest (Graham Burnett suspected that most of the time this was the shed at the back of the under-taker's yard) had already seriously alarmed him. As an account-ant he was accustomed to breaking bad financial news and he did not relish it. The prospect of adding fiduciary complaint to Norman's personal grief did not appeal to him at all and he accordingly took the responsibility for arranging his sister's prompt cremation – as Norman had been sure he would.

On his visibly distressed return from Milwaukee, via New York where sad messages had awaited him, Norman Pace had listened to a long account of illness and death with suitable mien.

'I can assure you, Norman, everything that could be done

3

was done,' said Graham in careful, neutral – but unctuous – tones that he could only have picked up from the undertaker.

'The doctor . . .' said an apparently broken-hearted Norman.

'He was marvellous,' said Graham swiftly. 'He couldn't do enough for poor Millicent.'

Norman had bowed his head. 'I'm glad to hear it.' In fact his brother-in-law had never said a truer word. The only thing the old fool had been able to do for Millicent had been to write her death certificate. The really important thing was that he had not associated any of her symptoms – abdominal pain and vomiting leading to heart failure – with poisoning by thallium.

Even more importantly, neither he nor the other doctor who subsequently also signed the cremation certificate, had associated those everyday symptoms with Norman, by then in faraway Milwaukee. One of the undoubted attractions of thallium as a poison was the valuable delay in the onset of symptoms – it could be as long as forty-eight hours – as well as the peerless advantages of its being odourless, tasteless and colourless.

The only drawback of thallium known to Norman was that it was not only detectable in bone after death but that it survived in cremated ashes too. The disposal of Millicent's ashes at sea thus became more than mere ceremony. Graham Burnett and his wife, not being privy to the real reason for the scattering of the ashes at sea, saw it only as an occasion. Hence the discussion about what to wear.

'I'm hoping for good weather, of course,' said Norman, 'but don't forget that it's always colder at sea than ashore.'

'That's what Neil says too,' said Graham. Neil was his son, a bright lad with all the cleverness of a born clown. 'I don't know about you, Norman, but even so I don't think a yellow sou'wester is quite right.'

'No,' agreed Norman, adding judiciously, 'but then neither is my black. Not at sea.'

'I hope you won't mind,' said Graham, 'but Neil says he's going to wear his cagoule.'

'I think,' said Norman with unaccustomed magnanimity, 'that

everyone should put on whatever they feel most comfortable in.'

'So shall we say that dignified yet practical wear is the order of the day?' said Graham Burnett, who liked summing up.

Horace Boller, boatman, wore his usual working clothes for the expedition. Whether he knew it or not, the fisherman's jersey which he had on complied with a long tradition of Aran knitting where each seaman's jersey was of a slightly different pattern, the better to identify the drowned.

Horace's deplorable garment could have been confused with no one else's – dead or alive. Norman Pace regarded him and his cluttered boat with distaste.

'You do understand, don't you, that we must be outside the three mile territorial limit before it is legal for me to scatter my wife's ashes in the sea?' said Norman, who had his own reasons for being well out to sea before unscrewing the flask containing the mortal remains of Millicent. The said flask was nestling safely in the inner pocket of the new raincoat which Norman had seen fit to purchase for the occasion.

'Leave it to me, guv'nor,' said Boller, whose regard for the letter of the law was minimal and for its spirit non-existent. 'And watch that bit of coaming as you come aboard, if you don't mind. I've been having a peck of trouble with it. Now, be very careful . . .'

Conversation on board, stilted to begin with, thawed a little as Boller's boat turned out into the estuary from Edsway and headed for the open sea and Neil Burnett revealed himself as knowledgeable about birds.

'Common sandpiper,' he said in response to a question from his mother. She had settled on a tasteful grey outfit with plastic raincoat handy. 'And that's a ringed plover.'

'I suppose that one's a little twit,' said Angela, Neil's fiancée, who had insisted on joining the party to underline her new status as a potential member of the Burnett family. She, too, was wearing a cagoule.

Family solidarity on Norman's side was represented by two

late-middle-aged sisters who were his cousins. Old enough to be veteran funeral-goers and therefore experienced mourners, they were kitted out in dark slacks and blazers left over from a Mediterranean cruise of long-ago.

'I think it's a silly little goose,' responded Neil, giving Angela a quick hug.

This by-play on the part of the young ostensibly passed Norman Pace by, although he was obscurely gratified by the presence of Enid and Dora, who had not heard about the cremation in time to attend. He had taken up a rather aloof stance at the prow of the boat, looking out to sea, and letting his back give every appearance of a man thinking his own thoughts – if not actually communing with the deep. Horace Boller very nearly spoilt this *tableau vivant* by opening the throttle of the motor-boat without warning just at the moment when they left the saltmarsh estuary behind and hit the open sea.

'Tide on the turn, I expect,' said Graham Burnett knowledgeably. He audited the books of several fishing enterprises in Kinnisport and thus felt qualified to give an opinion.

'Why are we going east and not straight out to sea?' demanded Norman who was more observant.

'Got to get the church at Marby juxta Mare in line while I can still see Cranberry Point, haven't I,' said Horace Boller glibly. He paused, craftily waiting for the contradiction which would indicate that anyone on board *The Nancy* knew anything about nautical miles. It was not forthcoming so he went on, 'Otherwise I shan't know exactly how far out I am, shall I?'

Norman turned back to the bow. He'd struck a hard bargain with Boller but he didn't want the fisherman telling the whole party so. Horace Boller was still smarting from it, though, and had no intention of going half a mile further out to sea than he could get away with.

When he had gone nearly as far from land as he deemed necessary Horace put *The Nancy* about just enough to make the motor boat pitch fractionally. Mrs Burnett was the first to notice.

'It isn't going to get rough, is it?' she asked timorously. 'I'm not a very good sailor.'

Horace Boller throttled the engine back before grunting non-committally.

One of the effects of slowing the motor-boat's speed was that it also began to roll ever so slightly.

Cousin Enid unfortunately chose to be bracing. 'Remember the Bay of Biscay, Dora, that time we were on our way back from Lisbon?'

'Don't remind me,' pleaded Dora. 'It was dreadful, simply dreadful.'

Horace Boller went through a charade of examining the sea and sky and looking anxious. He reduced the speed of the motor-boat until it was scarcely making any headway at all, saving fuel the while.

'Haven't we gone far enough?' said Graham Burnett.

'Distances at sea are very deceptive,' observed Cousin Enid. 'It's always further than you think.'

'And later,' hissed Neil irrepressibly to Angela.

Norman Pace, standing in the prow, was aware that the boat was now beginning to wallow in the water. He patted the flask containing the ashes. How right he had been not to scatter them on land where they might one day have been sought by a diligent constabulary. Strewing them on the waves met every possible requirement . . .

'Should be all right now,' said Boller. 'Can't see St Peter's spire at Collerton any more.'

That this was because it was behind the headland he did not see fit to explain. Instead he put *The Nancy* about, switched off the engine and suggested to Norman that he came and stood at the lee side. 'Can't strew ashes into wind, can you?' said Boller grumpily. 'They'll only blow back at you.'

Nothing loath, Norman clambered back into the well of the boat and then, helped by Graham, stepped up onto the seating which ran round the inside of the tiny deck. He took out the flask from the crematorium, still slightly disconcerted that that fine white dust could contain all that had come between him and the young lady from Personnel.

'Steady as she goes,' quipped Neil unnecessarily. The nautical double entendre went unappreciated, all eyes being on Norman as he held the flask between his hands for a decent moment before unscrewing it. Enid and Dora, he was happy to see, were standing at attention – at least as far as they were able to in the rocking boat.

In fact, Cousin Enid, always game, appeared to be saying some private prayer – for which Norman was grateful since he found no words coming spontaneously to his own lips and the silence was a bit unnerving.

It was unfortunate that just as Enid had got to 'Eternal Father, Strong to save, whose arm doth bound the restless wave . . .' a very restless wave indeed caught *The Nancy* amidships. It was even more unfortunate that this happened just as Norman was about to unscrew the flask containing Millicent.

He lost his footing and the flask at the same moment.

'Butterfingers,' murmured young Neil, not quite sotto voce enough.

'Oh, my God!' said Norman, losing his cool as well as his footing and the flask, which was now bobbing briskly away from the stationary boat.

'It's not God's fault,' said Dora quietly in the eminently reasonable tones that must have accounted for the deaths – should they have used them, too – of quite a number of Early Christian Martyrs. On religious matters her docility was always trouble-making.

Any naval disciplinary court would have had no difficulty in holding Horace Boller – rather than God – to blame since he should never have allowed the boat to drift in the sort of sea he did, being, amongst other things, a hazard to shipping. As their Lordships of the Admiralty were not called upon to pay for Horace's fuel – and he was – he remained untroubled.

Until, that is, Norman turned on him. 'Quick, start the

engine . . . Look, it's floating about . . . just there. Hurry, man, hurry, or we'll lose her.'

With maddening calm Horace Boller applied himself to the engine. Everyone else on board rushed to the port side of *The Nancy*.

'Mind that coaming!' shouted Boller.

'Never mind your blasted coaming,' shouted back Norman, who had turned a nasty shade of puce. 'Get that engine going. Quickly, quickly . . . keep your eyes on her everyone.'

The engine of the motor-boat gave a little cough and then reluctantly sprang to life.

'Follow that flask . . .' Norman implored Boller urgently.

'Yoicks! Tally ho!' said Neil.

'Neil, you are awful,' said Angela.

'She went that way . . .' said Norman, since the flask could now be seen only intermittently bobbing on the waves.

'That way,' said Cousin Dora, pointing in a different direction.

'She's over there,' said Graham's wife distantly. She'd always rather liked her sister-in-law and thought the whole expedition unseemly.

'Where?' Norman clutched her arm. 'Which way?'

Graham Burnett said nothing at all: but his brother-in-law's patent dismay gave him furiously to think.

So did his next exchange with Boller.

'What sort of a tide is it?' Norman demanded, advancing on the boatman.

'Flow,' said Boller testily. 'Now, which way is it you want me to go?'

It was too late. Of the little flask containing the mortal remains of Millicent there was now nothing whatsoever to be seen.

'If we don't catch her,' Norman asked the fisherman, 'where will she fetch up?'

'De profundis,' murmured Enid.

'Dead man's reach,' whispered Neil to Angela, who gave him a little shove in response.

'Billy's Finger,' said Boller without hesitation. 'Spit of shingle in the estuary where the tide turns . . .'

'A dead spit . . .' murmured Neil in Angela's ear.

'You'll find her there by morning, guv'nor,' promised Boller. 'No problem.'

There was a problem, though.

For Norman, anyway.

Millicent's ashes had indeed fetched up on Billy's Finger in the estuary of the river Calle by morning but then so had Detective Inspector Sloan and Detective Constable Crosby, advised (Graham Burnett would never have used the expression 'tipped off') by Millicent's brother that there might be a message for them in the bottle.

There was.

As Millicent, his late wife, would have said, it was just like Norman to spoil the ship for a ha'porth of tar.

ERIC AMBLER

THE ONE WHO DID FOR BLAGDEN COLE

Felix Everard Cole, the English painter who signed himself Blag or Blagden Cole, has been dead for over sixty years; yet only now is he beginning to be recognised as one of our century's masters. The catalogue notes of last year's retrospective at the Royal Academy attempted somewhat obscurely to explain the delay.

'He was a draughtsman to be compared with Constantin Guys whom Monet admired and whose praises were sung by Baudelaire. As a painter he developed, as did other young Post-Impressionists of the Julian school, in the long shadow cast by Puvis de Chavannes, but he soon became drawn to the Intimisme of Vuillard. He even studied for a while with the Synthetiste Paul Sérusier, an influence that may have contributed to the later richness of his palette and the charm of his Bonnard-like interiors. None the less, it was as a portrait painter that he fulfilled himself; and it was, perhaps, his commercial success as a theatrical portraitist that suspended and then postponed judgement on his work as a whole. He died, absurdly and mysteriously, at the height of his powers.' And so on.

Now, God help us, there is to be an official biography.

There is nothing absurd about a shotgun blast at close range. The note writer is wrong, too, about the dangers to a painter of commercial success. Those who deal in the reputations of dead artists – art historians, curators, senior auction house appraisers – are rarely moralists but they are inclined to take themslves and their work seriously. They despise the snap judgements of popular taste. They hate to see art written about and hear it spoken of as if it were a branch of show business or the women's fashion trade. They are intellectual snobs, of course, but they are not fools. In our day there have been few good artists who have been able to avoid the attentions of the press or tried very hard to do so. Publicity has usually brought work. But the young Blagden Cole had sometimes gone too far. He had seemed to court publicity and controversy for their own sakes. Moreover he did so at a time before the 1914–18 war when popular newspapers were building national circulations. Their stock-in-trade was the common touch, but the touch had to be firm and sure of itself. To the fringe editorial staff of Harmsworth's *Daily Mail* informed jokers like Blag Cole were invaluable. When Blag made fun of Clive Bell and the Contemporary Art Society readers could understand the jokes. When Bloomsbury hit back by describing Blag Cole's talent as 'the fine commercial knack of making rich grocers look interesting' the *Mail* printed that too. Some of its keenest readers were grocers. All Blag achieved was notoriety.

It was about then that he took to signing his work 'Blag'. He had never liked his given names. His mother had been a music teacher and the Felix had been her salute to the memory of Mendelssohn, one of her favourite composers. Blagden was her family name and Blagden Cole looked and sounded more interesting than Felix Cole. The abbreviation to Blag developed after the death of his sister Cécile, named after the other favourite composer Chaminade. Blag liked the abbreviation pronounced with a long a, as in the French word *blague* meaning a bad joke or trick. He made other enemies in those early years, and not just in Bloomsbury. Appointed as War Artist to the British expeditionary force on the Salonika front, he was the direct cause of a diplomatic incident.

The Army of the Orient based on Salonika was a multinational force. Besides the two British divisions, mostly survivors of the Gallipoli campaign, there were French, Serbian, Italian and Greek troops. The army commander was General Sarrail, an affable Frenchman with a soldierly bearing and a taste for political intrigue. He lived in a small palace in some state with his mistress, a Russian princess of great beauty with an astonishing taste in hats. The troops lived in tented camps among the malaria swamps of the Vardar valley with sand-fly fever and dysentery for company. A large Bulgarian army was dug in on the heights above, and although most of the Allied casualties were caused by disease, Bulgarian sniper fire added substantially to the account. Morale was low: the troops thought of themselves as forgotten; and not without reason.

The nearest the General ever went to a forward area was the Cercle Militaire, a French officers' club near their corps HQ. It was at this club that Blag heard from a correspondent of the Havas news agency about a review of troops planned for the Fourteenth of July. It was expected that, despite advice from Paris that the lady was spying for King Ferdinand of Bulgaria, the General's noble mistress would be beside him on the reviewing stand. Photographers would be forbidden but who would notice a sketch artist in British uniform sitting on the edge of the parade ground?

No one did, and the pen-and-ink drawing Blag made from his sketch was smuggled to the Havas office in Paris via the Italian diplomatic bag. The magazine *L'Illustration* gave it a full page. They dared to publish it partly because it was strongly reminiscent of Guys at his best, partly because Havas had declared (truthfully) that none of the allied censors in Salonika had objected to the work and partly because it was felt that Clemenceau the new Prime Minister would not object to British criticism of a French general whom he was known to despise.

The drawing shows Sarrail taking the salute at a march past of high-stepping Senegalese infantry. He is standing, hand at kepi, in an open horse-drawn carriage. Hovering over him, however, are the plumes of an enormous hat, that of his princess. She is standing slightly behind him in all her statuesque glory, protecting him from the sun with her parasol. The drawing has a caption in English: 'General Sarrail reviews his presidential guard.' It is signed 'B. Cole '17'.

Unfortunately, Clemenceau did object, strongly. The British prime minister had chosen that moment to write to him personally about Salonika. Not only did he question Sarrail's fitness for command (as everyone else did) but he had also had the impertinence to suggest that the British and French colonial components of the Army of the Orient would be better employed on the Western front in place of the French divisions there which had recently mutinied. Coming on top of the Blag drawing, with its insulting use of the phrase 'presidential guard', the whole affair looked like a planned provocation and an attempt to humiliate France. French intelligence agreed and blamed the British secret service in Athens. Who but the British could employ their official war artist in Greece to discredit their French ally?

Blag was threatened with a court martial, but lied his way out of it. His story was that he had been asked to do the drawing by the French Cercle Militaire to hang with other pictures on the wall of their bar room, and since he was an honorary member of the Cercle he had been glad to do it. He had not been paid for the drawing. Its removal to France and reproduction in *L'Illustration* had nothing to do with him. The British force commander, himself an occasional guest at the Cercle, confirmed the findings of a Court of Inquiry in Blag's favour. He had escaped the military danger, but the offence given had been almost wholly political and the politicians were not disposed to let the prank go unpunished. His accreditation as an official War Artist was withdrawn and he was sent home.

There Sir Alfred Harmsworth had been translated into Lord Northcliffe and his *Daily Mail* had become a power in the land. Blag's old editorial acquaintances were not really pleased to see him, even when he told them the truth about the Sarrail affair. The word from on high was that he should be regarded as Bolshie, a new term then used to describe those likely to become mutinous. Besides, Sarrail had already been replaced by General

Franchet d'Espèrey who didn't live in a palace with a Russian mistress. Blag was advised to watch his step and do something ostentatiously patriotic, like a royal portrait. No, of course he couldn't get a commission to paint royalty just at the moment. The black mark would have to fade. Perhaps he should volunteer to do war work of some sort, for the Society of Friends, maybe, or the Red Cross.

He seemed struck with the idea and asked for an introduction to a committee member of the Red Cross. They gave him one. The result, however, was not at all what they had expected. When Blag had been sent home he had taken all his sketchbooks with him. Nobody had tried to stop him taking them, not even the censors at base. So now he took the sketchbooks to the Red Cross. He had an offer to make and a proposal. If the Red Cross committee would choose one hundred sketches from the hundreds in the books he, Blag, would make a hundred finished pictures of them. Most would be on double demy board, some line-and-wash, some gouache, some pastel. With the hundred pictures the Red Cross could mount an international fundraising exhibition.

That it has such an extraordinary success was only partly due to Blag and his work. Timing and the fortunes of war were on his side, for it was in the late summer of 1918 that the forgotten Army of the Orient came into its own. The faces of the men Blag had sketched in 1917 were the faces of those who next year fought their way through the Balkans to the first Central Powers surrender of the war. There were the faces of Frenchmen and Englishmen, of Chasseurs alpins and South Wales Borderers, of the Scottish Brigade and Moroccan Cavalrymen, of pilots of the 47 Squadron RAF who won the Kosturino Pass and Spahis watering their horses in the Struma River. The exhibition catalogue became a collector's item and sold well at charity auctions. Blag's name became very well known. An eccentric British peer tried to sue him for unlawfuly disposing of Crown copyrights. The French gave him a Légion d'Honneur. In London he was offered accreditation as an Official Artist to the Paris Peace Conference. He refused on the grounds that the spectacle of allied politicians drawing battle maps for the next war was a job for a caricaturist. He was going back to painting portraits.

And he did. By the twenties he was, undeniably, the most fashionable portrait painter. He also dabbled in the theatre. He designed a ballet for Diaghilev and collaborated with Komisarjevsky in the design of a production of *Peer Gynt*. He experimented with lithography. It is possible that he did too much and that some of his work then did not show him at his best. Most of it did, though, and in the last year of his life he was certainly at his best. He did indeed die 'at the height of his powers'. It has been only the manner and mystery of his death that have obscured the fact. But the work has survived that long expert scrutiny and his reputation is at last secure. His messy death is no longer seen as an admission of artistic failure comparable with that of Benjamin Haydon. It is now seen as an act of voluntary euthanasia committed to terminate a life of mental suffering which had become intolerable.

Seen by the pundits that is. But not by the biographer. Now, all the old lies and the old agonies are to be dredged up and picked over again by this youthful, less fastidious seeker after truth. She says that, as the only surviving witness and as the subject of the last portrait Blag painted, I have a moral duty to unburden myself.

She does not say 'spill the beans'; but that is what she means. I have been expecting something like this to happen ever since the picture with that tell-tale date on it turned up at Christie's last year and fetched that huge price. I had been hoping, in the way the old do, that I would be dead before someone started asking questions and that my executors would be left to cope. But the biographer invites me to 'unburden myself'. Some years ago a publisher asked me to write a piece about Blag's last days and I refused easily. I am a truth-teller of sorts but the theatre is my medium. Still, there is a need in the old to unburden which can become as urgent as the need to confess guilt.

As a boy I knew Blag as a friend of the family. After my father died Blag became for a few weeks a benefactor.

My parents were actors, Harry and Kitty Blagden, and they spent most of their working lives on tour or in provincial rep. My brother and I lived with Grandma Blagden in Clapham. It was there, when our parents were at home resting, that we heard all the gossip. In the autumn of 1919, after the treaty of Versailles was signed, they were in Birmingham doing a season of rep. One of the plays was Ibsen's *Ghosts*, still a very daring play then. My mother played Regina and my father Pastor Manders. The local bishop preached against it. It was quite a hit. The theatre was next door to a municipal art gallery and the curator there was stage struck. It was he who made the connection between Blagden Cole and the production of *Ghosts* with my parents in it. Part of the gallery was devoted at that moment to an exhibition of modern portraits and among them was a portrait of his mother by Cole. The picture was signed but not dated. What only the curator knew was that on the back of the canvas were scrawled the words, 'Portrait of Mrs Alving by her son Oswald'. That was dated 1912.

That was the year *Ghosts* had its first public performance in a London theatre and audiences had been deeply shocked. The subject of hereditary disease had until then been strictly taboo. Ibsen used it as a symbol for moral corruption, but the disease he had had in mind was generally assumed to be congenital syphilis. An artist who signed a portrait of his mother as Mrs Alving's doomed son Oswald was making a harsh statement. My father already knew Blag well. They had met in the dog days of 1917 at the base hospital in Salonika, my father a convalescent subaltern in the Welsh fusiliers. He had become friendly enough with Blag and one of the doctors there to know that Blag believed himself the potential victim of a disease that 'ran in the family'.

In Birmingham my parents tried to persuade the rep management to forget the curator's amusing little discovery, but in vain. Blag was news and they could use the publicity. A London paper picked up the story from the local rag and asked Blag to comment. He denied all knowledge of the *Ghosts* inscription on the portrait and wasn't too sure that he remembered the portrait itself. He would ask his mother what had happened to it. But he was delighted to hear that his old army pal Harry Blagden had survived the war. No, no relation but the same family name. A fine actor, Harry. He himself meant to go up and see the play.

He went the following week. It wasn't *Ghosts* he saw, but the Frederick Lonsdale comedy that alternated with it. For that my father was thankful. He had not believed Blag's denial of the *Ghosts* inscription. He knew that for Blag 1912 had been a bad year in more ways than one. He had heard Blag telling a friendly doctor all about it in the Salonika hospital. During the year ending in the spring of 1912 Blag's sister Cecile had died in a mental home; and Blag had witnessed the process of her dying. The thought of Blag sitting in the stalls watching the final scene of *Ghosts*, with Oswald centre stage, deserted by Regina and watched only by his mother, crying out for the sun as he sinks into imbecility, would have been unbearable.

My mother liked Blag from the first. 'They talked about the war, of course, and about amoebic dysentery and malaria being better for an actor than losing an arm or a leg. But Blag knew why your father wasn't playing leads. He knew that Harry's illness was worse than serious. He said that us Blagdens ought not to trust army medical boards. He said that the only medicine they understood was a disability pension table. He was right too. He knew all about the Blagden families and which lot came from where. His came from Lancashire. Your father's came from Yorkshire via London, as you know.'

'But Blagden was his mother's family.'

'His father had no family to speak of. Anyway he was no good. When Blag was only six Mr Cole ran off to America without a word and died there. Old Mrs Cole made a living of sorts teaching music but it was the Blagden drapery business that paid most of the bills. That's how Blag started as an artist you know. He went to a Manchester art school to learn textile design.'

'Was his father an artist, the one who ran away?'

'Not him. He was a piano tuner by trade. I think he sold insurance too, as a sideline. Blag doesn't like talking about him.'

That was just after my own father died in 1922. It was the undiagnosed diabetes that killed him, not the ailments they had been treating him for. Not that it would have made any difference. Insulin was discovered just too late to help him. It was a terrible year but it became a year of decision. Granny couldn't keep house for all of us with no money coming in. Mother had marvellous legs and could move beautifully on a big stage. She had been asked to go into panto before but couldn't because of my father. Now she accepted.

Her first principal boy was Prince Charming in the Moss Empire production of *Cinderella* at the Grand, Leeds. And that was when we discovered what a good friend Blag could be. The show was rehearsed in London but dress-rehearsed in Leeds. Blag talked to the London management publicity people and arranged to attend the Leeds lighting and dress rehearsals. There he did croquis and drawings of all the principal actors. They were the sort of drawings and sketches that Lautrec might have done – simple, sad and wonderfully elegant. The drawing of Kitty Blagden as Prince Charming was particularly fine. It was published with a page to itself in the *Bystander*, a London magazine that reported the doings of the smart set and the bright young things. Her agent always said that it was his astute use of the Prince Charming drawing that promoted her from the provinces to the West End stage. Agent or no agent, she began to get flattering work in musical comedy and then in a series of Charlot revues. Blag lived in the country just outside London and for a year or two we saw quite a lot of him. It was my younger brother who had the temerity to ask one evening, after Blag had taken her to lunch at the Savoy, if they were going one day to get married.

If I had dared to ask such a question I would have been

damned for my impudence. My brother was only told not to be silly and to go and do his homework. My grandmother had gone to her Thursday whist drive. We were sitting at the kitchen table where I had supper and my mother had tea and a sandwich before leaving for the theatre. When my brother had gone she gave me a look.

'Did you put him up to that, Charlie? No? Then what's he been reading? *Peg's Paper?*'

'He asked me, I didn't know what to say. I still don't.'

'Well, I suppose I'd better tell you. The answer is no. Blag would like to get married but not to his old friend's widow even if she was willing. What he needs is a young wife who'll give him a good time. He could have that, but that's not what he wants. What he wants is a young wife who'll give him children. And that he can't have – mustn't have.'

'Sins of the father? *Ghosts?*'

'Not the sins that you mean. There are other things beside VD that people can inherit. Things that run in a family for generations like red hair or blue blood. Only some of them are killers. The one waiting for Blag is called Huntington's Chorea and I'd rather not talk about it at table.'

'You said that it's waiting for him. Does he know?'

'He can't know for certain. It got his father when he was in his forties. The father's mother died of it while he was still an infant in arms. Blag's sister was just thirty. He's lasted the longest. If it was only syphilis he could have a blood test and know. But there's no test for Huntington's and he could still be a carrier. There's no need to tell your brother all this, of course. Heaven knows what fairy tales he'd invent. Your father told me most of it.' She glanced at her watch. 'Which reminds me. About a year ago Blag sent your father the synopsis of an idea for a play. If it survived the nursing home tidy-up he'd like it back. But I'm not going to go through your father's papers. You're the man of the house now. You find it. It'll be in one of the big suitcases. I must be off, I'm late already.'

I found it eventually, between his army papers and a war

diary. It was written on two pieces of Elm Park Farm letter paper. The provisional title of Blag's play was *A Respectable Woman's Guide to Murder* and it was based on the life of Madeleine Smith. She was tried in 1857 for poisoning her lover, escaped the gallows by looking invincibly respectable and lived happily ever after, with a succession of legal husbands, until well into the nineteen twenties. What caught my eye first, however, was the folded paper to which the synopsis had been pinned. When unpinned and unfolded this turned out to be an art gallery reproduction of Toulouse-Lautrec's famous poster portrait of the cabaret singer Aristide Bruant. In the margin there was a scribbled note in Blag's writing.

'You asked why I never did self-portraits. Here's one reason. I never saw Bruant or heard him sing and I never wore a big black cape with a red scarf like this. Far too actory. But I must admit to finding that somewhat Napoleonic profile an astonishing likeness. More so as I grow older.'

And it was indeed an astonishing likeness. No doubt the cape was a prop designed to conceal short legs and a pot belly. Blag didn't need it. He was tall and lanky. The Bruant profile, though, was just right. I went back to the play synopsis. On a space at the foot of the second page my father had pencilled a note.

'Madeleine Smith is an interesting subject and there have been several attempts to dramatise her. At the moment, I hear, a Hollywood producer wants to make a film about her. She objects. She now lives in America, is over ninety, still highly respectable and will have the law on anyone who says different. Better wait a bit. The theme will keep.'

I put the synopsis in an envelope, addressed it to Blag at Elm Park Farm, near Pinner, Middlesex, and wondered if I could find some inexpensive way of delivering it in person instead of sending it by post. I had always been curious about Elm Park Farm. My mother had spent weekends there and had been very enthusiastic. 'It's neither a park nor a farm,' she had explained once; 'but it used to be both. Now, it just shows you what a good architect can do with a walled garden, a Victorian stable yard and a fire-gutted Regency house.' For guests it was 'deliciously comfortable', though she didn't much care for old Mrs Cole, the 'eternal music teacher'. However, Aunt Alice, her sister, wasn't a bad sort, 'Tweedy. Plays golf.'

Luckily, I remembered something else my mother had said. 'It's easy to get to. You take the Metropolitan line to Pinner and Blag has a hire car waiting at the station to pick you up. Or you can go to Rickmansworth and get a country bus.' I posted the synopsis with the Lautrec repro to Blag and consoled myself with the diary.

It wasn't really about the war; it was about the efforts of a professional actor with a 'hostilities-only' commission in the Fusiliers to run an army divisional concert party in northern Greece. This was between courses of treatment at a military field hospital. There were long lists of names taken at auditions with comments on the participants – most *nbg*. There were the occasional discoveries – 'Cpl Hughes R. fair baritone, better pianist, can sight-read and transpose.' The times he spent in hospital seemed, on the whole, more enjoyable. The doctors had a mess tent to themselves which he was allowed to use; an actor who can tell funny stories well is always good company. It was there that he got to know Blag, who had done a lot of sketching in the hospital. Blag was popular in the mess because he brought the high command gossip he picked up from the Italians and the French. He also liked talking medical 'shop'. The doctors didn't mind this because, for a layman, he was well informed, particularly about the diseases of the central nervous system. On the subject of child-birth, however, he could make a fool of himself. My father recorded a boozy Burns night dialogue between Blag and the Scottish senior surgeon.

Blag: Jock, I tell you this with my hand on my heart. I was born two months premature and I weighed nine pounds.

Surgeon: You can put your hand where you like, Blag

my boy, but you canna have it both ways. Nine
pounds you may have been, but if so you
weren't premature. Or if you were premature
you didna weigh nine pounds. Who told you
this fairy tale? A midwife? Ah, those old bidd-
ies will say anything if they think you want to
hear it.

Blag's reply was to get up from the dinner table and leave
the mess without another word. My father noted that this was
the only time he saw Blag behave less than well. As it was
Burns night none of the Scots there took any notice. On Burns
night anyone was likely to behave badly. 'Poor Blag,' had been
my father's comment; 'he must have known the date of his
parents' wedding day.'

Why poor? In the end I asked my mother. She sighed. 'Really
Charlie, I should have thought it was obvious. When there's
something that runs in the family, even little things, everyone
wants to know what he or she was like as a baby. Even in
normal families there's a lot of lies and careful talk about such
things. If he was born a nine-pound baby boy, the doctor says,
he wasn't premature. So, mother Cole was nine months pregnant with him. She had been pregnant on her wedding day.
These things happen all the time. It was a wicked world, Charlie, even in good Queen Victoria's day, God rest her soul. What
are you grinning at? It's not funny. Young Emma Blagden,
the sprightly little music teacher, had a romp before she was
supposed to with person or persons unknown.'

'The piano tuner?'

'Who doubled as an insurance agent? The Huntington's carrier? Poor Blag must have hoped that it was someone else.
Especially after the death of his sister.'

'He could have asked his mother. I mean, she'd have to tell
him the truth, wouldn't she?'

My mother gave me an extra-long look. 'Tell you what,

Charlie,' she said; 'if you're ever invited to Elm Park Farm and you meet old Mrs Cole, you can ask her that question yourself.'

My young brother James got to the Farm first. Nineteen twenty-six was a bad year for our family. Granny Blagden, whose house we had always lived in, had to go into a nursing home for a minor operation. It went wrong and she died there. Mother was in one show and rehearsing for another. Things had to be done like paying the nursing home in order to get the death certificate. Blag came to the rescue. He dealt with the nursing home then took me to the undertakers who had the body in their mortuary. With them he was equally firm. Just the motor hearse and one car for mourners. A plain oak coffin is what your grandmother would have wanted, eh, Charles? and not those fancy bronze handles, please, the ordinary brass ones. He gave the name of his own solicitor in Covent garden as the one who would be probating the Will. He did not mention that she had drawn it up herself on a form bought at the local stationer's.

We buried Granny in the morning three days later. When we got back to the house we were joined by Blag's lawyer who said that Granny had read the Will form instructions carefully and followed them. The house was the major part of her estate and she had left it to mother. For her there were two immediate problems. The first was that of finding a live-in cook-house-keeper to replace Granny. The second, to my surprise, was that of my matric. I was due to sit for it in two weeks' time. If I didn't sit for it, my mother declared, and if I didn't pass with honours, I couldn't go to college. She had promised my father that I would do both. She knew of an out-of-work dresser who could be trusted to keep house for a week or two if one strictly rationed the gin. Blag said that if I were to be kept busy preparing for an exam and keeping an eye on the gin, my brother might like to spend some time at the Farm. As it was getting near the end of term he was sure the school would agree. All James wanted to know was whether there was a piano at the Farm. On being told sharply by my mother that Mrs Cole had two pianos and that if he behaved himself she might let him try the Broadwood grand James gave Blag a beatific smile. At thirteen my brother was already a practised charmer.

Of course, we all knew by then that he had a musical talent. He wasn't a prodigy but he was clearly exceptional. Mother knew people at the Guildhall School and the professor who had heard James play had assured her that there would be a scholarship for him a bit later on. Obviously, a few weeks in the country playing on a good piano before an audience as experienced and sympathetic as Mrs Cole (herself a Blagden) would be weeks well spent.

According to James it was time wasted and a set-back to his career as a musician. The stables, studios and gardens were all right, spiffing indeed, but Mrs Cole, Auntie Alice and their house were all *ghastly*. 'Don't misunderstand me, Charlie, it's a very *pretty* place. There's a small river that runs through it with willow trees along the bank and a path to the village. The real farm, the old eighty-one acre one, is on the other side of the river. It belongs to a real farmer now. The real old house was commandeered in the war as a convalescent home for the shell-shock cases. Jack Hunter says that it was the shell-shock cases who set fire to it on Armistice night.'

'Who is Jack Hunter?'

'He was one of the shell-shock patients. He and his wife Annette run the whole place for Blag. Annette does the cooking. She's Belgian.'

'What's the cooking like?'

'Oh, I was at Mrs Cole's house. Auntie Alice does the cooking there. They have a girl in from the village to do the cleaning and the beds. The Lancashire hotpot was all right.'

'But not the piano?'

'The piano was all right. It was her. The moment I got there she said she was going to give me lessons. And she'd even bought me a party piece to learn.'

'Chopin. Something flashy.'

'She gave me a choice. One of Mendelssohn's Songs without

Words – she called it The Bees Wedding – or else Kitten on the Keys by Zez Confrey. Auntie Alice had a gramophone record of that. She called it ragtime.'

'Which did you choose?'

'Kitten. It's not really difficult but it does need what Professor Brant calls dexterity. Besides, Mrs C. wanted me to choose the other one. She's weird. She gives a concert recital every evening at six. She always has the lid of the piano right up and all the windows open. It's always when Blag's walking along the river path to the village pub for a drink. She plays Chaminade's Autumn at him full blast. She says it's to remind him of Cécile. Who's Cécile? He never takes any notice unless he has someone with him, like Jennifer or Rowe. Then he just waves. Jack Hunter shoots the rabbits because they're pests. If I were Blag I'd ask him to shoot her. You know, she even marked the fingering for me on the music.'

I asked mother who Rowe and Jennifer were. My brother had banished Elm Park Farm to an outer limbo. My mother made sense.

'Didn't I tell you? One side of the old stables has been converted into two biggish studios with living quarters attached. Tom McGowan has one. He's an engraver and an old friend of Blag's. Jennifer, his daughter, keeps house for him and does a little book illustrating. Nice girl. Lost the boy she was going to marry on the Somme. Ruskin Rowe has the other studio. He's a commercial photographer. Things not people. Very clever I'm told. It's a bit like a Mayfair mews down there. Without Blag it could get artsy crafty.'

'Where is his studio then?'

'Behind the garden wall. As far away from his mother and his Aunt Alice as he can reasonably be. You'll see. He's bound to ask you down. He said he'd like to draw you. He sees your father in you. So do I, come to that. You've got to go to college.'

There was no help for it; I had to work harder. Just over a year later I jumped through the necessary hoops, passed the right exams and acted my way past an interview board. In

September, when I was eighteen, I could go to college and read law at the taxpayers' expense. My mother was very pleased. Since she was in the new Noël Coward revue she was also disposed to be generous. She bought me some new shirts and underwear and decided that I had grown enough to wear one of my father's Savile Row suits. She also said that when my last term at school ended I should have a holiday. The invitation from Blag came two days later. It was in the form of a job offer; that of temporary assistant gardener. The pay offered was two pounds a week plus bed, full board and beer money.

'But two pounds is a lot,' I protested. 'I'm no gardener.'

'He knows that, silly. It's just a way of giving pocket money. Besides, think of the food. Annette runs her kitchen like a French bistro. All you'll have to do for yourself is make your bed.'

I didn't know what a bistro was, but I soon found that I was going to have a better time at Elm Park Farm than my brother. I had one of the guest rooms built over the old coach house with a view of the river, and its own bathroom next door. It was entered from a balcony that ran the length of the stable yard from the walled garden to 'The Lodge', the small house with the clock tower in which the Hunters lived. The balcony was reached by an iron spiral staircase. Blag himself showed me the way.

'This place is run like a boarding house,' he explained, 'with Annette as the landlady. The studios, mine included, all have their own kitchens but artists and craftsmen don't always feel like cooking. Some of us aren't very good cooks anyway. Sometimes we prefer to eat in dear Annette's kitchen, which is conveniently next door to the Lodge where you met Jack just now. Lunch is at one o'clock, dinner at eight. Annette doesn't do breakfasts though, just tea and toast. What do you drink now, Charlie? Wine? Beer?'

'I had a glass of sherry last Christmas.'

'I ask because I'm in the habit of walking along to the village pub for a drink before dinner. I dare say your brother told you.

I'm always glad of company. You're allowed to drink in pubs, aren't you? You're eighteen.'

'Almost.'

'It's five now. By the time you've unpacked and found a book to read it'll be sixish. I'll give you a shout.'

The path along the river bank was cool and pleasant in the shade of the willows, but as we came abreast of the monkey puzzle on Mrs Cole's lawn the shade thinned and we had the evening sun directly in our eyes. At the same moment the sound of the piano, of which I had been dimly aware, suddenly became louder. It was the Chaminade all right. I knew because James had picked out the melody on our piano at home the night before. He hadn't wanted me to be caught out if challenged.

Blag wasn't challenging anyone just then, not even his mother. Out of the corner of my eye I saw him raise his arm in acknowledgement of the music as we walked on.

'I dare say your brother told you what to expect,' he said.

'Yes, but I thought the music might have changed. That's not the only piece that Chaminade wrote.'

'Oh, the music changes from time to time. We had Mendelssohn last week. But it's the same old tune really, if you see what I mean, Charlie. By the way, she rechristened your brother Zez. After the composer of 'Kitten on the Keys'. Did he tell you?'

'No. He's rather touchy about his music. He's going steady with Schumann at the moment.'

At the end of the river path there was an iron footbridge across to the farm side of the river. There we joined the cart track that the farmer used to get his milk churns down to the road. Two hundred yards or so further on another footbridge took us back across the river into the rose garden behind the Anglers' Rest. There were people sitting at tables on the lawn by the river.

'The flies get in your drink out here,' Blag said and led the way inside.

It wasn't a pub but a gentrified village inn with a courtyard in front and cars with chauffeurs waiting. The owners of the cars were standing in the saloon bar drinking pink gin and whisky on their way home from the day's work. Blag nodded to one or two of them as he led the way through to a room labelled BAR PARLOUR. Here there were tables and chairs and, on the walls, hunting prints and stuffed fish in glass cases. A pretty woman with a nice smile came in to serve us. Her name was Dolly and I was introduced as a kind of nephew.

Dolly beamed. 'Are you Kitty Blagden's boy? There was a lovely picture of her in *Play Pictorial* last month. What'll you drink?'

'How about the draught cider?' said Blag.

'The stuff we've got will give him collywobbles. He'd be safer with a nice long Pimm's. We've got fresh borage. Oh, I was forgetting.' She pulled a letter out of her apron pocket. 'This came for you today by post care of us. Dad said you'd asked him if he minded.' She handed him the letter. 'Gin and tonic for you?'

'Thanks, Dolly.' He looked at the letter. 'Sorry, Charlie. I'd better see what this is.'

I watched him open it. The address on the envelope was typed. I was puzzled. In those days typewritten letters were not as common as they are now. Even business letters were sometimes written by hand. Love letters always were. But why would the master of Elm Park Farm want to use the Anglers' Rest as an accommodation address?

When Dolly brought the drinks Blag had his pocket diary open beside the letter. 'I've got a man from Manchester coming down to see me weekend after next,' he said. 'I can't do with him at the Farm. Could you put him up here for a couple of nights? Mr D.J. Bristow. He's a lawyer, quite respectable.'

As we walked back we met Jack Hunter with a shotgun under his arm. He had been a troop sergeant in the field artillery and in the breeches and leggings which were his weekday work clothes he was still a soldierly figure. He said he was going to shoot rabbits in the farmer's lower field.

'Does he know?' asked Blag.

'He won't argue. If that cowhand of his can't be bothered to keep the rabbits down he'll be getting no more fresh vegetables from us. It's our cold frames those little bunnies like to get into. Talking of which, Mr Blag, your Auntie Alice has been practising her mashie shots again. Broke two panes in the tomato house this evening.'

'I thought you put up some netting for her.'

'She says that's for tee shots, not short approaches. Better watch out as you go by.' He nodded to me and went on his way.

I had no trouble identifying Auntie Alice. She was a white-haired, stubby little woman wearing a pleated tweed skirt, a canary-yellow jumper and low-heeled brown brogue shoes. She was now practising chip shots from the edge of the lawn. Sitting at a rustic table by the monkey puzzle tree, and unmistakably mistress of all she surveyed, was Mrs Cole. Her right hand rested on the tasselled handle of a pink parasol which, as we approached, she raised above her head and brandished slightly as if she were hailing a taxi. It would have been difficult for us to have ignored her.

'Better get it over with,' Blag said.

'So this is Zez's big brother Charles,' she said as we approached her. 'Welcome to Elm Park Farm, Charles Blagden.'

'Thank you, Mrs Cole.'

'I never met your father but your mother says you're like him, just as handsome. Are you musical like your brother?'

'Not in the least, Mrs Cole.'

'Modest as well as handsome. You must come to supper with me, young man.'

'That's enough, Em,' said her sister firmly, 'you're making him blush.'

Lancashire still came through clearly in the way Aunt Alice spoke. Mrs Cole had sounded like a drama school elocutionist.

I was relieved when Blag took charge again and moved us on. Mrs Cole's affectations on top of the Pimm's and an otherwise empty stomach had given me an uncontrollable desire to belch. Luckily we were out of earshot before I had to give way. Blag was sympathetic. 'You must be hungry,' he said. 'Annette will soon take care of that.'

Leek and potato soup followed by a chicken casserole with braised endives took care of it very well; and the fact that I can still remember after all these years exactly what was cooked should speak for the quality of Annette's cooking. She was inventive but her dishes were mostly of the pot-au-feu kind, simple but tasty, soups and stews. Since she cooked for so many this was understandable. Her 'kitchen' was two stables knocked into one big room and it had four small tables in it. These could be placed together and she could seat ten if necessary. Usually there were no more than six or seven including her and her husband Jack. They had no children. The real kitchen, where the cooking was done, was in the Lodge next door; an arched doorway connected the two. A sideboard with spirit lamps and hot plates kept the food warm. Everyone, including guests, helped themselves.

I was the only guest that evening but all the residents were there. Tom McGowan, the engraver, and his daughter Jennifer sat at the next table, Rowe, the photographer, was by himself and the Hunters were at the end.

Over the years the portraits Blag did of Jenny have made her beauty as familiar a measure of that quality as Manet's Olympia or a Rembrandt portrait of Saskia. At the time, I regret to say, all I saw was a pretty woman with a nice smile and a talent for illustrating children's books.

'What are you going to do with yourself down here?' she asked. 'In Clapham you could have gone to the pictures twice a day.'

'I was hoping he was going to help me plant out the September lettuce,' Jack said loudly. 'Right, sir?'

'It was discussed,' Blag admitted.

'I thought that I was to be allowed to help with the lettuce,' said Rowe and sounded as if he really meant it.

'When I reminded you, Mr Rowe, you said you had a bad back.'

'I'm going to be busy with a sitter for the next two days,' Blag said. 'I'm sure Charlie won't mind giving you a hand, Jack.'

'Of course,' I said. Everyone smiled. The formalities were over. A temporary assistant gardener had been engaged. Supplies of September lettuce could now be relied upon.

'You're trapped,' said Jenny; 'mornings from nine to twelve. We can go to the pictures in the afternoon, though, if you like. I can drive us into Rickmansworth.'

'What's on there?' her father asked.

'*Scaramouche* with Ramon Novarro.'

'Face like a Rue Blanche pimp,' he said and then turned sideways on his chair to look directly at me. He had a fierce bristly moutache and very sad blue eyes. 'I saw a Henry Blagden on the stage just before the war. He played Marchbanks in Shaw's *Candida*. Was that your father?'

'Yes, sir. Did you enjoy the play?'

'The play, no. Tiresome, I thought. Your father seemed to make sense of it. Curious.'

'He told me that he played the long speeches as if he were trying to correct a stammer. It took the literary curse off them.'

He grinned. 'There speaks the actor.' He turned back to his plate.

'Charlie's going to be a lawyer, Tom,' Blag said; 'his mother thinks he ought to have a trade.'

They all laughed a little, as if in disbelief. There was both wine and water on the table. I took a little of each. When I got up to my room that night there was an envelope on the dressing table. In it there was a note with two pound notes folded inside it. The note read: 'Congratulations on a skilful performance before a difficult audience. I'll bet you made up that bit about taking the curse off *Candida* – B.'

32

Several days went by before I saw Blag again. His sitter was a distinguished actor-manager who lived in Henley and drove over every day in a beautiful Rolls-Royce coupé de ville, the kind of car in which only the chauffeur and front-seat passenger get rained on. Annette sent lunches of smoked salmon sandwiches and chilled Chablis across to the studio. Blag was doing preliminary sketches. The process could go on for days. In the mornings I worked with Jack Hunter, mostly in the greenhouses. These were on the far side of Mrs Cole's house by the vegetable garden where Jack's battle with the farmer's rabbits was fought out. They even got under the wire into the strawberry patch. Jack had to have his shotgun handy. There was a broom cupboard just inside the back door of the house where Auntie Alice cleaned her golf clubs, so he kept the gun there. The boxes of cartridges he kept in a bag hanging behind the door.

The mornings weren't all gardening. Blag had given the Hunters a four-seater Morris-Cowley in which they used to go shopping for the things that couldn't be delivered, like blocks of ice and boxes of kippers, from a fishmonger in Pinner, and wine that had to be fetched from a warehouse near Watford. Jack taught me how to lift cases of wine, as he had taught me how to use a heavy shovel, without doing myself a mischief. The afternoons were restful. I read Aldous Huxley's *Crome Yellow* and browsed through a stack of old *London Mercurys*. To sustain my impersonation of a law student I had bought a copy of Maitland's *Constitutional History* found secondhand at Foyle's, and became quite fascinated by it. And, of course, I went to the pictures with Jenny. She would have gone every day if there had been enough changes of programme within reasonable driving distance. We went in Blag's car, the old Crossley tourer that Auntie Alice also drove when she went to her golf club. Jenny was a good driver, but the moment we got inside a cinema she became an emotional mess. At least I thought so. She sympathised with the wrong characters. When we saw *Scaramouche*, for instance, she mooned over Lewis Stone who played the wicked marquis, wept for the wooden prettiness of Alice Terry as the heroine and thought nothing at all of Ramon Novarro as the lead. When she had dried her eyes and we were back outside again she seemed quite sensible. I found it disconcerting.

The threatened invitation to supper from Mrs Cole was conveyed by Jack. I was given a choice, Friday or Saturday, so I asked his advice. 'I'd make it Saturday,' he said; 'on Friday it's only high tea with fish cakes and you get the new curate as well. On Saturday it's always a pie from Fortnum's.'

At first it wasn't as bad as I feared. Of course, the recital seemed endless. Raff's Cavatina was added to the usual programme for that week. With the Chaminade finale Auntie Alice poured us both another glass of sherry and brought forward her sister's whisky and soda. Grand-piano lids are heavier than they look, but Mrs Cole closed hers with surprising ease. Then, picking up her drink, she sat down with a smile facing me.

'Such a nice cosy woman your mother,' she said; 'has she ever thought of marrying again do you think?'

I was speechless but Auntie Alice filled in for me.

'That's enough, Em,' she said sharply. 'We'll have none of that. You promised.'

It gave me time to become pompous. 'My mother is a highly successful actress,' I said; 'and a highly respected one. She enjoys her work. She has no intention of marrying again. She has told me so.'

'How lucky you are to be trusted with her secrets.'

'No more now, Em. It's time for supper.'

The pie was all right, but I had no appetite.

The following Saturday Mr Bristow arrived. Blag sent Jack with the Morris into Pinner to meet him at the station and take him to the Anglers' Rest. Annette and I were having tea when Jack returned. The errand had puzzled him. This Bristow had turned out to be a well-spoken north-country officer type. Why did he have to stay at the pub? There was a spare guest bedroom that he could have had. Of course, there was one thing that was odd; the man had two suitcases with him and one of them, the larger, was practically empty, as if it had no more than a well-wrapped picture in it. Could it be some work that Mr Blag had been asked to identify? Bristow could be an insurance investigator, a dealer or even some kind of policeman.

'Or a lawyer?' I suggested.

'He could be. Naturally Mr Blag wouldn't want anyone like that in the house.'

But Blag had surprises for everyone that day. Towards six o'clock he came out of his studio, banged on the ironwork of the staircase to bring me out and asked if I fancied a walk to the pub. Jenny was with him clutching a handkerchief to her breast and looking like Alice Terry on her way to the duel. As I reached the bottom of the stairs she blew a kiss, cried a strangled 'Good luck' and ran back to her own studio. 'Let's go and have a drink with Mr Bristow,' Blag said.

D.J. Bristow was indeed an officer type, but to my mind more navy than army. He had the smooth pink complexion, the tight blue serge suit and the starched collar with the skinny black tie. He was sitting at a table in the rose garden with a glass of beer in front of him and he stood up when he saw us approaching. He and Blag shook hands as if they had met before. I was introduced as one of the London Blagdens. Bristow smiled and nodded. 'Son of Henry? Yes, I thought so.' He turned to Blag. 'Is this young man your photographer?'

'No, Charlie's here to lend moral support. The photographer's waiting inside, all ready to go to work making the copies.'

Bristow pursed his lips. 'Well now. I hope you're not going to be too disappointed, Blag. I was able to bring only one of the pictures. The Town Clerk was very helpful but it was one or none. You see, these photographs are, in a sense, part of the furniture of the council chamber. They are also of some historical significance. Our man held office as a councillor for eighteen years and there are five group photographs with him in them, the last one dated eighteen ninety-five. He was the architect of the Preston town hall annexe completed in that year. I chose that one to bring because it's the sharpest and because he has more facial hair in the earlier ones.'

'I'm sure you did your best.'

'It wasn't easy. I had to promise the Town Clerk that I would have it back in the Town Hall council chamber by Monday morning. And I had to promise that it would not be removed from its frame. It's glazed of course.'

Blag sighed. 'Well, let's go inside and have a look at it.'

Rowe was waiting for us in the oak-panelled dining-room. Jack was in the Morris outside. Bristow went upstairs to get the picture.

'It's framed and glazed,' said Blag, 'and must stay that way. Mr Bristow will not let it out of his sight.'

'I've got a polarising filter that should take care of the glass,' Rowe said; 'and if the filter doesn't work I'll manage somehow. Is it really valuable?'

'Only to me. You see . . .' He broke off. Bristow had returned. The picture was wrapped in corrugated paper and tied up with tape from a lawyers' office. The frame inside was about twenty inches by twelve made of ebonised hardwood with gilt beading. A yellowing white mount surrounded the photograph which showed the steps up to the portico of a town hall. Lined up on the steps and standing in two ranks of nine were eighteen gentlemen all formally dressed for the occasion. Some of those in frock coats had mutton-chop whiskers. The rear rank stood two steps above the front so that all were clearly visible. Their names were inscribed in copperplate style in two ranks along the mount below.

'Which is the one we are interested in?' asked Rowe.

Blag reached out and pointed to the second figure from the right in the front row. 'That's the chap,' he said; 'Councillor T.C. Everard. I'd know that face anywhere, wouldn't you? Now let's see if you can blow the good man up. Shall we, Rowe? Eh?'

He was so excited that he could scarcely get the words out.

Rowe and Bristow seemed infected too. They bundled the picture back into its wrapping and took it out to the car where
Jack was waiting. As they piled into it Blag rememberd me and
looked back. 'Have a strong drink, Charlie,' he said. 'We'll see
you back at the studio.' They drove off.

I didn't want a drink but I wanted badly to talk. It was six
thirty on a Saturday, a matinee day then. My mother would be
having a sandwich in her dressing-room at the theatre. The
Anglers' Rest had a phone box in the hall. I had the stage door
phone number written in my pocket diary, for emergency use.

When my mother discovered that there was no emergency
she was cross but prepared to admit that what I had to report
was of interest.

'So, it wasn't the piano tuner she had a romp with, but some
sparkly young architect from the town hall.'

'It could be.'

'Who did you expect it to be, the Prince of Wales? I say lucky
old Blag. He's found the father he always wanted, the one who
wasn't a carrier of Huntingdon's disease. What do you say?'

'I just hope so.'

'What's wrong, Charlie? Speak.'

'I think the Lautrec poster of Bruant looks more like Blag than
that man in the photograph, Councillor Everard.'

'Well, let me tell you something, Charlie. Blag once asked his
mother why his middle name was Everard. She told him that
it had been a mistake, a clerical error by the parish clerk who
had bad eyesight. She had wanted his middle name to be Erard
after the French piano manufactuers from whom her father had
bought her first piano. What's more, the late Mr Cole had
served an apprenticeship at Erard's London works. Everard is
only an old north country spelling of the name Edward. Of
course she could have been covering up with the wrong spelling
story. Are you listening, Charlie?'

'Yes, mother. Mrs Cole would be capable of anything.'

'Yes, but don't you start getting mixed up in Blag's or Jenny's
love lives or start taking sides. Come home if you like. We'll

manage. But don't start thinking things over and dreaming up stories like your brother. Promise?'

'All right. But Jack says Blag wants to do a portrait of me.'

'I'm sure he'll make you look exactly like your father. Be good, darling.' She hung up.

I did not see Blag again for over a week. Jack said that after Bristow had left with his precious picture Blag and the McGowans had gone up to London, on business. They were staying at Brown's Hotel, all three of them. I knew about Tom McGowan's business. He had been elected a member of the Academy that year and a Bond Street gallery was giving him a show. The picture-framer favoured by the gallery was widely disliked by etchers and engravers for his conceit. The man believed, according to Tom, that a picture frame could have as much as or even more artistic importance than the work it adorned. He looked forward to a hard struggle with the bastard for the integrity of his work. Jenny? Jack thought she would be seeing that publisher of hers, and of course the new films.

The McGowans returned first. Jack met them at the station with the Crossley. They had a festive air about them and that evening at dinner Rowe was bold enough to comment on it. 'You've been shopping for a dress,' he told Jenny; 'I know the look. Is it to be in a church or a registry office?'

Tom McGowan bridled. 'If you knew what a special licence cost you'd not be asking such a damn fool question.'

'Then it's to be a registry office, eh?'

I am sure that neither Jack nor Annette uttered a word to anyone, but the idea of a wedding was now abroad at the Farm and the village girl who did Mrs Cole's housework also went in twice a week to the McGowans. Word must have reached Auntie Alice very quickly.

I knew when Blag was back because I heard the hire car from Pinner drive away and saw a light in the wall door of the studio. When I went down next morning to make myself tea and toast Jack had a message for me. 'He wants to work. He'd like you to model for him. Gardening togs. Ten o'clock.'

I had been in the walled garden before to do weeding and other odd jobs but I had not seen inside the studio. It was bigger than it looked from the outside. From the inner doorway you saw a deep lofty room with a broad skylight at least thirty feet long, and tall windows with slatted blinds on the garden side. It seemed full of light. There was a tilted drawing table as well as easels and work tables. One of the easels carried a large pin board with drawings and photographs tacked to it. The drawings were mostly sketches of the actor-manager's head and hands and bits of them. The photographs were glossy and more difficult to see from where I stood.

Blag came through a doorway at the other end of the studio. There was a faint smell of cooked kippers. That seemed to be his kitchen with the bed-sitting room beyond.

'Hallo, Charlie,' he said; 'did they get off to the framer's all right?'

'Those boxes of Mr McGowan's wouldn't all go in the Morris.'

'I told Jenny they'd need the big car. Who helped her?'

'Jack and me. Jenny said they'd be back late but not to worry.'

'The framer's in Fulham. They're having dinner with Tom's sister in Chelsea. What do you think of it?'

He had caught my eyes wandering to the biggest photograph pinned to the board. It was the blow-up Rowe had done of the Everard head.

'From that fuzzy old print it's amazing.'

'I expect you're right. Charlie, why don't you try sitting on that bar stool over there. Yes, the one with the arms. Now, lift your head a bit and look out of the window. Head right a bit. What do you see? A flower bed, but what flowers? Geraniums. All right. Relax, but hold still.'

He had a double-demy sheet of cartridge paper pinned to a board on the smaller easel. The easel was on castors. He wheeled it into a position somewhere behind my left shoulder and began to draw. He used charcoal at first, then crayon. Then there was a smell of turpentine and he began dabbing at the paper with a sponge. He caught me looking at him and told me to keep still. 'Relax but keep still,' he said. 'I'll tell you when you can move. I'm working in pastel now but I'm using turps as well. You'll look like something by Dégas.'

It was a long time before he spoke again and the cramp in my neck was becoming really painful when there was a hammering at the door to the yard, the one I had come through, and the sound of a woman shouting.

Blag said: 'You can rest for a bit, Charlie, but don't go away. Stay where you are.'

He went to the door and opened it. The noise was coming from Auntie Alice and the golf club she was using as a hammer.

'What on earth are you doing Alice?'

She pushed past him into the studio. 'The car,' she said. 'That McGowan girl's taken the car. And on my club day. What right has she?'

'I told her to take it. It's a family car. Everyone uses it.'

'The McGowans are not family.'

'They're part of *my* family, Alice,' he said, 'whether you and Mother Autumn like it or not.' He said it very distinctly.

'You're breaking her heart,' Alice sobbed, and then burst into tears. The worst was over. With her grey shingled hair, her tweed skirt and her golfing brogues Alice wasn't dressed for grief, not the persuasive kind. Blag gave her his handkerchief to dry her eyes. 'Jack'll drive you in the Morris,' he said.

'But you'll come and talk to your mother tonight? Blag, you did promise.'

'Oh yes, I promised. Off you go, Alice. Talk to Jack.' He shut the door behind him and returned to the easel. 'All right, Charlie,' he said; 'let's get back to work.'

He worked another hour and then sent me off to lunch. He said that I could have a look at the picture the next day.

I was late for lunch and tired. Annette made me an omelette. After that I went up to my room meaning to read Maitland. Instead I fell asleep. When I woke up I had a bath and changed into my father's Savile Row tweed. Then I walked to the pub, not along the river path because I didn't want Mother Autumn to see me, but along the road. At the pub I met Rowe who had used the road for the same reason as I had. I experimented with a gin and ginger ale.

We were late back for dinner which was Annette's superb rabbit casserole with the white wine and basil sauce. All of us, including the Hunters, drank a lot of wine with it. After dinner they taught me to play nap. It was quite dark when the party broke up. To get some air I went for a walk along the river bank. Then, when it began to drizzle with rain, I quickly walked back.

The studio lights were all on and spilling into the yard. Blag, I thought, would be waiting for Jenny to return home. I was at the top of the spiral staircase when I heard the shot. It was quite a loud bang. I went back down the stairs. As soon as I reached the door I recognised the fired cartridge smell. I called to him. 'Are you there, Blag? Are you all right?' Then I went in.

He was lying on his back at the foot of the easel he had been using that morning and the blood was still pumping from the huge wounds in his chest and neck. The padded end of a mahlstick I had seen him use that morning was clutched in his right hand. In the few seconds I stood looking at that ghastly red bubbling mess my only thought was that the heart must still be beating. So I blundered out into the yard and ran for help.

It took me an age to get it. The Hunters were sound asleep and hard to wake. I knew that Rowe also had a telephone so tried shouting at him to call a doctor. The noise I made brought Jack downstairs with a raincoat over his pyjamas. I did *not* say 'Blag's shot himself.' I said, 'Blag's been shot.' Jack said, 'Dear God Almighty,' and ran to the studio door. As I followed him I was chattering about getting a doctor.

Minutes must have elapsed between my finding Blag wounded and re-entering the studio with Jack. The second time was quite different. I could not stand where I had stood before.

There was the family shotgun lying on the floor just where I had stood.

Jack was crouched over the mess on the floor. He glanced up at me sharply. 'If you're going to puke, Charlie,' he said, 'you'd best do it outside. It's not the local doctor we'll be needing but the police surgeon.'

Blag had thrown a cloth over the portrait on the easel. Now Jack pulled it off to cover the dead man's face. That left my face looking at me from the easel. As Jack had suggested I should, I went outside to be sick.

I was still doing so when the lights of the returning Crossley swept into the stable yard of Elm Park Farm. Jenny had returned. The bad dream entered its horror phase.

The coroner's inquest was at Isleworth near the hospital at which the autopsy had been performed. The courtroom was a territorial drill hall with not enough seating to accommodate the press. The place was packed.

The Coroner was a local medical officer of health with some forensic qualifications. I was among the first to give evidence. I told the court about hearing the shot, about finding Blag wounded and about running for help to the Hunters.

'That is Mr Jack Hunter who called the police?'

'Yes, sir. There was nothing I could have done for those wounds, but Jack had been in the war.'

'Thank you, Mr Blagden. I'm sure you did all you could. You saw Mr Cole that morning. How would you describe his state of mind?'

'Impatient, sir. He wanted no interruptions of his work or of his life.'

That was the end of me. Jack Hunter came next. The star turn, however, was Dr Lionel Benton-Black who had an address in Harley Street and who was consultant neurologist at a London teaching hospital. Blag Cole had been a patient of his for nearly twenty years.

'Suffering from what disease, Doctor?'

'I don't know for certain, sir, and now I never shall. His

sister had died of Hereditary Progressive Chorea when he was referred to me. That is the disease of the central nervous system which is now generally known as Huntington's disease. The disease is hereditary and genetically transmitted through either parent or both. There is at present no blood or other body fluid test that can detect its presence. There are Huntington familes – I know too many of them – and they are in a sense doomed. If the disease is there genetically, it can always strike, most commonly in the third, fourth, fifth and sixth decades of a person's life. There are family histories of Huntington's going back ten generations. It has been described as the most vicious of hereditary diseases. Vicious is not a scientific term but I can understand its use in this context.'

'When did you last see the deceased?'

'Three weeks ago. He said he had firm evidence to show that his father, the proved Huntington's carrier in that family, had not been his natural father. He claimed that he had been con-ceived illegitimately before his mother's marriage to Mr Cole. He could not, he argued, be a Huntington's carrier. There was no reason, therefore, why he could not marry and beget children.'

'Did you believe him, Doctor?'

'He had a good case, and photographs and other documents to support it. Probably all fantasy. With those who reach middle age it often happens. They have fantasies. Then they commit suicide. With men that is the most common outcome. I told Blagden Cole that on the subject of marriage he must use his own judgement.'

The verdict, of course, was suicide, 'while the balance of his mind was disturbed'.

On the way out I felt a tap on my shoulder.

'Hello, young man.' It was Mr Bristow. 'You look as if you could do with a beer.'

I was glad to see him. I needed someone to share my awful secret. When I told him about the shotgun that wasn't there when I found Blag but *was* there when I returned with Jack

Hunter he nodded approvingly. 'Not suicide, you think, but murder. What did the police think of the idea?'

'They were patient and kind. Naturally, when I found Blag with those terrible injuries I would be in a state of shock. It was quite understandable that I hadn't noticed the gun first time.'

'And it was understandable.'

'It was also understandable that Blag would hold the mahl-stick by the wrong end. The police say that he used the stick to press the shotgun trigger and kill himself.'

'And you don't?'

'I think that when he saw the gun pointing straight at him he grabbed the stick to try to deflect the gun barrel. He almost succeeded. The wounds were mainly on the right side.'

He sipped his beer. 'And who pointed the gun? Mother Autumn?'

'Blag went to see her that evening to confront her with that picture of Councillor Everard that you found for him and to announce his marriage. When he left she took the gun, which was kept with Alice's golf glubs, and followed him. She shot him. Then, still holding the gun, she walked back to her own house. On the way she met Alice who had heard the shot. It was Alice who took the gun from her and left it on the studio floor for us to find.'

'You'll never prove any of that, young man.'

'I won't be trying, Mr Bristow.'

He had been fumbling in his briefcase. Now he pulled out a print of the Councillor Everard blow-up. 'You may like this as a souvenir,' he said. 'The case for Everard as Blag's natural father is about as sound as the verdict of suicide to which we have just listened. Everard married twice but had no children. His fault, probably. As a young man he had a commission in the Yeomanry and, in the year before Blag was born, attended an Officers' Ball at Preston Barracks at which Miss Emma Blag-den was also present. That is recorded in a local newspaper of the time. I say no more. Good luck with the law, young man. I have a train to catch at Euston.'

When I got home I showed the photograph to my mother.

'That one never fathered Blag,' she said. 'Nothing like him. Wrong bones. The only good portrait I've ever seen of Blag was the one he did of his mother. I mean the nasty one he wrote on the back of, the one he said was of Ibsen's Mrs Alving.'

It was over twenty years before the subject of Blagden Cole came up again between us. In the mid-fifties a play of mine was opening in New York and she came over to see it. Of course, she had pieces of gossip.

'Do you remember that girl Jenny, the one Blag Cole was going to marry? Well, after the suicide I kept in touch with her. Blag had got her pregnant you know. Well, you wouldn't know. You were away.'

'What happened?'

'She had a daughter. Nice child. Died in her twenties, poor thing.'

'Huntington's?'

'Yes, I thought you'd be interested. My new doctor says they think now that in ten or twelve years' time they may be able to tell if someone's a carrier. Gene-mapping they call it. Yes, Jenny herself is all right. Children's book illustrating. I had to admit, though, I've always found her a teeny bit silly.'

SIMON BRETT

THE MAN WHO GOT THE DIRT

To have killed Bartlett Mears from motives of jealousy would have been a small-minded, petty crime; but fortunately Carlton Rutherford had a much more respectable, wholly practical, reason for eliminating his old rival.

Murder had not been involved in his original plans for settling old scores, but Carlton Rutherford felt not the tiniest twinge of regret when he realised it would be necessary. In a sense, it would tie together a lot of ends otherwise doomed to eternal looseness.

The rivalry between the two writers had lasted nearly forty years, and though Bartlett Mears, had he been questioned on the subject, would have dismissed it with a characteristic shrug, for Carlton Rutherford the wound had never healed, and its scab required daily repicking.

Both had written their first novels at the end of the fifties. By then Kingsley Amis, John Osborne and others, burglarising the shrine of pre-war British values and shattering its first hollow images, had declared the open season for iconoclasm.

Carlton Rutherford, at that period climbing the North Face of a doctorate on George Gissing at the University of Newcastle, had used his spare time to good effect and written his first novel, *Neither One Thing Nor The Other*.

This was a work of searingly fashionable nihilism, the story of Bob Grantham, a working-class genius, son of a postman in Salford, who struggled, against the odds of misunderstanding parents and virginity-hugging girls, all the way up to university.

The book contrived to pillory traditional educational values, and at the same time potentially to alienate everyone with whom the author had come into contact in the twenty-five years he had been alive.

And therein lay its problem. Bob Grantham was so patently the *alter ego* – in fact, not even the *alter ego*, just the *ego* – of Carlton Rutherford that all of the book's other characters became readily identifiable.

Dashiel Loukes, the lean and hungry literary agent to whom (randomly from a reference book in a Newcastle library) the manuscript had been sent, confided to its author over a boozy lunch at Bertorelli's in Charlotte Street, that, though he was 'excited, but very excited' about the book, he was 'just a tidge worried' about the libel risk. And thought a little bit of rewriting might be prudent.

That had been in 1958. Though simplified by the death of both Carlton Rutherford's parents in a charabanc crash soon after his meeting with Loukes (you cannot libel the dead), the rewriting had proved unexpectedly difficult and time-consuming.

Eventually, a year later, at another Bertorelli's lunch, the author presented the agent with a revised manuscript, announcing that he had contrived to disguise all of the living characters save for that of Sandra, the toffee-nosed solicitor's daughter who had proved so tragically insensitive to the exceptional genius of Bob Grantham and so provincially unwilling to be the recipient of his extremely tenacious virginity.

Dashiel Loukes, thin and acute as a greyhound, had asked how closely this character resembled its original, and dragged from Carlton Rutherford the unwilling admission that, except for the detail of having had her eyes changed from blue to brown, Sandra was identical in every particular to Sylvia, a toffee-nosed solicitor's daughter who had proved tragically insensitive to the exceptional genius of Carlton Rutherford and provincially unwilling to be the recipient of his extremely tenacious virginity (still, though Carlton did not mention the fact, intact in 1959).

The agent, aware that in *Neither One Thing Nor The Other* he had a fashionable and marketable commodity, suggested an extreme solution to the problem. The author should send a copy of his manuscript to Sylvia/Sandra and ask her to give a written undertaking that she would not take any action if the book were published. They had nothing to lose; it was worth a try.

Sylvia/Sandra was not for nothing the daughter of a solicitor. Now married to another solicitor, she was appalled by the manuscript and announced her firm intention to put an immediate injunction on the work if it was ever scheduled for publication.

Another gloomy Bertorelli's lunch, and Carlton Rutherford returned to another year's rewriting. In his new version, the Sylvia/Sandra character was virtually erased from the text. The dynamics of the novel were somewhat weakened by this alteration, but at least *Neither One Thing Nor The Other* could now be published without fear of litigation.

But a new shadow stretched over the 1961 Bertorelli's lunch at which Carlton Rutherford handed over his newly-sanitised manuscript to Dashiel Loukes. The Sunday papers that week had been full of rave reviews for *Chips On The Elbow*, a first novel by a hitherto-unknown author, Bartlett Mears.

This was a work of searingly fashionable nihilism, the story of Ted Retford, a working-class genius, son of a milkman in Stockport, who struggled, against the odds of misunderstanding parents and virginity-hugging girls, all the way up to university. The book contrived to pillory traditional educational values, but what distinguished it from the novels of the other voguish 'angry young men' was that it told the story with a sense of humour.

According to *The Sunday Times*, 'It is spiced with a refreshing wit, and, whereas other contemporary novelists have used their tongues to lash outdated institutions, Mr Mears keeps his firmly

– and wisely – in his cheek. *Chips On The Elbow* contrives to express its own distinctive anger while at the same time deflating the pretensions of the other "angry young men". In Bartlett Mears the arrival of a major new literary talent must be celebrated.'

The ensuing events were predictable. When, in 1962, *Neither One Thing Nor The Other* was finally published, its launch caused only minor ripples on the surface of literary life. *The Observer* referred to 'yet another whining catalogue of the ways in which the working-class misunderstands the hypersensitive artist in its midst', and *The Spectator* even spoke of 'a self-regarding diatribe in the manner – but without the wit – of Bartlett Mears'.

All this was gall and wormwood to Carlton Rutherford – particularly because he knew he had finished his novel before Bartlett Mears had even started his.

Another spur to fury was the discovery, from the deluge of newspaper profiles, radio and television interviews of the new genius, that Bartlett Mears was not even the genuine article. He was not the son of a milkman in Stockport, but of a bank manager in Guildford. He had been educated at a minor public school and – of all places – Oxford University.

Chips On The Elbow had not been written in the light of bitter experience, but as a patronising satire by a Southerner on the kind of life that Carlton Rutherford had led.

Given such a start, it was perhaps not surprising that the relationship between the two writers should end in murder.

The reception of their first books set the pattern for the future. Carlton Rutherford, having made a borehole into it in *Neither One Thing Nor The Other*, continued to mine the rich seam of his own childhood hardship and consequent feelings of alienation. The heroes of his subsequent novels were not all *called* Bob Grantham, but they all *were* Bob Grantham. Or, to put it another way, they all *were* Carlton Rutherford.

However, the vogue for gritty Northern realism passed. Other authors moved on to new subjects. Only Carlton Rutherford continued to produce the same tales of unrecognised genius. And, in an ironically self-fulfilling prophecy, his genius was recognised less and less with each succeeding book.

The novels, laborious to write, became even more laborious to read. Those reviewers who had found promise in *Neither One Thing Nor The Other* found it thereafter in decreasing measure, and eventually applied their ultimate destructive sanction – by not reviewing Carlton Rutherford's books at all.

Dashiel Loukes, initially such a champion of his author's cause, also proved a fair-weather friend. Through the sixties the agent grew fatter and more sleek, as he gathered under his banner an ever-increasing troop of ever-more-popular novelists. His early commitment to what he had described to Carlton Rutherford as 'really sensitive literary fiction' gave way in his priorities to the pursuit of the dollar.

Publishing changed, going through yet another of those recurrent attempts to shake off its image as the last refuge of a gentleman and prove it really *is* a hard-nosed commercial business. This involved, among other economy measures, the shedding of a large number of middle-list 'literary novelists'.

The British film industry began to disappear. The vogue for films of the type that might have offered Carlton Rutherford hope, *Saturday Night and Sunday Morning* or *A Kind of Loving*, gave way to breathlessly trendy reflections of Swinging London, which in turn gave way to nothing.

Dashiel Loukes, fatter but still as sharp, trimmed his sails accordingly. He began to specialise in cold-war thrillers, which offered possibilities of lucrative American film deals.

Carlton Rutherford became more and more a dinosaur in the agent's stable of fleet-footed winners.

The crisis came in 1967. Dashiel Loukes was unable to find any publisher willing to take on the latest novel, in which Bob Grantham (by now named Sid Doncaster and working as a novelist) had another disastrously unconsummated love affair and suffered from writer's block.

For Carlton Rutherford, though it still continued to strain constipatedly off the typewriter, the writing was on the wall.

His agent broke the news in a pub one evening after work. Carlton Rutherford no longer justified the expense of a lunch. Indeed, had the author not insisted on a face-to-face meeting, Dashiel Loukes would have made the perfunctory severance by telephone.

(As things turned out, though, the encounter was not without its uses for the agent. He was at the time in the throes of a very heavy affair with an editor from Hamish Hamilton. Telling his wife he had to meet 'that dreary old bellyacher Carlton Rutherford' gave him the perfect alibi. So long as he kept the actual meeting brief – which he ensured that he did – Dashiel Loukes efficiently managed to carve out two hours of uninterrupted bliss between the editor's satin sheets in Notting Hill.)

Such categorical obliteration of his hopes might have turned a less resilient author away from the literary life for good, but it did not have that effect on Carlton Rutherford. Partly, he was made of sterner stuff; and partly, his doctorate on George Gissing having been abandoned some years before, there was nothing else he could do.

So Carlton Rutherford set about constructing something which a surprisingly large number of other literary folk have managed – a career as a writer that does not involve the publication of books. He gave lectures on the theory and practice of writing. He attended seminars and symposia on writing. He joined writers' committees. He wrote reviews of an increasingly waspish nature, deploring the decline of British letters since . . . well, since his own books had been regarded as publishable.

And, of course, he taught creative writing courses.

In spite of all these activities, he still found time to go on writing his own novels, which charted further the conspiracy of an unfeeling and philistine world against Bob Grantham.

And he lived in daily anticipation of a change in the fickle tastes of the literary marketplace. The revived career of Barbara Pym in the late seventies prompted hopes for a similar rediscovery of Carlton Rutherford. When these were unrealised, he began increasingly to rely on thoughts of posthumous acclaim like that accorded to Gerard Manley Hopkins.

And when such thoughts proved inadequate to check his spleen, Carlton Rutherford comforted himself with fantasies of revenge on the man who had blighted his entire career. Bartlett Mears.

It might have been easier for him if Carlton Rutherford could have been unaware of his rival's activities, but the career of Bartlett Mears continued to maintain the high profile initiated by the success of *Chips On The Elbow*.

Mears, unlike Rutherford, had not allowed himself to be trapped into rewriting the same book time and again. Each of his publications was different from the last, each one attacked a new target, and in each the author's wit was more venomous. The books themselves did not get better – indeed, they undeniably got worse – but they did get reviewed.

And they got talked about. Bartlett Mears had an instinct for subject-matter that would prompt controversy. His books gave rise to passionate love and passionate hatred in equal measure, but they always gave rise to some reaction. Each new publication was derided as evidence of a sad falling-off in the author's former talents, as each one made its inexorable way into the bestsellers' lists.

It was impossible to be unaware of Bartlett Mears.

He became a media pundit, never far from the centre of literary debate. His opinion was sought on every innovation. His reactions were frequently ill-considered and bad-tempered – sometimes even infantile – but they were always quotable. His favourite weapon was inadequately informed blanket condemnation. He genuinely did not care what people thought about him, and as a result, whether with relish or disgust, people thought about him a great deal.

The profile of Bartlett Mears' domestic life was equally high. *Private Eye* would have been lost without him.

A few well-publicised affairs with glamorous literati preceded a very public divorce from his pre-celebrity wife. More well-publicised affairs preceded his very public courtship of, and marriage to, the dauntingly attractive and intelligent novelist and critic, Mariana Lestrange, another potent magnet for gossip columnists and press photographers.

The stormy course of this marriage, its public rows, separations and ultimate collapse in a spitting crackle of recrimination were known well outside the literary world – even in households where nothing was read more taxing than *The Sun*. Bartlett Mears' subsequent vituperative attacks on his ex-wife and general misogyny added further fuel to the blaze of his publicity.

And all this before one even mentioned the drinking.

Bartlett Mears had started his literary life as an *enfant terrible* and stayed *terrible* long after he had relinquished all possible right to be called an *enfant*.

He was a selfish, drunken loud-mouth of diminishing talent, with the physical allure of a warthog, the tact of a rhinoceros, the morals of a sewer rat.

And the public loved him for it.

The more he abused them, the more restaurants he was banned from, the more television programmes he appeared on incapable through drink, the more the public loved him.

Try as he might – and after a while he didn't try that hard – Carlton Rutherford could not be unaware of Bartlett Mears and his latest outrage.

Soon, rather than trying to escape references to his rival, the less successful writer was positively seeking them out.

He was well placed to do so. He moved in the same literary world – albeit on its fringes – as Bartlett Mears. The two were frequently in the same room – in restaurants, at book launches, publishers' parties, writers' seminars, newspaper offices – and Carlton Rutherford witnessed many of the famous author's more spectacular misdemeanours.

All of these he chronicled in a notebook, which over the years became a series of notebooks. Soon, in addition, he started building up scrapbooks of newspaper cuttings, and after a while began the practice of soliciting scurrilous gossip about his rival whenever the opportunity arose. So extreme was Bartlett Mears' general behaviour that such opportunities arose frequently. All this adversarial anecdotage was also punctiliously recorded.

Gradually, over thirty years, was built up an exhaustive archive of misbehaviour.

There was no doubt that Carlton Rutherford had got all the dirt on Bartlett Mears.

It was early in 1991 that the idea came to him, and he was immediately impressed by its simplicity and wholeness.

He rang Dashiel Loukes the same day. 'There's a project I want to put to you.'

The agent, who thought he had permanently shaken off Carlton Rutherford some twenty years before, was instantly evasive. He was very busy, he had all the authors he could cope with, the current state of publishing was too depressing for him to offer any hope to another saga of North Country misunderstanding.

'Ah, but what I'm talking about now is non-fiction,' Carlton Rutherford announced triumphantly.

'Well, the state of the non-fiction market is not a lot more encouraging at the—'

'Come on, we must meet and talk about the idea. It's a sure-fire commercial proposition.'

Dashiel Loukes tried valiantly to escape, but eventually succumbed to a meeting. He suggested the author should come to his Mayfair office the following Thursday at eleven-thirty, an appointment whose timing proclaimed 'not only am I not offering you lunch, but also I am having lunch with someone considerably more important than you'.

'What I'm suggesting,' Carlton Rutherford pronounced, once he was safely ensconced in the agent's office, 'is a biography of Bartlett Mears.'

Dashiel Loukes looked up, his face purple from its daily marinade in the good wines of the Garrick and the Groucho. Time had treated his business kindly. Three of his espionage authors were now international bestsellers, and his principal daily task was to sit and work out his percentage of their money as, unprompted, it came rolling in.

'An official biography?' he asked.

'No, no,' Carlton Rutherford replied slyly. 'An extremely *un*official biography.'

'Hm . . .'

'You can't deny that Bartlett Mears is the kind of person the public wants to read about.'

'I'm not denying that. It's a matter of *what* they want to read about him. A literary biography of a living author's bound to be a minority sale.'

'I'm not talking about a *literary* biography of Bartlett Mears. I'm talking about a *scurrilous* biography. I've got all the dirt,' Carlton Rutherford concluded smugly.

Dashiel Loukes was thoughtful. 'It's actually not such a bad idea . . .' he conceded.

The author smiled.

'Trouble is . . .'

'What?'

'*You*, Carlton, I'm afraid.'

'What? At the absolute lowest, I'm a perfectly competent writer.'

'I know, but your name's not . . .'

'Not what?'

'Not *sexy*.'

'I don't see what sex has got to do with it,' said Carlton Rutherford, who was always embarrassed by the subject.

'Look, for a project like this – which, as I say, is actually not a bad idea – if I'm going to sell it to a publisher, I'd be on much stronger ground if I was selling it on the name of a well-known journalist or—'

'But you don't want a well-known journalist, you want someone who knows the facts. And I can assure you – I've got all the dirt,' Carlton Rutherford reiterated.

'Hm . . .' The agent looked at his watch. 'Got to be off soon, I'm afraid. Tell you what – I'll have a ring round some publishers this afternoon – see if I get any nibbles – can't say fairer than that, can I?'

The author considered the agent could say a lot fairer than that, but was in no position to argue. Meekly he left the office and went home to his flat in Upper Norwood to eat a boiled egg and wait for the phone to ring.

It rang at a quarter to five. The mellowness of Dashiel Loukes' voice suggested he had only just returned from lunch. 'Had a ring round, old boy, like I said I would,' he announced bonhomously. 'Got quite a positive reaction to the idea of a book about Bartlett, but sorry, your name didn't win too many coconuts.'

'How do you mean?'

'I mean there's no chance of my getting a commission for this project with your name attached.'

'Oh. But I'm the one who's got the dirt,' Carlton Rutherford insisted.

'Maybe. I'm afraid that didn't seem to carry much weight.'

'So what do you suggest I do?'

'Well, nothing. Nothing you can do, really. Unless, of course, you want to write the whole thing *on spec* . . .' The agent's voice was aghast at the alien nature of his own suggestion. 'I mean, if you did come up with something really scurrilous, I might not have too much problem placing the completed manuscript. But it'd have to be pretty strong stuff . . .'

'Yes . . .'

'And you'd certainly have to talk to Mariana Lestrange. No book on Bartlett's going to be complete without a few shovelfuls of shit from her.'

'Hm. Right . . .' Carlton Rutherford was silent, until an unpleasant thought came into his head. 'Meanwhile, I suppose, your calls will have planted in a few publishers' heads the idea of doing a book about Bartlett Mears . . .'

'Possibly, yes . . .'

'*My* idea of doing a book about Bartlett Mears!'

'Well . . . They could have come up with it on their own . . .'

'No, they couldn't! They'd never have thought of it if I hadn't asked you to—'

'Carlton, Carlton . . .' the agent remonstrated. 'There is no copyright in ideas. Now you know that as well as I do – don't you, old boy . . . ?'

It didn't take Carlton Rutherford long to make his decision. He had no other means of revenge at his disposal. Besides, if he did not publish his findings, nearly thirty years of chronicling the misdemeanours of Bartlett Mears would have been wasted.

And there was a new spur to action. Now that Dashiel Loukes had spread around London publishers the idea of a book on Bartlett Mears, it was only a matter of time before some suitably 'sexy' journalist was commissioned to write one.

Carlton Rutherford reckoned that, because all his research was already done, he had a head start. But only if he got down to the writing straight away. He knew that experienced journalists could – and frequently did – paste-and-scissor together celebrity biographies over a weekend.

He was greatly reassured as soon as he started the actual writing. So exhaustive had been his chronicling of Bartlett Mears' life that he could copy out most of his notebooks verbatim. The book was virtually written; all it needed was a little judicious editing, to take out the only-mildly-scurrilous incidents and bring the thoroughly-scurrilous ones closer together.

He worked flat-out for three weeks and the draft was done. It was the most searing indictment of a human being he had ever read.

One thing still niggled, though. Dashiel Loukes had been right. No biography of Bartlett Mears would really be complete without an infusion of Mariana Lestrange's distinctive vituperation. Her public set-tos with her former husband were well chronicled; but she was bound to have a store of character-destroying reminiscence of their life together. That was the dash of venom which the biography required.

He got her phone number from a literary editor who gave him occasional reviewing work. She answered the phone with the brusqueness of someone who jealously guards her privacy, but when Carlton Rutherford announced his mission, her manner changed.

Yes, she would be delighted to tell him anything he wanted to know. No fate was bad enough for that bastard Bartlett Mears.

Mariana Lestrange lived in Hampstead. Of course she did. Bartlett Mears still lived in Hampstead, come to that. So did the majority of the glamorous literati with whom he had had affairs before, during and after his second marriage. The supply of them in Hampstead was so constant, he'd rarely felt the need to look elsewhere.

She received the biographer in her imposing sitting-room. One of its walls was shelved with British and overseas editions of her novels; another with international awards and citations.

'So,' Mariana Lestrange purred in her famously sexy voice, 'you want all the real dirt on Bartlett Mears . . . ?'

She must have been nearly sixty, but was still very beautiful. Tall, slender, with a surprisingly ample bosom, she wore her artfully blonded hair as a frame to the small face whose nose would have been too large on someone less striking.

Carlton Rutherford felt a little uneasy in her presence. He always reacted that way to women of obvious sexual attraction. The state of his virginity remained precisely as it had been in 1959.

'Yes,' he said nervously. 'Anything you're prepared to tell me. Obviously, I know all the stuff that's been in the papers, but, er, anything more intimate would be . . . very welcome . . .'

'Hm. Who's publishing your book?' she asked sharply.

'Well, er . . . The thing is, that's not quite decided yet . . .'

'Ah, I see. You mean it's going to be auctioned.'

Carlton Rutherford did not disabuse her of this error. For a writer of Mariana Lestrange's stature, auctions would be a regular occurrence. She knew nothing of the end of the market where publishers don't fight over books, but have to be cajoled into accepting them, and even then frequently don't.

'Well, where shall we start . . . ?' Mariana purred on. 'Impotence the first night I agreed to make love to him . . . ? Or Bartlett peeing over the bed in our honeymoon suite . . . ? Or the time he hit me so hard he broke my jaw . . . ?'

'Oh, any of those. All of those. It all sounds wonderful!' Carlton Rutherford responded gleefully. 'Fire away!'

So Mariana Lestrange fired away. She produced a savage catalogue of meanness, drunkenness, sexual malpractice, infidelity, theft and cringing deceit. She enumerated her former husband's disgusting personal habits – his practice of stubbing out cigarette butts in coffee cups, his self-pitying hypochondria, his pill-gulping, his nose-picking, his farting, his belching, his snoring, his halitosis and the revolting state in which he left his underwear.

The resentment born of five years' cohabitation seemed not to have mellowed one iota with the passage of time. Only the tiniest of prompts was required to bring it once again bubbling to the surface.

Carlton Rutherford's pen could hardly move quickly enough across the page to record this cataract of domestic villainies. With each new revelation he hugged himself, gleefully envisaging where it could be inserted into his narrative.

Dashiel Loukes had been right. This was the secret ingredient that the biography needed. There is nothing like total character assassination to send a book rocketing up the bestsellers lists.

At times Mariana Lestrange's account sounded so vicious, the antics she described so evil, that Carlton Rutherford almost suspected her novelist's instinct was fictionalising for his benefit, but if ever he asked a hesitant 'Did he *really* do that?', she snapped back, 'Of course! I know. I lived with the bastard!'

He'd thought he was doing all right before, but after the interview with Mariana Lestrange, he knew he'd *really* got the dirt.

It took him less than a week to thread this new vein of vindictiveness into his text. At the end of that time, Carlton Rutherford checked carefully through his manuscript before delivering it personally to Dashiel Loukes' office. According to the agent's unnervingly pretty assistant, her boss was still out at lunch. Carlton Rutherford thought this slightly odd at five forty-five in the afternoon, but did not question it.

He went back to Upper Norwood to await the reaction to his literary bombshell.

At least this time their meeting merited lunch. Dashiel Loukes took him to the Groucho Club and, bathed in the sunlight of the upstairs Dining Room, gave his verdict.

'Sorry, old boy. Not a chance in hell of placing it.'

'But come on, it's good. All that detail – fascinating stuff. You can't say I haven't got all the dirt, can you?'

'No. Certainly not. No, it's the most compulsive manuscript I've read for years. I was up half the night reading it – absolutely riveting.'

'Well then . . . ?'

'It's your old problem, Carlton. Just like it was with *Neither One Thing Nor The Other* . . .'

'What do you mean?'

'Libel, old boy, libel. Your manuscript has got something actionable on every page.'

'But it's all true! It's all substantiated. I actually witnessed a lot of it.'

'Surely you didn't witness the incident in the gents' lavatory with Joe Orton . . . ? Or the benedictine-drinking contest with David Niven . . . ? Or that business with Malcolm Muggeridge and the spatula . . . ?'

'No, I wasn't actually there, but it's all true! I got it from

Mariana. Anyway, Joe Orton's not going to pop up from the grave to deny it. Nor's David Niven likely to—'

'I agree, old boy. No problems with *them*. They're all safely dead and you can't libel the dead. No, it's Bartlett himself who's likely to make a stink – absolutely guaranteed to make a stink, I'd say.'

'But it all happened! Mariana Lestrange said he even used to boast about a lot of it.'

'Boasting in private about it is very different from sanctioning the printing of this kind of unsubstantiated gossip.'

'Dashiel, how many times do I have to tell you – it's all fully substantiated!'

'Carlton, the bottom line is that I've consulted a top libel lawyer whom I've used many times before. He's read your manuscript and he says it's absolute dynamite.'

'But it's *good*,' the author wailed plaintively.

'I'm not denying it. It's very good. Easily the most readable thing you've ever done.' Carlton Rutherford decided not to rise to this implied slight to the rest of his *oeuvre*, as the agent went on, 'But the fact remains that it's good *dynamite*. No publisher will touch it.'

'But—'

'No, old boy, you have to face the truth. There is no chance of publication for this book while Bartlett Mears is alive!'

From that moment Carlton Rutherford realised that he would have to commit murder.

The idea didn't worry him at all. In fact, the more he thought about it, the more he relished the prospect.

The manner of Bartlett Mears' killing did not really matter, so long as he ended up safely dead. But self-preservation dictated that Carlton Rutherford should use a method which could appear to any investigating authorities as an accident.

He did not have to look far to find it. Details that he knew of his quarry's personal habits – his smoking, his drinking, his addiction to a variety of pills – they all pointed in the same direction.

Bartlett Mears would die in a fire at his home.

It was hard for Carlton Rutherford – or anyone else – to avoid knowing his victim's tall Victorian Hampstead house, so frequently was it featured in colour supplements and television profiles of its owner.

Bartlett Mears took the image of the impractical artist to extremes and was nationally known to live in a state of paper-strewn chaos. Coupling this fact with his heavy drinking and smoking – not to mention his reliance on sleeping pills – what was more likely than that a casually discarded cigarette butt should ignite a pile of papers in his house and cause a life-ending conflagration . . . ?

Carlton Rutherford began surveillance of the murder scene, and soon discovered that Bartlett Mears never walked any-where. If he was going out, a taxi would arrive to take him to his destination; and on his sodden return a late-evening taxi would pour him out on to his doorstep. Then he would presum-ably take a few more drinks to anaesthetise himself further before falling into bed and – usually – remembering to turn out the light of his first-floor bedroom.

Obviously the fire would have to take place at night. At that time its victim's stupor and the lack of witnesses would give the conflagration a chance to take a good hold before emergency services could be summoned. But a little planning was required to ensure that a really good blaze was quickly achieved.

One day, when Bartlett Mears had been taxied away for a long lunch (all his lunches were long ones), his nemesis – Carlton Rutherford – slipped through the side gate of the house and examined the dustbins in the passage.

He quickly found what he wanted. In common with many other writers, Bartlett Mears was a member of a whole raft of literary organisations like the Society of Authors, PEN and the Writers' Guild. Also in common with many other writers, Bart-lett Mears immediately consigned the literature of these organisations – *The Author, Pen International, The Writers' Newsletter* – unopened and unread into his dustbin. Carlton Rutherford did not have to search long to find a sheaf of solid envelopes all printed with his quarry's name and address.

Once he had secured these, and bought vodka, cigarettes and matches, his preparations were complete. It was just a matter of waiting for the right moment to put his plan into action.

The television gave him his cue. One Tuesday he was watching the end of *Newsnight* and heard the presenter say, 'Tomorrow evening in *Newsnight* we'll be discussing the pros and cons of the Net Book Agreement, and amongst those giving his – no doubt trenchant – views will be the author Bartlett Mears.'

It was typical that the BBC should try to enliven an extremely dull topic by bringing in Bartlett. Whatever the subject, he could always be relied on to say something outrageous – particularly at such a late hour when his day's drinking would really have started to build up. He was bound after the programme to have a few more drinks in one of the BBC Hospitality Suites, before rolling into the car that would decant him in Hampstead.

Carlton Rutherford felt almost uncannily calm the following evening as he sat in his little flat in Upper Norwood, watching *Newsnight*. Bartlett Mears behaved predictably. He was rudely dismissive of other eminent authors, gratuitously offensive to the rather pretty girl conducting the interview, and he used the word 'shit' twice to ensure that the BBC switchboard would be briefly jammed by offended listeners. It was in fact the performance for which he had been booked.

Carlton Rutherford was still calm as he got into his dilapidated Austin Allegro and drove easily across London to Hampstead. As he had anticipated, his quarry had refreshed himself for a while with BBC Hospitality, and Carlton had been parked opposite the house waiting for a full hour before the chauffeur-driven car arrived.

Bartlett Mears staggered out, with no word of thanks to the

driver, and fumbled with his keys for a while before managing to open the front door.

Still icy calm, Carlton Rutherford waited another full hour for Bartlett Mears' nightcaps to be consumed and for the bedroom light to be switched off.

He gave it another half-hour, then got out of the car and sauntered across to the house opposite.

He doused some of the envelopes of literary literature with vodka, and slipped them through the letter-box. Then, casually, he lit a cigarette, drew on it a few times to get it thoroughly going, and dropped that through.

He waited.

At first he thought he had failed and was on the point of starting again, when he was rewarded by a reflected orange glow on the hall ceiling.

Gently, he dropped through more of the envelopes to build up a substantial bonfire.

Then, even more gently, he trickled the contents of the second vodka bottle in through the letter-box, careful to restrict its flow so that it would not douse the growing fire, but rather spread across the carpet, warm up slowly and ignite.

He stayed on the doorstep for two more full minutes, until he could feel the heat of his blaze through the wood of the front door; then sauntered back to his Austin Allegro.

He was back in Upper Norwood, in bed and asleep, within the hour.

He slept well, and was wakened by the *Today Programme*'s seven o'clock news on his clock radio.

It was exactly as he had wished. The last item of the bulletin announced the death of the popular author Bartlett Mears, in a fire which had gutted his Hampstead house.

Carlton Rutherford leaped out of his lonely bed, and danced a little jig of triumph, which left him flushed and breathless.

It was agony to wait till ten, when he reckoned Dashiel Loukes would have arrived in his office. Back in the sixties,

when Carlton Rutherford had been one of the white hopes of
the agency, Dashiel would have encouraged the author to ring
him at home. But those days were long past, and the agent had
moved upmarket through a good few addresses since then. His
favoured espionage authors were granted his current home
number, but for lesser mortals it remained firmly ex-directory.

Eventually the hands of Carlton Rutherford's clock radio
moved round to ten o'clock, and he rang through to Dashiel
Loukes' office.

'I'm afraid,' said the dauntingly pretty assistant, 'that Mr
Loukes is busy on another call.'

'Well, get him off it!' snapped the author, confident of his
sudden value to the agent. 'Tell him it's Carlton Rutherford on
the line!'

His confidence had not been misplaced. Dashiel Loukes was
through to him immediately, almost fawning in his delight to
have made contact with one of his most potentially lucrative
authors.

'Carlton, terrific to hear you! Just about to ring you! I assume
you're calling about what I think you're calling about . . . ?'

'I would imagine so. Rather changes the situation, doesn't
it?'

'That, old boy, is the understatement of the year! Wonderful
thing is – there'll now be a whole rash of Bartlett Mears books
commissioned, and we've stolen a march on the lot of them,
because our manuscript is already finished!'

It was interesting to hear how *your* manuscript had suddenly
become *our* manuscript, but Carlton Rutherford was too excited
to comment. 'So what's the next step?'

'The next step, old boy, is that I set up the most almighty
auction that London has seen for a long time. Bartlett Mears
sells in the States too, and he's translated everywhere. We are
talking about a really big international book here. It's going to
be *the* title at Frankfurt, no question. We are talking big, big
bucks. You've really come up with the goods this time, Carlton
Rutherford!'

Those were the words that all of his literary life, the author of *Neither One Thing Nor The Other* had longed to hear.

Radio and television were heavy that day with reminiscences, assessments and tributes to Bartlett Mears. Death changes many people's tunes and all of his fellow authors spoke with inordinate affection for 'the old rogue'.

Carlton Rutherford hugged himself as he listened. Just wait, he thought deliciously, just wait till my book comes out. That'll really set the record straight.

More details emerged about the accident which had so prematurely robbed the eminent author of his life. The general view seemed to be that, given the chaos in which Bartlett Mears had always lived, the only surprise was that an accident of that sort had not happened before.

The one shocking piece of additional information that emerged was that Bartlett had not been the only victim of the conflagration. He had not been alone in the house at the time of his death.

There had been a woman with him.

Her body had been so charred that immediate identification had not been possible.

By the end of the day, however, news bulletins carried the startling news that the other victim had been Mariana Lestrange.

Carlton Rutherford was surprised by this information, but strangely unmoved. So . . . he had murdered two people rather than one. The literary world had lost another of its stars. It was something for which he could not grieve.

He did wonder idly what Mariana had been doing in her ex-husband's house. He favoured a theory that she had been there to sort out some financial detail left over from their marriage, which Bartlett, typically inefficient, had neglected.

The strong rumour around literary circles that the two writers had actually been found in bed together, Carlton Rutherford refused to countenance.

He was not going to admit any thought to his mind that might threaten the sunny feeling of satisfaction that so benignly reigned there.

The following Sunday, needless to say, the quality papers – and even much of the gutter press – were full of tributes, appreciations and assessments of Bartlett Mears.

Carlton Rutherford bought all of them, and read them all with relish. Again, he was comforted by the knowledge of how his forthcoming bestseller would upturn all of these charitable assessments.

It was while he sat there in bliss that the phone rang.

Dashiel Loukes. 'Sorry to bother you on a Sunday . . .'

Carlton Rutherford did not mind at all. No doubt the agent had received the first 'ball-park figure' from which the forthcoming book auction would start, and was anxious to tell his author without delay.

'. . . but something's come up,' the agent continued, in a voice which suggested he might be the bearer of less pleasing news.

'Oh? What?' asked Carlton Rutherford, instantly alert.

'Something which I'm afraid may rather put the kibosh on our scheme, old boy.'

'What!'

'Apparently Bartlett Mears wrote his own memoirs. Did you know that?'

'No, I didn't. But that needn't worry us. By the time they've been edited and got ready for publication, my book will have been out a long time and we'll have cleaned up.'

'No, I'm afraid we won't.'

'Why not?'

'Bartlett Mears' *Memoirs* have been all ready for publication for the last three years. His publishers can have them on the bookstalls in a couple of months if they want to.'

'But how? I mean, if they're ready, why haven't they been published before?'

'They were all set up – pre-publicity about to start – announcement in *The Bookseller* about to be made – when suddenly they had to be withdrawn.'

'But why?'

'Libel risk, old boy. Most of the people in the book were either dead or unlikely to sue, but there was one who held out. They tried sending her the manuscript to read, but that only made her even more determined to sue.'

'Who was it?' asked Carlton Rutherford weakly, knowing all too well the name that Dashiel Loukes was about to pronounce.

'Mariana Lestrange,' the agent replied. 'But, of course, now she's dead, there's nothing to stop them publishing as soon as they want . . .'

The agent went on for a while, explaining why this news invalidated the chances for their book, but Carlton Rutherford heard no more. He felt a sudden stab of pain in his chest, then his breath seemed to be sucked painfully out of his body until, moments after, blackness descended.

He collapsed, still holding the telephone, and died on the pile of newspaper tributes to his great rival, Bartlett Mears.

The death of Carlton Rutherford did not merit any newspaper obituaries. Memories of any promise contained in *Neither One Thing Nor The Other* had long been swamped by recollections of the subsequent turgid annals of Bob Grantham. There wasn't a lot to say about a novelist who hadn't published a book since the sixties.

The British edition of Bartlett Mears' *Memoirs* was published with great éclat in the autumn of 1992. It shot straight to the top of *The Sunday Times* bestsellers' list, and stayed there for many weeks. The American and foreign language editions looked set fair to repeat this success.

Part of the appeal of the book was that it was extremely scurrilous. The author made no attempt to whitewash himself, and indeed his account of his own life was infinitely more offensive than anything contained in the forgotten manuscript of Carlton Rutherford. There was lots of dirt, which was why the book proved so phenomenally popular.

The public, as they always do, loved a rogue.

Incidentally, there was no mention in Bartlett Mears' *Memoirs* of Carlton Rutherford. The famous author had been completely unaware even of the existence of his rival.

LEN DEIGHTON

THE MAN WHO WAS A COYOTE

From somewhere beyond the tall chain-link fence, the brittle sound of Mexican music punctured the Texas night. A trumpet fanfare and a rapid succession of triplets was overlaid by the tenor singing a melancholy petition of love. It was probably a car radio: there were no houses in this desolate place. It was more than sixty miles south to the Mexican frontier but this was the only route out of the Rio Grande Valley. This was the place the illegal immigrants had to pass to get to the USA.

The three US Border Patrolmen had dark complexions and black shiny hair and had grown up speaking the nimble sort of Spanish that you needed to communicate with people who would walk a thousand miles from distant regions of the Americas. The men were not in uniform: they wore olive-drab fatigues and woollen hats. All had powerful flashlights clipped to their belts. Their high boots were caked with dry earth and it was under their nails and in their hair. The eldest man had a sniffer dog named Rambo on a short leash. They'd been assigned to check the freight train that came through every night. It was not a job anyone sought. Searching the box cars – from roofs to rods – usually put the team in a bad temper, especially when they found nothing.

They walked past a brightly lit compound packed tight with cars and trucks. Having been used for the transport of drugs or illegals, the vehicles were now confiscated. Some were old and battered but some of them were fine new cars – BMWs, Mercs, even a shiny new Cadillac – better than anything a Border Patrolman could afford from his pay.

The music stopped.

'What's this?' said the man with the dog, as he watched a smart taxicab coming down the track. It stopped outside the battered huts that the Immigration and Naturalisation Service provided as office, sleeping quarters, waiting room and cells. Alongside the huts a trailer acted as a storeroom for bales of marijuana and other illegal substances.

'Fancy looking guy,' said the second man, not without a hint of admiration. A tall man in a well-fitting grey suit climbed out of the taxicab and told the driver to wait. He went to the windows of the dark bus and stared. Inside it he could see twelve Mexicans. They were still and silent breathing in the soft wet Texan air. Having studied the bus without finding what he sought the tall man looked round in that proprietorial way that visitors did when they were about to announce that they were tax-payers who didn't like what they were paying for.

'A lawyer,' pronounced the dog-handler. He'd been doing this job for nearly twenty years.

'How so?'

'You'll see. I can smell them. So can Rambo.' The dog heard its name and gave an appreciative little whine.

'It will be about the kid,' said the second man. No one had to ask which kid he meant. A few hours previously, just as it was getting dark, this same team had arrested a young man leading a party of ten men and two women. Some careless or tired member of the group had blundered across one of the buried seismic sensors. When the computer squeaked, it was a simple task to roll out there in a truck and bring them in. The illegals had had no papers, no money and no explanations. Weary and despondent, the women sobbing – they had laboriously scrawled their signatures on the I-274 forms, agreeing to be 'Voluntarily Returned'. Silent now, sitting in the bus with lattice windows, they were dreaming other dreams. They'd be back in Mexico – in police custody – within three hours, four at the most. But

71

their guide had been separated from his charges. He'd not been offered a I-274 form to sign. He was locked up in a small cell with three other illegals who were wanted for further questioning. The kid had made an obnoxious nuisance of himself. He'd called the Patrolmen 'fascists' and 'Gestapo' and said the sort of things they regularly read about themselves in the liberal newspapers.

The fly screen banged as the tall man went inside and the taxi driver drew in closer to the tall fence. The driver switched on the radio again and the same music came more softly. Having watched the lawyer going into the hut the three Patrolmen found tasks to keep them busy. Men in business suits usually meant trouble of one sort or another. It was better to leave it with Pete Lopez, the man down there at the desk in the trailer. He knew how to deal with outsiders.

'Hello, Pete.'

'Hello, Mr Dawson.' Lopez was thirty years old, and handsome, with a tanned face and large slightly greying moustache that made him look like the star of some old Hollywood Western. He got to his feet and picked up some papers from his desk in a flurry of activity that he hoped would disguise the consternation he felt at seeing the senior partner of one of the county's most successful law firms dragging the visitor's chair across the floor at five o'clock in the morning.

Despite the wide-open window, the trailer was blue with cigarette smoke and fluorescent light. The visitor could now be seen as a tall, frail-looking old man who walked with the aid of a silver-topped cane. Even at this hour of the night his turnout was impeccable, with perfectly starched white shirt, silk polka-dot tie and cuffs that only just revealed the heavy gold links. Having pulled the chair into a position he liked he lowered himself into it.

'You don't mind if I smoke?' he said, wetting his lips and putting a cigar into his mouth without waiting for the affirmative grunt that came eventually.

Pete sat down on his swivel chair and tossed the papers into a wire tray. The two men knew each other to some extent. Pete

Lopez regularly saw photos of the Dawsons in the social pages and once, many years ago, Pete had backdated some paperwork to legalise a live-in domestic that some nosey reporter from Dallas had discovered was in the Dawsons' employ. It had been a gesture of dislike for the newspaper man, as much as a favour to Dawson.

'What can I do for you?' Pete asked, now it was clear that he wasn't to be offered a ten-dollar cigar.

'You know, Pete,' said Dawson in a drawling voice. 'You must know.'

'The *coyote*?'

'Coyote?' said Dawson as he let the smoke trail out of his half-closed mouth. It was the word they used to describe the men who, for a fee, led parties of wet-backs over the border to the USA and sometimes robbed, raped and murdered them if that proved expedient.

Pete looked down and read from a card on his desk. 'White Caucasian: twenty-five years old: five feet eight: weighed in at one hundred and sixty pounds.' He looked up. 'Is that it?' When Dawson, after a long pause, gave an almost imperceptible nod, Pete added, 'We think he was carrying narcotics. Cocaine. Cocaine is the big cargo lately. As soon as it's light I'm taking a party out to search the area near the sensor. Could be they buried it.'

'Don't play games with me, Pete. It's late and we both need our sleep.'

'It's the truth.'

'It's INS bullshit and you know it. If you thought there was anything buried out there you wouldn't be sending the rest of those wet-backs home. You'd be holding them if only as witnesses. I want to see the prisoner.'

'Detainee, not prisoner, Mr Dawson. And you're wrong in thinking that I wasn't going to send the boy back across the border with his amigos.'

'You'll do nothing of the kind!' He spoke quietly but for the first time showed real concern.

Pete grinned. 'Why not, Mr Dawson? Why not send the kid back where he came from?'

Dawson got his feelings under control and smoked his cigar and didn't answer.

'Let me tell you why you don't want him sent there. Because you know the Mexican cops will bust his head open. And if he yells at them the way he's been hollering at my boys he'll end up cold and floating head down in the big brown river. And that will suit me just fine because he's an insolent, aggressive little bastard who needs to learn a lesson or two.'

Pete Lopez stood up. He was angry now, angry at the way the Dawsons of the world treated him, angry at the way the whole nation treated him when all he was doing was the job that the President and Congress sent him here to do: stop the whole population of Latin America coming here to take jobs from Americans and bring the whole economy tumbling down. He could see that the boy was important to Dawson and Pete couldn't resist letting him know what it was in his power to do. 'You know how the cops work over there, do you, Mr Dawson? They got seventy-two hours to get a confession or let a suspect go. Most of them sign a confession after a couple of hours or so. Of course those cops over there have got a whole year before an accused person has to be brought to trial. It's a long year. Or so they tell me.'

Dawson listened sadly and nodded and tapped ash into a tin lid that was overfilled with squashed cigarette butts. 'That young man's father is one of my most respected clients: a man of substance,' he said as if nothing else need be said.

'What is a man of substance, Mr Dawson? What kind of thing does he do? I've often wondered about that.'

There was a more serious note in Dawson's voice as he said, 'A man of substance winters in the Caribbean, Pete. He makes contributions to political funds. He places a call to Washington DC and he burns your ass, Pete. That's what a man of substance does.'

For a moment Pete sat there, his face devoid of expression.

Then he sighed: 'Goddamned Ivy League kids: they are a pain in the ass.'

Dawson smiled too.

Pete leaned over to get a big bunch of keys from a drawer in his desk. Once in his hands he bounced the keys on his open palm so that they jingled. 'I see a lot of different people coming through here. Not just Latins . . . Just in the past few weeks we've processed nationals from Egypt, Iran, Albania and a dozen or more Germans. But I've got to tell you that your boy is just about the meanest little critter I ever remember throwing into the slammer.'

Dawson's smile had not faded.

'Do you want to see him?'

'Not particularly,' said Dawson. 'I share your views to some extent, Pete. Never did like these rich troublemaking kids. My own boys never went off the rails. Did he have any money on him?'

'Three hundred and twenty US plus some Mex small change. Are you taking him with you?'

'With that kind of dough he can call for a cab,' said Dawson. He got to his feet slowly and carefully using his cane to steady himself. 'I work for his Dad and I do what I'm told. But that don't include riding into town with obnoxious kids.'

Pete remained in his chair while Dawson walked out of the hut. His footsteps crunched on the dirt path and there was the sound of the taxicab door slamming very loud. Then the engine started and the Mexican music from the car radio was very loud. 'Tu Solo Tu': it was one of Pete's favourites. They'd played it at his wedding.

The music faded as the taxi went back down the trail the way it had come. The eastern sky was lightening. It was still very hot. Pete decided to get a cold Pepsi from the machine and drink it before going out to release the coyote. It was good to have a few minutes to himself.

ANTONIA FRASER

THE MAN WHO WIPED THE SMILE OFF HER FACE

I think of her smiling and certain catch-phrases, songs, will always bring her back to me. Even that cheerful refrain roared out: 'Pack up your troubles . . . and smile, smile, smile.'

Then I remember my Lara with her soft upward curve of the lips. And I weep.

Of course, long before it happened, he had tried to wipe the damned smile off her face. His language not mine; and rather cleaned up. (He didn't say damned.) He simply exploded out of the blue, in that way he had, over nothing.

'I'll wipe that – damned – smile off her face, you see if I don't. And yours too, for that matter, yours too–' He stopped. I waited. What was he going to call me? That was the clue.

Finally he pronounced it sarcastically: 'Yours too, Mother.' Medium bad. Definitely worse than Virginia, much worse than Ginny (used only in a *very* good temper, that is, after two drinks and no more), but not as bad as 'Mummie'. He hated that word, hated to hear it, that is, so it was look-out time when Tom called me that. I once went so far as to ask Lara privately not to use 'Mummie', in front of Tom. After all he was her husband, and for the sake of harmony, what did a little thing like a name matter? Lara laughed: real laughter this time, not just a smile.

'Oh, Mummie! Sorry *Mother* – no that's too formal. Sounds as if we didn't love each other. Kind of Victorian and respectful. As if you're my aged parent. Whereas, on the contrary . . . I'll call you "Darling" – how about that? If I remember. That way I'll call you both "Darling", you and Tom. But I can't call you Virginia, let alone Ginny. The trouble is, for twenty-three years I've been calling you Mummie.'

I suppose, looking back with as much detachment as I can – not a great deal under the circumstances – that was indeed the trouble. She had been calling me Mummie for twenty-three years, and she had been calling Tom 'Darling' for only two years one month at the time of this conversation; two years and a half when *it* happened.

When Tom first met my Lara, she was twenty. Or rather that was when he saw her, and as he put it, fancied her something rotten, those long legs in her little white shorts, her figure (not the word he actually used) in her skinny T-shirt. His language was always so coarse! And the man matched the language.

He saw Lara at the Plantagenet Tennis Club where she some-times worked as a pro. She'd have liked to work there all the time, and heaven knows, the members would have been happy enough. I can tell you, everyone always wanted to book Lara. But the other girls got mean behind her back, said she pinched other people's clients, that sort of thing. Wouldn't let her be permanent on the staff. Pure jealousy; it upset me, but Lara ignored it. She concentrated on other things.

'Oh Mummie, forget it. Trust me,' she'd say jokingly, 'I'm working on our future.'

Then the day came when Tom did manage to play with Lara: thus infuriating Sam, his regular coach, I believe. But it was simply a mix up. Tom got the impression Sam was sick, and Sam never got his message that he wanted to play that day. Lara was available and so quite naturally she filled in. Nothing more to it than that.

Lara came rushing home to me with the news: 'Mummie, let me tell you about this brilliant man I just met. He's fabulous. Tall, dark and handsome. Well, to be honest, quite tall, very dark and not particularly handsome.'

'And rich?' I asked lightly. It was a bit of fun between us.

One day Lara would find a fellow who was tall, dark, handsome and rich. He'd look after her and she'd look after me. I regarded her expression. The famous natural smile made it difficult to read sometimes, even for me. She'd had it since babyhood, even in repose, so that at school they ticked her off.

'Stop smiling, Lara.'

'I can't, Miss Hopkinson, it's my natural curve.' Plenty of hilarity at that! Even at eleven years old, Lara was an eye-catcher.

'I believe he is quite rich,' said my Lara, deadpan. 'He's called Tom Barney.' Lara certainly knew how to deliver a punchline. *Tom Barney*. Phew.

'He's a member?'

'He doesn't play regularly. Of course he's abroad a lot. The boat. The plane. The deals. You know.'

'I know. Or rather I can guess.' It was my turn to smile.

After it happened, people pretended that Lara hooked Tom Barney, went out to get him and duly made the catch. Everything had been carefully planned: so that we, or rather I, deserved what came to me. How ridiculous!

Jealousy again. People are so cruel. As you can see, Tom was the one who made the first move, went after her. In those days he loved her, worshipped her, adored her. No blows, no rages. It took him ages to persuade her to marry him – after all, he was twice her age. To put it another way, he was old enough to be her father, or rather her parent, her surviving parent, me. Tom Barney was exactly the same age as I was.

Then it changed. All the things he shouted at her! 'You cold-hearted bitch, I gave you everything, you—' Bitch was the least of it. The anger always came very suddenly. Right to the last, I never learned to read Tom Barney's moods. Oh yes, it would certainly have been better for my Lara if I had . . . And did she? Even now, I can't tell you that. I can weep for her and I do, but I can't tell you about her secret heart. Like her it's lost to me for ever.

We were so close as mother and daughter, too close many

people said. She was born when I was twenty, and her father – least said about him the better. An older man, a married man. He took advantage of me, forced me – then left me when the baby came, said he had never wanted that, blamed me. The lawyers gave me enough money to bring her up on condition no more demands were made. I had to sign something. So Lara never knew her father. But just because we were so close, Lara kept one precious bit of herself completely private. Lara was like her smile: she tantalised you and she charmed you, and you could never be absolutely certain – but I mustn't think like that. I must go back to thinking about her as she was. My Lara.

I'll go back to the beginning. Did she love Tom? An unlikely thought perhaps, my lovely young girl and that gorilla with his long hairy arms. He used to make me shudder looking at him in the pool at Stair, the house in Kent. But of course I kept the shudder to myself. Yet Lara may have loved Tom – at the beginning, before the anger. After all, he was so crazy about her and she had a loving nature. Everything she wanted was hers: including having me to live with her, to live with them. That was no problem, not really. Lara spoke to him so sweetly about it, and then Tom came to me.

'Ginny,' he said – those were the good old days. 'You've had a tough life. Lara's been telling me about it, your struggle, all you did for her. Come and live with us. You'll have everything you want, your own flat, self-contained, your privacy. Besides, Lara will be travelling with me a lot. She's looking forward to that, her new life. So never fear, we shan't always be on top of you. And then when the babies come—'

'Babies,' I said sharply, more sharply than I meant, 'I don't know about that.' It was a mistake. I just blurted it out; me, usually so controlled, as I've had to be in my life – a struggle indeed, as Lara had told Tom. But Tom made light of it at that point. We were still in the merry days.

'You may not know about babies, Mother' – that was the first time he used the word and then as a sort of joke – 'but I do. And so does my little Lara. Or she will.' I should explain that

Tom's first wife never had any children. She died just about the time Tom made all his money. Just as well, perhaps. She didn't look much from the photograph I saw: they'd been childhood sweethearts or something. After her death, there were a series of women, girls really, all quite young – but of course none quite as young or quite as pretty as my Lara.

So how long were we all three happy? When did Tom's rages really start? The idea of babies – was it that? He certainly went on about babies a good deal, did Tom. I learnt my lesson from that first unfortunate remark and held my peace, although to me of course Lara was still just a baby herself. But Tom was always talking about 'babies before he was too old to enjoy them', sentimental stuff like that. Was it Lara's fault he was so much older than she was? Hardly. No wonder Lara began to say no – no to babies, and no to, well, what makes babies.

Were there any good things to be said about Tom? Yes. Tom was generous. I can be honest enough to say that. The man was a brute – the mere sight of their wedding photograph told you that: him so broad, those heavy shoulders, and Lara so slight, childish even, in the Valentino suit he bought her for the occasion. (I got a Chanel handbag and a pair of shoes too, the real thing – I'd never had anything but imitation before.) A brute, yes, but he was a generous brute.

He worried about me, too, when they were away. It wasn't just me who was forever ringing up, whatever Tom shouted at me later: 'Let her go! Let her bloody well go!' (But the word used was stronger than that.) Tom used to ring me up as well.

'OK there, Ginny? Keeping the home fires burning? Not lonely, I trust? I bet you've found a fellow in the pub and bring him back for a bit of nookie.' That was his idea of a joke – as if I'd ever had anything to do with any man at all once Lara was on the way. However, Tom's question about loneliness was natural enough. Stair was a big house. Any woman on her own might have been lonely there. There were no staff living in: plenty of cleaning ladies, but they came from the village. (Tom saw to it that Lara had to do nothing around the house.)

A secretary came and went. That was Eileen Farleigh, who'd been with him for years: a rather prune-faced woman who had probably hoped to marry Tom when his wife died. Then there was the Greek chauffeur Dimitris (but Tom called him Jimmy).

Maybe the real trouble began when Tom got this idea into his head about Dimitris. When Lara didn't, how shall I put it, respond, Tom began to imagine that Lara actually preferred Dimitris! Another mad jealous notion. Dimitris was pretty enough, I'll grant you that, a pretty boy. He made a lovely pair with Lara. Sometimes they played tennis together with Tom watching.

At first Tom enjoyed that. He'd play with Lara first, then sit there by the court, sweating, not even bothering to shower first. Gazing at Lara as she played a single with Dimitris, wearing the brief white tennis dress with the pleated skirt which he loved. He'd ask for 'that sexy pie-frill one'. Then he just lay back there commenting on the game.

'She's knocking you all over the court, isn't she, Jimmy? How do you like that from my gorgeous girl?' He'd shout things like that. I noticed that Dimitris never answered. But sometimes following that kind of remark he'd suddenly hit one very hard shot which would go just a little too close to his boss. That was all. Nothing, nothing whatsoever for Tom to complain about. And Lara never let anything like that ruffle her. She just smiled.

Later Lara swam in the pool with Dimitris. To relax when it was hot. Not a stitch between them. Skinny dipping, Lara called it. (That was when Tom was away but Eileen Farleigh must have reported it: a troublemaker, the secretary, from the first; jealous of Lara for being so pretty, and yes, so young.) Two children together: Lara and Dimitris. It was all so innocent.

But Tom couldn't believe it was innocent. He wouldn't. To the coarse, all things are coarse. When Lara stopped wanting to travel with him it was because she found it tiring, and frankly business trips, however luxurious, are rather dull for a young woman, aren't they? Nothing to do with me in the first place and nothing to do with Dimitris after that.

So Tom got rid of Dimitris. Couldn't handle it so he sacked him, the beautiful young man. Couldn't stand the competition. The handsome young body being compared to his own. There was an idea that Lara kept in touch with him; I'll never know the truth about that now. If she did, it was probably just kindness, worrying about him. Nothing more to it than that. As for the crazy jealousy, at first Lara just ignored it all. The smile, the famous smile came in handy. The more she didn't answer, didn't fight back – how could she? She had no weapons – the angrier he got.

'I'll wipe the fucking smile off your angelic face.' The fucking smile. I've said it now. Not so bad perhaps – so many people talk like that nowadays – but you should have seen his face, the eyeballs bulging, the hands, the forearms knotted. 'You and your Mummie, the pair of you, scheming icy bitches.' And obscenities followed. A great many of them. 'As for Jimmy,' he used to rant on, 'if I hear that he's been back here again. Sneaking around . . .' More of that frightful language.

'Tom, Tom,' I'd say sweetly. 'Sticks and stones can break my bones but calling names can't hurt me.' Then I'd go quietly to bed, hating to leave her – 'Don't go, Mummie,' she'd say or maybe 'Don't go, Darling.' But I did go, knowing that me remaining there just made it worse.

After all, my room, my little room wasn't so far away: within earshot. You see I soon left the separate flat: Lara saw I felt cut off and lonely. She tried to help me to bear it; even suggested that Tom should let me have one of his guns. (He was a gun freak, well, he would be, wouldn't he? It went with all the dreadful masculinity. And the violence.) All the same, gun or no gun, I felt happier once I was installed in my little nearby room. That way I could protect Lara.

That's how it came about that I heard the row, the bad one, the terrible one, the one that finally wiped the smile off my Lara's face.

It began as usual with the shouting. Something to do with Dimitris maybe: Tom had an idea that Dimitris had been seen hanging about the house when Tom was off in Switzerland. But sooner or later he got off the subject of Dimitris. By the way, if Dimitris did sometimes come back, in spite of being forbidden by Tom, as Eileen Farleigh testified later, he only did so to collect a few things. Even Eileen knew that he wasn't there that night – it turned out Dimitris was miles away, drinking in some pub or other (he did like his drink – but then he was a Greek, as Lara pointed out, and used to a hot climate). There were just the three of us in the house that night, Lara, Tom and me. And soon Tom was back to the same old theme. How cold Lara was to him. Hot shouts about coldness. After that he began to beat her up. I heard the sounds, her cries.

I swear it. They said they didn't find marks, except the marks where he clutched her on her wrists (my Lara always bruised easily). But I'm quite sure that when I rushed out, he was really hitting her. Even if it hadn't quite started he would have hit her sooner or later. It was all a matter of time.

'Mummie,' my Lara cried out. 'Help me! He's going to kill me. Save me. You know what to do.'

Tom looked at me. I had one hand behind my back.

'Oh here's Mummie,' he sneered. 'Mummie's feeling lonely, is she? Mummie's feeling sad. Come out of her burrow to look after her poor little girl . . . well, I can tell you, Mother, this is one little girl who can look after herself. Did you train her specially to be like that? Come to think of it, who better? You grabbing ice-cold—' Obscenities followed. 'Now look who's doing the grabbing,' he ended.

Then he put his hand, his big, dark, hairy hand on her breast. She was panting in the thin silk shirt she wore – he loved her in silk, no bra of course. I saw his hand on her breast, and the silk moving as though in time to it.

'Mummie,' screamed Lara, 'do it!' Then I took the gun from behind my back, the gun Lara had got Tom to give me.

Afterwards she told them that she tried to take the gun away from me, but that wasn't true. It happened as I've said. Lara looked at me and said for the third time: 'Go on, Mummie, do it.' Then she added an odd thing. I've never forgotten it. 'Make me free,' said my Lara. And for the first time the curve, the gentle upward curve I loved, was gone from her mouth. She looked hard, determined, a woman. My baby was gone. And I did it for her. I made her free.

I shot Tom Barney as he stood there, so his blood splashed on her clean silk shirt, soiling it, before he keeled over and fell, heavily at her feet.

The people who put me here, all of them, the judge, the jury, the lawyers, all wanted to establish that I did it out of jealousy. My own lawyer talked a lot about a jealous impulse, that sort of thing. Said that if I could make out I acted in a sudden fit of jealous anger, it would go down better in front of the judge. But what did he know about mothers? He didn't even have any children of his own (I asked him). He could never understand that I did it to make her free. As she begged me: 'Go on Mummie, do it.'

It wasn't my impulse. It was hers, Lara's.

And now my Lara is gone from me, won't speak to me, won't even come and visit me in prison. She said terrible things about me at the trial – well, I expect her lawyers made her do that. How I'd ruined her life with my demands! How she'd tried to help me, after my unhappy life (and her unhappy childhood) and Tom too had tried to help me. How in the end I determined to come between them, and in my mad jealousy – because I couldn't do that, and Lara really loved Tom – I killed him. I never betrayed her, not even when she married Dimitris. I had to read about that in the newspaper: Lara never told me, never sent me a message. But still I never betrayed her.

I can bear prison. My whole life has been a prison, in a way, with just my love for Lara like a bright window. But how can I bear life without her? I think of my Lara, and the gentle upward curve her lips once had, and I weep.

MICHAEL GILBERT

THE MAN WHO WAS RECONSTITUTED

Mrs Manisty heard the car coming when it was a quarter of a mile away.

The road she was walking along was a narrow one, serving Sibthorpe Village. At the point she had reached a much larger road came in on the right. The car was moving fast. Rather too fast, she thought, for that particular road, but the driver, who was evidently expecting the turning, slowed in good time and changed down before swinging round. At that moment there was a sharp detonation, not much louder than the noise her ancient Morris used to make when it back-fired. The car made no attempt to correct its right-hand turn, but continued its swing, hit the telegraph post at the corner of the road and burst into flames.

Mrs Manisty, who was not lacking in courage, started to run towards it, but was driven back by the heat. There was a telephone box at the exit from Sibthorpe Village. She started back to it, as fast as her middle-aged legs would carry her.

'Yes,' said Elfe. 'I remember reading the account of the inquest. They were referred to as scientists in the employment of the Ministry of Defence. Salmundsen and Prescott. Two of your men, Michael?'

'Yes.'

'That would be Dr Olaf Salmundsen. I know about him, of course. Who was Prescott?'

'Fred Prescott. Head of our Documents Section.'

'I see. Yes. I thought the coroner was being a shade tactful. I suppose you'd warned him not to dig too deep.'

'I did have a word with him,' said Michael Harriman. 'He promised to co-operate as far as he could. The trouble was that the only witness, a Mrs Manisty, had a mind of her own. He tried to get her to say that the car swung out of control, hit the telegraph post, exploded and caught on fire. She wouldn't be bullied. She was quite firm. She said the explosion came first.'

'Which of them was right?'

'The woman. When we took the car down we saw exactly what had happened. Someone had planted one of our latest incendiary devices underneath the petrol tank. Small, but immensely powerful. We call it Tiny Tim. It locks on magnetically. Also, the connecting rod in the steering linkage had been partly cut through. The first swing to the right activated the bomb *and* finished off the connecting rod.'

'I see,' said Elfe. 'Yes, I'm sorry.'

He said it sincerely, but a lot of things were puzzling him. He was not surprised that the discussion was taking place at his office. That was in accordance with protocol. Chief Inspector Harriman was head of the anti-terrorist section of MI5. Elfe, as an Assistant Commissioner, and head of the Special Branch, was greatly senior to him in rank and appointment. No. What was odd was that they should be seeking to involve him in a matter which, on the face of it, lay exclusively in their own field.

'Do you suppose,' he said, 'that this was an IRA riposte for the killing of Dr Quilty?'

Dr Quilty, as everyone knew, but no one could prove, was the main IRA explosives expert. His last exploit had been the blowing up of an SAS leave bus. When, some months later, the car Dr Quilty was in had swung out of control and met a lorry head on, his death had been brought in as an accident. Harriman, who seemed to be reading Elfe's mind, said, 'That's right. He was killed in the same way as Salmundsen and Prescott. Tiny Tim under the petrol tank and the brake rod half cut.'

'On your orders?'

'Certainly not. We were glad to see the last of him, but we didn't organise it. It was a solo effort by one of our men. Frank Oadby. His brother had been in that SAS bus.'

'He admitted it?'

'He was proud of it. We had to get rid of him. But somehow the truth got out, so he became target number one for the opposition. Even though he was no longer one of our men, we had to protect him.'

'Of course. You arranged for him to disappear.'

'Right. You'll understand that when we destabilise an agent the details are handled by as few men as possible. In this case two men only. Dr Salmundsen, who built his new face for him, and Fred Prescott, who did all the paperwork himself, personally. Made out his new passport and driving licence, set up the bank accounts and organised the insurance side. I knew what was being done, but none of the details.'

'After the accident, you examined their offices?'

'Of course. We went through Dr Salmundsen's records – against strenuous opposition from his lady secretary who knew nothing about the work he did for the Department. And we took Prescott's desk and office to pieces. We found nothing. Any relevant papers must have been in Salmundsen's brief-case.'

'Which was in the car?'

'We found the remains of one and some charred remnants of papers in it. Our lab boys have been working on them for the last month, but they're not hopeful.'

'So,' said Elfe thoughtfully. 'Old Oadby has vanished. New Oadby exists. Somewhere. And you know nothing about him. Why not let him rest?'

'And get away with the murder of two of our men?'

Elfe stared at him.

'We'd lodged him in a safe house at Sibthorpe while Prescott did the preliminary paper work. Then he and the doctor went down to finish the job. They were there for a week. Plastic surgery can't be rushed. Whilst they were there, their car was in the garage. Oadby kept his motor-bike there and had the only key. So the car was wholly at his disposal. Quite clearly he rigged up the same trap as he had for Quilty. The job had his signature all over it.'

'I see,' said Elfe slowly. The complications were beginning to dawn on him. 'So he got rid of the only two men who knew the actual details of his new identity?'

'That's right. When he got on to his motor-bike and rode away from Sibthorpe, he was riding into limbo.'

'But why?'

'Limbo's a useful state to be in, if you're planning to blackmail the government, wouldn't you say?'

Elfe, for once in his life, was past saying anything.

'He'd been voted ten thousand pounds – against Treasury opposition – to help him find his feet in his new life. He thought it totally inadequate. And said so. Now he's asking for more. His first suggestion is fifty thousand pounds.'

'Then he's been in touch with you?'

'Yes. By letter. On unidentifiable paper. Posted in central London.'

'And if you refused?'

'All he said was that he would make his presence felt.'

'You took his threat seriously?'

'When you realise that he not only knows a great deal about explosives – I wonder how many Tiny Tims he managed to help himself to? – but also possesses the most intimate knowledge of our organisation, why, certainly we took him seriously.'

'And you want Special Branch to find him?'

'It seemed to us that you were best equipped to do so.'

Elfe thought about it. He said, doubtfully, 'It's true that we have some experience in tracking down terrorists and cranks. But in those cases we usually have *some* lead. Something to start on.'

'We can give you all details of Oadby's past existence.'

'Details which have been efficiently and carefully rubbed out by your own experts. Correct?'

Noting the expression on Harriman's face he added, 'We'll do our best.'

Guy Horsey had recently been posted as second-in-command to Harriman. Don Mainprice, who was then heading MI5, had recommended him warmly. He said, 'He's a brainy chap, Michael. Full of ideas. Ex-RN.'

Harriman, who was sceptical about recruits, had a word with a naval friend, who had laughed immoderately. When he could speak he had said, 'Guy Horsey? He's a freak. Of course, you might find him useful. After all, most of your boys are mad. He should fit in well.'

Ignoring this, Harriman said, 'What's his particular form of insanity?'

'There were a lot of stories about him. The only one I know for certain is that when he was a junior sub-lieutenant he invented an improved quick-firing mechanism and sold it, through a third party, to the Admiralty. When they discovered that the money had gone to a serving officer they nearly had a fit. And tried to get the money back. They're still trying. It was about then that Horsey decided to quit. I wish you luck of him.'

In the short time he had been working with him, Harriman had discovered two things about Guy Horsey. That he talked a lot; and that he was constitutionally lazy. In spite of this he liked him and found him refreshing.

His first assignment had been to keep an eye on the Oadby investigation and to report progress, if any.

'Elfe and all the little elves,' he said, 'have been working their fingers to the bone trying to solve the problem you've set them. It's like a mad crossword puzzle with lots of clues, but none that lead to any actual words. They know his height and his weight and his age and the size of his feet and the length of his legs and where he was vaccinated and how many teeth he's had out—'

'How about his new bank account?'

'No luck there. He was paid off in cash. If it went into the bank, it probably went into accounts he'd already set up under different names. Oh, they found his motor-bike. Fifty miles away, in a pond. Another dead end.'

'Suppose we stop looking at the negative side and approach the problem positively.'

'Good thinking, Chief,' said Horsey insubordinately. 'But what exactly had you in mind?'

'He said he'd make his presence felt. I read that as a threat. The place he's most likely to attack is this office. He used to work here and knows all about our security measures. We'll have to change them and tighten them up. Have a word with Oliphant.'

Oliphant was head of office staff. With his red-cheeked face he looked, thought Horsey, more like Father Christmas without his beard than an ex-sergeant major in the Guards. He had already had one or two stately rebukes from him over papers left lying about and doors left unlocked. He said, 'Can I tell him what it's all about?'

'Yes. But no one else. If anyone else asks, blame the IRA. One other thing. Have you made anything out of that paper?'

The laboratory, after two months of patient work with screens and colour photography had produced one page from Dr Salmundsen's notebook which had been protected by its central position in that book. On the page, on separate lines, was what appeared to be:

Gee hct/mit m/br con t/30gr wx eacb/Haem/Tight mass/New Lst.

'Pretty cryptic,' said Horsey. 'And not helped by the fact that like all doctors his handwriting was almost illegible anyway. Would it be all right if I showed it to a friend of mine?'

'What sort of friend?'

'He's an American I met when I was in the Navy. His name's

Freund. Otto Freund. A most interesting man. As a matter of fact he used to do the same job for the CIA that Salmundsen did for us. He'd be just the chap to tell us what this means, don't you think?'

Slightly comforted by the thought that he'd be dealing with a fellow professional, Harriman said, 'As long as you're sure he can be trusted to keep his mouth shut.'

Fearful that even this qualified permission might be withdrawn Horsey hurried off, pausing on his way out of the office to talk to Oliphant, who listened patronisingly and then explained the additional precautions he had already taken. They seemed more than adequate. Horsey said, 'Excellent, excellent,' and sped out. He was making for the Special Services Club where Dr Freund could usually be found at lunchtime.

Harriman spent an uneasy afternoon regretting that he had allowed one more man to be brought into a secret which, if it became common knowledge, would make his department the laughing-stock of the security services in five continents.

He was still worrying about this when he reached his house in Twickenham, a small house in a street of small houses behind the Rugby Football Ground. It was not a fortress, but it was guarded, with mortice locks on the front and back doors and window locks on all the downstairs windows. The police, who knew about him, kept an eye on it.

He slipped his key into the lock of the front door and, as he opened the door, it came out to meet him, knocking him flat. He felt the impact almost before he registered the explosion. He climbed slowly back onto his knees, more dazed than hurt, as his nearest neighbour, a solid Scotsman, hurdled the intervening fence and came to his help.

He said, 'Would you care to use my house? Yours is in a bit of a mess.'

'Must telephone the police.'

'I've done that. Come along. I'll give you a hand.'

Harriman went gratefully. A crowd was beginning to collect. By the time Superintendent Naylor of the local force arrived, he had downed a glass of the Scotsman's whisky and was feeling better.

'We've alerted your people,' said Naylor. 'They're sending a team along. They warned us not to touch anything until they came.'

When the team had finished taking photographs and samples they gave the house a clean bill. The explosive packet, they calculated, must have been in the post box behind the front door. The door, a stout one, had absorbed most of the force of the explosion. The damage had not been excessive.

'We've talked to your neighbours,' said Naylor. 'One of them says she did notice a man. Just after your daily woman had left. He walked round to the back and used his own key on the back door. He did it all so openly that she thought nothing of it.'

'Did she describe him?'

'Not really. She only saw his back view. She said he was bulky. Incidentally, he seems to have left a note for you. It was on the kitchen table.'

The note said, 'Just a demonstration. One-way activator. Might have been two-way. Think about it.'

'Do you understand it?' said Naylor.

'I'm not a technical expert in the field of explosives,' said Harriman. 'But I can get it translated.'

At the office next morning he showed it to Horsey who grinned and said, 'He wasn't exaggerating, was he?'

'If you understand it, perhaps you could explain it.'

'It's simple enough,' said Horsey. He said it with such ineffable smugness that Harriman understood at once why the Navy had dispensed with his services. 'Activation can be one-way or two-way. In this case it was one-way. The opening of the door was all that was necessary to detonate the explosive. If it had been two-way the opening of the door would have primed it, the closing of the door would have detonated it.'

'By which time I should have been inside and standing over it. Yes. It certainly makes you think.'

'I've been doing a bit of thinking myself,' said Horsey. Noting the look in his superior's eye he added hastily, 'I had a talk with Freund. He was very interested in that piece of paper and took it away to work on it. He telephoned just before you got in to say that he'd reached what he called an arguable solution. He'd be glad to come round and discuss it.'

'The sooner the better.'

Otto Freund had the massive judicial appearance which seems to clothe Americans when they attain eminence in business or the professions. He had brought with him and spread out on the table an enlargement of the original page. Under six times magnification the scribbled letters stood out starkly. It was now evident that, in two places at least, they could have been misread.

'I would offer the supposition that the second group is "mil-m" rather than "mit-m" and if this is correct, then, again, when we substitute "l" for "t", the third group reads "br-con-l". This seems to produce a more logical sequence.'

'I'm glad you find it so,' said Harriman.

'I only assert that it's logical because in our trade, when one is making alterations to a subject's appearance, one always follows the same order, starting at the top of the head, with the hair. Then other hirsute appendages. Next, the eyes. Then the cheeks and general shape and colour of the face. Then the nose. Finally the jaw and lower frontal, always the most difficult feature. Assuming this to be so, "gee hct" will be some form of haircut. Unfortunately I am not acquainted with all the current English styles.'

'Guardee haircut,' said Horsey. 'Short back and sides.'

'Very possibly. In which case the next group calls for a military mustache. One of those short-clipped affairs, I assume, along the upper lip.'

'Then brown contact lenses,' suggested Harriman. 'Oadby had rather prominent light blue eyes.'

'That must be right. The next two groups are most important. They call for an injection of thirty grammes of wax – that's more

93

than an ounce by your measurements – under each cheek bone. The effect would be a rounding out of the cheeks, which would then be coloured with ochre. Haematite, you note, rather than limonite. This would produce a bronzed, open-air effect, with a tinge of redness. The nose they seem to have left alone. Then the last two groups relate to the chin. The tightening of the masseter muscle would bring the jaw forward, an effect which could be heightened by substituting a new and more prominent lower set of false teeth.'

There was a moment of silence. Harriman was trying to visualise the new Oadby. What he had heard was ingenious and almost certainly correct; but not entirely helpful. He said, 'I don't want to seem ungrateful, doctor. I'm sure you've read our riddle for us. But unfortunately the type they suggest – the military or ex-military man – is very common in this country.'

Horsey said, 'You haven't thought it through, sir.' The fact that, unusually, he added 'sir' to this impertinence made Harriman look at him sharply.

'I presume Oadby was photographed when he joined the Department. I know I was.'

'Of course. Front view and both profiles. Colour prints.'

'Then we can reconstruct him. Get a suitable skull from one of the teaching hospitals. We've got his dental records so we can fit in the appropriate teeth and build on that.'

'Bearing in mind,' said Freund, 'that the skin of your model can't be plastic. It will have to be expandable. Might I suggest the material out of an uncoloured child's balloon?'

Both men looked at Harriman. He said, 'All right. I understand what you're getting at. I'll put it in hand. It'll take a little time. Say a fortnight at least.'

Freund, who was consulting a massive pocket diary, said, 'I could manage October 15th. At least, I hope I'm going to be asked to carry out what looks to me like a truly unique experiment.'

'I think you've earned the right,' said Harriman, with a smile.

*

'By God,' said Harriman. 'It's him. Him, and no one else.'

It was an astonishingly life-like face that looked up at him from the table; the black hair worn rather long framing the pale cheeks, prominent blue eyes, petulant mouth and weak chin.

He decided that what made it so startlingly life-like was the rubber skin which had been painstakingly stretched over the wax base. Under it, the face of Oadby was alive; alive, saturnine and faintly amused.

'There's your patient, Doctor,' he said. 'Carry on.'

Freund, who had put on surgical gloves, was standing behind the table. He had brought with him an assortment of syringes, clips and tweezers. Horsey, like a theatre nurse, had taken post at his side.

'No need to waste time over the hair. We just remove the old wig and substitute the new one. The same with the mustache. That goes straight on.' He adjusted the adhesive strip delicately, without disturbing the lips which were smiling, as at some private joke.

'Then the contact lenses – the smallest tweezer, please. We'll deal with the chin next and leave the cheeks to the last. We can't do anything about the masseter muscle, because he hasn't got one, but a small wedge in the jaw will produce the same effect. The lower set of teeth can be changed now. Fine. This is where we reach the vital part.'

At which point the telephone on Harriman's desk rang. When he ignored it, it went on ringing. He strode across, started to say something brusque and cut it off.

'Sorry, sir. I didn't know it was you.'

Don Mainprice said, 'This is a warning order, Michael. The Prime Minister will be with you in about twenty minutes' time. He's asked to see all our sections.'

The shortness of the notice did not surprise Harriman. For obvious reasons the Prime Minister's movements were not advertised in advance. He said, 'Do you want us lined up outside with sloped microscopes?'

Mainprice laughed. 'No, just carry on. I gather it's some

experiment you're doing. He'll be interested in that, I'm sure. A new identikit arrangement, isn't it?'

'Something like that, sir.' Harriman replaced the receiver and said, 'Sorry you were interrupted, Doctor.'

'As I was saying, it's the sub-cutaneous injection of wax that makes the real difference. It alters the whole shape and character of the face. Actors achieve the same effect, temporarily, by wearing pads inside their cheeks.'

He drove in first one and then the other of the large hypodermic syringes and depressed the plunger. As he did so, the hollow gauntness of the face changed into a robust cheerfulness.

'A touch, now, of the ochre paint. The small brush, please.'

Freund was so engrossed in what he was doing that he did not notice the effect which the transformation was having on the other two.

'Father Christmas, without his beard,' whispered Horsey.

'It can't be.'

'It most certainly is. Or his twin brother.'

Harriman grabbed the telephone on his desk and dialled. 'Ronnie?' he said. 'Michael here. Tell me, how long has Oliphant been with us?'

'Not very long, sir. We had to get someone quickly, you remember, when Westcomb died.'

'How long?' It came out almost as a shout.

'Got the file here, sir. If you could hold on a moment. Seven weeks at the end of this week. I hope there's nothing wrong. We got him from Commissionaires Ltd. They're usually very reliable. They'd only had him on their books for a few days, but he had excellent references—'

But Ronnie was talking into a dead telephone. Harriman had rung off and was dialling again.

'Frank? Michael here. Listen. I want two of your heavies and I want them at the double. In my office. Must be here in five minutes.'

'Do my best, sir.'

There was nothing obviously menacing in the appearance of the two men who came in quietly. Both looked and carried themselves like men in high training. One had red hair, the other black. Apart from this, with their similar faces, white, flat and hard, they might have been twins.

Harriman said, 'One of our staff – I've sent for him – has very possibly planted explosives somewhere in this building. Maybe with a device for detonating them. If I give you ten minutes could you persuade him to tell you about it?'

'Depends on the man, sir. Normally five minutes would be enough. Is there somewhere quiet where we could operate?'

'There's a washroom at the end of the passage, through that door.'

'Just the job.'

At that moment Oliphant came in. He said, 'You wanted me, sir,' saw the two men and broke for the door. Black hair was there first, caught him by one wrist and jerked his arm up behind his back. Red hair said, 'Don't break his arm, Charlie. Not yet.'

Then the three men disappeared into the passage and the door was shut.

Horsey, who was at the window, said, 'There's a bit of a crowd beginning to collect. How do they always hear about these things?'

'Bush telegraph.'

'What are you going to do if the PM turns up before Oliphant has started talking?'

'We'll have to evacuate the building.'

'Difficult to explain why.'

'Very,' said Harriman. He had his watch in his hand.

The passage door opened and red hair appeared. He said, 'We've got what you want, sir. He wasn't very brave. The stuff is planted under the platform in the conference room. The switch is outside the door. There's a sixty-second delay after it's been activated. No doubt that was to let your chap get clear. When this function is finished you ought to get one of your experts to dismantle it. Tricky to interfere with it now. Might set it off.'

'But unless someone actually presses the switch, it's safe?'

'That's what he says. No reason to be telling lies about it now.'

Horsey said, 'Here comes the car.'

Harriman took a deep breath. He said, 'We'll have to play this straight down the middle. Look after that chap for us. He's wanted for at least two murders.' And to Freund, 'If the PM comes up here could you spin him some story about the work we're doing. Then we'll all go down and sit round the platform and pray.'

'And don't tell him about Oliphant – I mean Oadby.'

'Certainly not. Poor chap, he's got enough to worry about.'

The Prime Minister advanced to the edge of the platform and switched on a professional smile. He said, 'It has been a pleasure and a privilege to gain, this morning, some idea of the work you are doing. I was particularly gratified to find our American friends co-operating with you.' He smiled at Freund, who smiled back. 'Your work may sometimes seem to you theoretical and dull, but believe me, it contributes most materially to the safety of all of us—'

REGINALD HILL

THE MAN WHO DEFENESTRATED HIS SISTER

'Certainly, when I threw her from the garret window to the stony pavement below, I did not anticipate that she would fall so far without injury to life or limb.'

Inspector Bunfit glanced at his constabular scribe to make sure he was recording this incriminating admission. Under the weight of that benign gaze, a pencil point snapped, but the man had two more in reserve. It was a foolish officer who appeared unprepared in the service of Bunfit of the Yard.

Satisfied, the inspector returned his attention to the young man seated at the other side of the table. Slightly built, with thin, sensitive features, he had eyes of cerulean blue which met Bunfit's scrutiny with unblinking candour.

'So what you mean to say, Mr Arlecdon, is that it was your intention to kill her?'

'What?' The sky-blue clouded with shock. 'Of course it wasn't! Kill Alice? It would be like killing myself. She is my twin, Inspector, the other half of me. The better half. As children we seemed to have but one mind, one spirit. It was only as we left that innocent age that she started to draw a curtain between us.'

'A curtain? You mean like you shared a room?'

'No! I speak figuratively,' cried the young man. 'What we shared were thoughts and feelings. I felt this as a gift from heaven, a source of indescribable joy. But Alice, alas, as we grew older clearly came to find it an intolerable burden.'

The scribing constable was beginning to look lost.

Bunfit said, 'Yes, sir, I understand, sir. But you see my difficulty. It is my experience, born of more 'n thirty years observing the – saving your presence – criminal classes, that when a young man throws a young woman out of a fourth-floor window, his intention is generally homicidal.'

'I've explained all this. I was in a fury, a blind rage. I called her names. Foul names, God forgive me. She ran to me, trying to calm my anger, begging me to hear her defence. But I was beyond reason and I flung her from me with all the force I could muster.'

'Yes. I see. You flung her through the window.'

'Not intentionally, I swear. It was a warm night, the casement was open, the sill low. One moment she was there. The next, gone.'

He buried his face in his hands as if to shut out that dreadful vacuity.

Bunfit shifted his comfortable frame in his uncomfortable chair. It was late, and he would be lucky if he got to bed while it was still early, but he didn't mind. Soon he was to retire and a desert of uninterrupted nights stretched ahead of him. It was more than twenty years since he had risen to his present eminence on the back of his not inconsiderable part in solving the famous Eustace Diamonds case, and broken nights had always seemed a small part to pay for that tremor of respect and fear when Bunfit of the Yard appeared on the scene of a crime.

It occurred to him that this might well be his very last case. It would be nice if it turned out a good 'un.

'You all right, Mr Arlecdon?' he enquired with unfeigned solicitude. A sick suspect is to a detective policeman what a dead mouse is to a cat. You can poke it and prod it, but if you can't make it run, all the fun's gone out of the game.

The young man took a deep breath.

'Yes, yes. I'm sorry.'

'Good. Then why don't you carry on a-telling me what happened next?'

'Next?'

'That's right. You'd just been a-telling me how the unfortunate young lady tripped over the sill and fell through the window. What did you do then?'

'I don't know. I honestly can't remember. In fact I can remember very little from the moment Alice disappeared till the moment when your sergeant came to the Settlement and . . . arrested me. Am I arrested, Inspector?'

'Helping with inquiries,' said Bunfit cautiously.

'Then of course I'm very glad to help. And perhaps in return you can help me. To remember, I mean. How did it come about that you were able to find me so quickly at the Settlement?'

The Settlement was the bricks-and-mortar manifestation of a noble project whereby young men with a university education were enabled to exercise, and exorcise, their missionary zeal without the inconvenience of long sea journeys and tropical disease. The East End of London offering the nearest home-grown equivalent to a tribe of untutored savages, it was here the good work began. Once lured into contact by gifts of food and shelter, the benighted natives were given access to such revelations of culture and religion as the worthy young settlers were equipped to make.

Arlecdon's more material contribution was in the field of medicine. Still a student, he was devoting his summer vacation to this good work and making sufficient of a mark for his name to be remembered when other more etherial settlers remained in airy anonymity.

But Bunfit was not yet ready to reveal all the cards in his hand.

'As to that, we'll get there just now, sir,' he said. 'But perhaps this will help jog your memory.'

He plucked a sheet of paper from the table top and went on, 'This here's an account given by one of our officers, Constable

Cox, of his part in these strange happenings in Brawling Alley. I should like you to listen carefully, sir.'

He coughed behind his hand; then, adopting the tone and manner which made even eminent defence counsel hesitate to hint a doubt of such a self-evident Custodian of Truth, began to read.

'On Saturday twenty-eighth of July eighteen eighty-eight, at approximately fifteen minutes before midnight, I was proceeding down Brick Lane in a southerly direction at the end of my shift when I became aware of a hullaballoo, and shortly afterwards I observed a party of female persons come out of Brawling Alley. When I got up alongside of them, I realised as how several of these female persons were known to me, in my professional capacity, as common prostitutes. I also realised they had drink taken, and when I admonished them as to their hullaballoo, they became abusive and began to threaten me with assault. Upon which, I played my rattle, and Sergeant Gager who happened to be proceeding up Brick Lane in a northerly direction in company of my relief, Constable Vector, came running to join me. With their assistance I quelled the disorder and set about putting the women under arrest. Upon which, one of the prisoners, Mary Ann Nicholls, commonly called Polly, protested, "What's your game, fishface? Stopping a few working girls having a bit of a birthday party when there's corpses lying in the street!" I asked her what she meant, and she pointed into Brawling Alley and said, "Look there if'n you don't believe me." Upon which Sergeant Gager and I proceeded along Brawling Alley in a westerly direction, and in the light of my bull lamp, we observed a body lying on the pavement.'

Bunfit paused and examined Arlecdon keenly. The young man had the rapt expression of a child listening to a favourite bedtime story. Or a pet mouse anticipating cheese.

'Go on, Inspector,' he urged.

Bunfit laid the statement on the table and, never taking his eyes off Arlecdon's face, he said, 'This body was lying precisely where it might have been anticipated your sister, Miss Alice, would be lying after her fall from the garret window.'

'Yes. Yes.'

'The only thing is, sir. This body as Constable Cox and Sergeant Gager discovered. It was not the body of a young woman, sir. It was the body of a young man.'

Arlecdon's blue eyes opened wide, not in surprise but in recognition.

'Ah. Of course. Purley!'

'That's right, sir,' said Bunfit, rather disappointed to find his mouse so co-operative. 'George Addison Lestrange Purley, Esquire. You know . . . knew him, sir?'

'Yes. At Cambridge. God forgive me, it was through me that the swine met my sister.'

'He knew Miss Alice as well then?'

'Knew her? Do you understand nothing? He was her seducer! It was in order to meet him that she went to that dreadful place last night.'

'Ah, I'm with you now, sir,' said Bunfit. 'You surprised them, is that it? So tell me, sir; did you throw Mr Purley out of the window before or after the defenestration of your sister?'

He produced the word modestly. Promotion had made him conscious of certain educational deficiencies and he had surreptitiously followed a programme of self-improvement at the Institute. His historical studies of the origins of the Thirty Years War had introduced him to the concept of defenestration, but hitherto he had had no occasion for the actual use of the word.

Arlecdon was now regarding him in amazement, but it was not at his vocabulary.

'What are you suggesting?' he demanded. 'I don't deny I would have gladly taken a horsewhip to the rogue, but I certainly never threw him out of any window.'

'Then how do you account for his presence on the pavement, sir?' demanded Bunfit.

'Because God is not mocked,' cried the young man, his eyes purpurescent with religious fervour. 'And sometimes He reminds us of His immutable laws with a most savage irony. How else may we explain that Purley, coming late to his evil assignation, should have been occupying precisely that spot necessary to break Alice's fall and thus preserve her life?'

Inspector Bunfit rose. It was an old maxim of his that when God appeared on the scene, a wise detective left. Though clearly responsible for much, the Deity was not indictable under Common Law.

'If you'll excuse me for a moment, sir, I'll see about some refreshment.'

'Good idea,' said Arlecdon. 'It must be nearly time for breakfast. We rise early at the Settlement, you know. Too early for me, if truth be told. I don't have much of an appetite till luncheon, so don't fuss. Couple of lightly poached eggs and a devilled kidney will do.'

Out in the corridor, Bunfit proceeded in a sou' sou' westerly direction (Cox's style was catching) till he reached a door marked DETECTIVE DEPT – *Knock and Wait*.

He went straight in. A fresh-faced man some ten years his junior, with his feet on a desk and a half-eaten ham sandwich in his hand, greeted him with a grin.

'What ho, guv. Popped out for breakfast?'

Sergeant Gager had risen on the same tide as Bunfit, but had not felt the same need for self-improvement. He was still as indiscriminate with his aspirates as in his Angel infancy, and his head was still glossy with the same oil he had used to dazzle the youthful beauties of Islington in his minority. In contrast to Bunfit's clerical grey suit, he wore a hacking jacket of amber and ochre maculae, and his Doric neck was garlanded with a celluloid collar white enough and a floral necktie bright enough to make the rash gazer wipe his eye.

Bunfit sighed a reproof of his subordinate's posture, language and tailor, but he had learned from long experience that against the incorrigible, even a corrective sigh is wasted breath.

'Don't talk to me of breakfast,' he said. 'Lightly poached egg and devilled kidney his lordship fancies. Some hope!'

'So what's his yarn?'

'He says as how he followed his sister to that crib in Brawling Alley, had a row with her about her fancy man, accidentally threw her out of the window into the alleyway where her fall happened to be broke by this here Purey, hot-footing it below on his way to meet the lady. Did you ever hear the like?'

Gager laughed, not allowing a mouthful of sandwich to inhibit him.

'More 'n 'ot-footing it, I'd say. Seems he wasn't going to hang about saying 'owdidoo when he met her. He was all unbuttoned and his John Thomas was sticking out! Mind you, might 'ave been them there tarts when they found 'im.'

'For heaven's sake, Sergeant,' said Bunfit with distaste. 'Not even them debased creatures would stoop to abusing a dead man.'

'Dying, not dead, remember? He 'ad enough strength to say *Arlecdon*. But I don't mean they was playing with his parts, just 'aving a looksee if 'e were wearing a money belt. There weren't a penny piece in his pockets, so there's no prize for guessing where the poor sod's geldt went.'

'Bloody vultures. You'll be a-charging them with theft then?'

'Not I,' grinned Gager. 'I know a thing worth twice that. Once charged, them gals will clam up tighter 'n a flea's fanny. It's knowing as 'ow they *can* be charged that'll keep 'em co-operative.'

'You'll go too far one of these fine days, Gager,' said Bunfit gloomily. 'Any word from the sawbones yet?'

'Cause of death, fractured skull, is all. Details to follow.'

'You have a word with him, Sergeant. Tell him to keep a sharp eye open for any sign Mr Purey might have been hit by a large falling object. Not that but I'm thinking he'll need a very sharp eye indeed.'

'You ain't hinclined to believe our Mr Arlecdon then?' said Gager mildly.

'If there's plain and if there's fancy, it's my experience you don't go far wrong by sticking to plain,' intoned Bunfit. Then something in Gager's expression alerted him.

'You got any reason to think different, young Gager, you just spit it out,' he said sternly.

'Well, guv, now as you comes to mention it, there may be a couple of reasons you should hang back from calling the young gent a liar to 'is face,' said Gager, tossing the remains of his sandwich on to the desk and swinging his feet on to the floor. From a drawer he plucked a battered volume of Burke's *Peerage and Baronetage*.

'It was 'im being a medical student as rang a bell,' he went on. 'I reckon he ain't just any old Mr Arlecdon, but the son and heir of Sir Ambrose Vasey Arlecdon who just 'appens to be the private and very personal physician of his Royal 'Ighness, the Prince of Wales. That being so, then our Mr Arlecdon, if the gen'lemen of the Press 'ave got it right, is a boyhood chum of young Eddie, the Prince's eldest.'

He's enjoying this, thought Bunfit. He resents me taking the case off of him, so he thinks to embarrass me. Right, lad, you need to get up very early in the morning to embarrass Bunfit of the Yard!

He said, 'I don't care who he may be, Sergeant. You shouldn't need reminding that it's our job to administer the law without fear or favour.'

'Which I takes to mean there's not much fear we won't do them as deserves it a favour. Just my joke.'

'Not funny. You said there was two reasons?'

'That's right. The other is Polly Nicholls. She weren't so pissed as the rest or she 'olds it better, and I've got a sort of statement from 'er.'

'A sort of statement? I've told you, I want no doxies' gossip. What sort of statement's a sort of statement?'

'The sort where I've made notes but she ain't signed anything, not till I'm sure she's saying what we want her to say. Here, take a look.'

'Just give me the gist,' said Bunfit.

'The gist is this,' said Gager, openly enjoying himself now. 'The gals were 'aving their birthday party in the room one of 'em has in Brawling Alley. Balling Alley they should call it, it's a real whore's nest that place. Anyway, they runs out of booze, and one of 'em says she's got a flask of mother's ruin in her crib at the top of Brick Lane, so they all tumble out into the alley, and there in the light from the door they see Purey's body. Only Nicholls now recalls as how there was someone else there, a woman in white sort of kneeling over the body.'

'A woman in white?' said Bunfit sceptically. 'She been reading that what'sit Collins book or what?'

'Don't do much reading, our Polly,' said Gager.

'So why didn't she mention this woman in white before?'

'Says she forgot, but I reckon she thought as how she was another working girl and din't want to nark on her, less'n she had to.'

'Loyalty among whores? You'll make me cry,' sneered Bunfit. 'So what did she do, this woman in white?'

'When she saw the girls, she got up and ran off towards Commercial Street. Polly says she ran sort of funny. Like she was 'urt? I asks. And she says, yes, it could 'ave been that. So it all fits, don't it, guv?'

Bunfit looked down again at the entry in Burke's which confirmed that Lady Arlecdon had given birth to twins, Arthur Ambrose and Alice Victoria, in 1866. There was no getting away from it. It all fitted.

Gager said, 'How's he want his eggs, Inspector?'

'He'll get no eggs till I see things a bit clearer,' said Bunfit furiously. 'Howsoever you look at it, there's a man dead. And where's this woman in white got to, that's what I want to know. But I suppose, seeing as he is who he is . . .' he tapped Burke's accusingly, unhappy at having to make any concession in front of the sergeant '. . . we'd best send word to the Major.'

The Major was Sir James Sholto Mackintosh, head of Scotland Yard these past thirty years and with a title to show for it the past ten, but still known to his subordinates by his old military rank.

'Done,' said Gager complacently.

'Done?' echoed Bunfit.

'I knew as how that's what you'd want, and as I didn't like to interrupt you in the pulpit, I took the liberty.'

'Seems to me you take a lot of liberties, young Gager,' growled Bunfit.

He returned to the interview room feeling he'd lost another round in his long battle with Gager. Though the sergeant was now well in his middle years, in Bunfit's eyes he was still a young upstart whose flash must one day die out in the pan.

But the inspector gave credit where it was due, at least in the privacy of his own thoughts, and though he'd not hesitated to take over what seemed like a promising case, he had to admit it was Gager who'd made all the running so far.

It had been the sergeant who responded to Cox's rattle, the sergeant who heard Purey's last word, the sergeant who sensed a reaction when he repeated the name to the riotous whores.

As Gager put it, getting information from drunk women was like drawing teeth, but by the use of God knows what threats he'd learned that some of them, attracted by curiosity and the promise of a good meal, had tried the University Settlement. The moral diet they'd found less tasty, and after a few days they'd drifted away. But they'd remembered a handsome young doctor who'd shown a lively interest in their occupational ailments and offered not preaching but practical advice and medication.

The Settlement was at the bottom end of Commercial Street. Bunfit, despite his asseverations on the high impartiality of the Law, knew he himself would probably have been much more circumspect in pursuing this line of inquiry. Behind the Settlement project there were powerful, influential people who didn't like the even tenor of their days, and still less of their nights, disturbed.

But Gager hadn't hesitated. He'd hurried down Commercial

Street and hammered at the Settlement door till an irate porter opened up.

The main door, he learned, was locked at nine thirty, after which hour presumably evil stalked the streets like a roaring lion. There was however a side door to which some of the young gentlemen, Mr Arlecdon among them, had keys.

Without more ado, Gager had brushed the porter aside and gone up to Arlecdon's room.

He had found the young gentleman fully dressed though somewhat dishevelled, and in a state of considerable agitation.

Gager had come straight to the point. Had Mr Arlecdon been out tonight? Yes, he had. Had Mr Arlecdon been in the vicinity of Brawling Alley? Yes, he had. In that case, would Mr Arlecdon do Sergeant Gager the favour of accompanying him to Scotland Yard?

It was the decision to have everyone and everything centred at the Yard rather than the local nick which had been Gager's downfall. Bunfit had found himself more and more reluctant to make for home as retirement approached. Tonight after his supper at a chop house in Villiers Street, he had returned to his office to deal with some unimportant business which could quite easily have waited till morning. His reward had been that he was on the spot, perfectly placed to pluck this ripe apple of a case out of his subordinate's hand.

Only now he was beginning to wonder if the wily Gager had not already begun to suspect the worm at the fruit's core and deliberately brought his prize back to the Yard in order that it might be claimed from him!

Perhaps the clever thing would be to follow this good example and put the lid on things till the Major showed his face.

But Arlecdon himself forestalled this discreet course of action.

He rose to his feet as Bunfit re-entered the room, his thin face flushed with excitement, and said, 'It's coming back to me now, Inspector. After Alice fell from the window, I of course rushed to the casement and peered out. It was Stygian gloom out there and I could see nothing. I wanted to hurry straight downstairs and see what had become of her, but my legs were turned to lead. It was, I believed, some form of sympathetic paralysis, by which I mean a condition in which, without physical cause, the body responds to a strong mental stimulus and behaves as if a physical cause were present.'

He paused as if fascinated by the clinical details, then hurried on.

'How long I remained like this I cannot say. But finally I cast off these emotional fetters and ran down the stairs, terrified at the prospect of what I might find. Imagine then my amazement when, instead of the broken body of my beloved sister, I found the corpse of her seducer!'

'Not the corpse, sir,' corrected Bunfit. 'Mr Purey was mortally injured, true, but not yet totally gone from this life.'

'Not dead?' Arlecdon looked at him with consternation. 'If only I had realised . . .'

'So you could have finished him off, you mean?' said Bunfit in a sudden fit of rashness.

'How can you say so? True, he was of all men the one I had least cause to love, but I am training to be a doctor, Inspector, and to men of our profession, all life is sacred.'

He spoke so earnestly Bunfit felt abashed.

'So, thinking as how he was dead, sir, what did you do then?'

'Naturally I cast around for sign of Alice. You can imagine my relief when I found none. For her to have vanished so quickly meant that she must have been uninjured, or only very slightly hurt. My heart sang, believe me, Inspector.'

'I can understand that, sir. What did you do next?'

Arlecdon's face screwed up in the effort of memory.

'I must have gone back to the Settlement,' he said.

'Indeed, sir? It didn't cross your mind that the proper thing to do, the civic thing, was to report this matter to the authorities?'

'I believe I did consider that. But how could I? Think of what it would have meant revealing about my dear sister.'

'I can see as how that might have weighed heavy against it, sir,' agreed Bunfit. 'But in that case, how was it you didn't go a-searching of the lady? I mean, there she was . . . there she may still be a-running round in an hysterical condition, and you don't go a-looking for her!'

Arlecdon subsided into his chair.

'I feel your reproof strongly, Inspector. I was in a state of panic. Like a wounded beast, all I wanted was to get back to my lair. But very quickly a consciousness of poor Alice's plight reasserted itself and I was on the point of going in search of her when your sergeant arrived at my door. You never explained how he got there so quickly, Inspector.'

'Mr Purey spoke your name before he died,' said Bunfit, seeing no reason to withhold this information now. 'Some female persons who first came across him had been clients of yours at the Settlement, it appears, and the name rang a bell.'

'Indeed. How fortunate.'

'Fortunate, sir?' said Bunfit suspecting an irony.

'Because it enabled you to find me so quickly. I would of course have come forward voluntarily once my rationality had returned, but by that time rumours of this sad business might have been bruited far abroad.'

Bunfit was getting his drift. He said, 'I fear, sir, that when it comes to sudden death, there's no keeping quiet about such things.'

'I understand. But there is surely no need to drag an innocent woman's name into the public gaze? A man found dead in an East End alleyway can hardly be so remarkable?'

'Perhaps not, but the coroner will have to be informed, sir.'

'Old Ferdie Sackloe? Then there's no problem. He's a particular friend of my father's.'

It was hard not to respond to the young man's pleasure in a problem solved, and hardly worth not responding, thought Bunfit gloomily. He could see no way this wasn't going to be settled by a typical upper-crust job. So much for his hopes of one last big case to make his exit on.

'Breakfast on its way, is it?' inquired Arlecdon.

'I'll just check, sir,' said Bunfit. It was an act of surrender, no less humiliating for being symbolic.

The Yard did not run to devilled kidneys, but he was promised boiled eggs and toast. At least Gager was no longer around to see his superior's capitulation. As Arlecdon tucked into his breakfast, Bunfit took the scribing constable to prepare the young man's statement. Hushed up the business might be, but he would make sure there was something on the official record.

He was on his way back to the interview room with the document ready for signature when his name was called. He turned to see Major Mackintosh hurrying towards him in the company of a stout, florid man of middling years whose expensively cut clothes looked as if they had been rather hastily thrown on.

'Mr Bunfit,' said the Major. 'This is Sir Ambrose Arlecdon.'

'How do you do, sir?' said Bunfit. 'I hope as how Miss Alice has returned safely.'

'You do, do you? Then you're a fool, sir,' said Sir Ambrose. 'Where's my son? In here? Right.'

And without further ado he went into the interview room, slamming the door behind him.

Bunfit turned indignantly to the Major, but Mackintosh merely compounded the eminent physician's rudeness by snatching the statement out of the Inspector's hand and glancing quickly through it before crumpling it into his pocket.

'Shan't be needing this,' he said. 'Where's Sergeant Gager?'

'He's around somewhere, sir,' said Bunfit, struggling with difficulty to repress his personal outrage. 'He's been a-questioning of the ladies as found Mr Purley.'

'The prostitutes, you mean? Call a spade a spade, man. Get him. I'll be in here.'

Bunfit watched the long, gaunt figure of his superior pass into the main office of the Detective Department. In the long years of his acquaintance with the Major, he had never known the man treat his subordinates with anything but courtesy. Something must be troubling him deeply.

He made inquiry after Gager and discovered that the sergeant had been seen going down the stairs at the main entrance. As he descended the last flight, he saw Gager's glowing face rising towards him like the sun which in truth was already gilding the chimney pots of the sleeping city.

'There you are then,' said Bunfit. 'You're to come with me. The Major's here and he's brought Sir Ambrose Arlecdon.'

'Yes, I know,' said Gager running lightly up the stairs. 'That's where I've been, to 'ave a chinwag with Sir Ambrose's coachman.'

'Why on earth should you want to do that?' grumbled Bunfit.

'Just you listen and you'll soon see,' said Gager. 'I've been a-talking to them girls, off and on, ever since we brought 'em in. Very friendly we got, specially after I promised 'em I'd see there were no charges . . .'

'You promised them what?' exclaimed Bunfit.

'No charges. Stands to reason. Case like this, the nobs ain't going to risk some tart standing up in court and wafting a nice scent of scandal up the news-hounds' noses. Right?'

Bunfit couldn't deny the logic.

'Anyway, I'd got all I could out of 'em with threats, so it made sense to try gratitude.'

'And what did you get from these grateful whores?' demanded Bunfit, urging the sergeant up the stairs.

'All sorts, and not just likorish either. Seems like this woman in white, Miss Alice by her brother's account, 'as been around Brawling Alley for a few weeks now. That 'ere garret is rented out to her, not to Mr Purey, who incidentally is well known to the gals as a young gent with a prodigious appetite for their favours.'

'What are you saying, Gager? That this weren't no romantic assignation, but a common pick-up? That Sir Ambrose Arlecdon's daughter has set herself up as a common Whitechapel whore?' said Bunfit aghast.

'No, I hain't a-saying that.'

'I'm very glad to hear it.'

'What I'm a-saying is far stranger than that.'

'What?'

'Listen to this. Couple of these girls 'ave 'ad clients recently who mentioned picking up a new girl, pretty young thing, only when they got down to the job, turned out she weren't no girl after all!'

'Good God. And what did they do, these clients?'

'One of 'em said things had gone too far for turning back, and a change was good as a rest anyway, so he just went ahead and wouldn't mind trying it again. Takes all sorts, don't it? Another cut up rough, though, and wanted to give the "tart" a good kicking, only before 'e can get fairly started, "she" hollos out, "Eddie!" and some fellow, must've been her ponce, comes running up, waving a pistol. All the gals 'ave been talking about it. They thought as 'ow it was a good laugh. I mean, they don't reckon a fellow playing charades is going to be any competition, do they?'

'Are you trying to tell me . . . what is it makes you think that . . .?'

'That the woman in white and our Mr Arlecdon might be one and the same? Well, the gals all reckon from what their clients said that this 'ere lady works out of Brawling Alley. And it'd explain 'ow no one saw Arlecdon, only the woman in the alley, wouldn't it? It makes sense, guv, don't it? "She" picks Purey up. Perhaps "she" don't recognise him, or perhaps "she" do and thinks it a bit of a joke. They gets up to the garret, "she" unbuttons Purey – which 'ud explain how we found him all ready primed – 'e sticks 'is 'and up her skirt, and he gets the shock of his life! But what really turns out fatal for 'im is that the shock triggers the memory of his old college chum. He says, "You're Arlecdon!" And that does it. Perhaps Eddie the ponce is 'iding in a cupboard and lends a hand. Whatever, next thing Purey finds 'isself flying through the window. Our "girl" runs downstairs to make sure she's done a good job, gets interrupted by the other tarts and takes off. Remember how Polly Nicholls thought she ran awkward because she was 'urt? I think she ran awkward because she was running like a man!'

They were at the door marked Detective Department, and Bunfit had about five seconds to decide how much of this nonsense to trouble the Major with.

He said, 'If'n I was you, Gager, I'd be very careful as to your tongue. Flights of fancy is all very well between colleagues, but if once you go shouting your mouth off without evidence . . .'

'Evidence you want, guv?' said Gager, stung. 'Ow about this? I spotted the Major coming up the stairs with Sir Ambrose so, like I said, I went down to have a chat with Sir Ambrose's coachman. Very casual, I mentioned Miss Alice and wondered if she were at home just now. 'E laughed sort of 'ollow, and said Miss Alice was always at 'ome in one manner of speaking and never at 'ome in another. Naturally I asked 'im what 'e meant. Seems that ten years back Alice and 'er brother were playing out on Sir Ambrose's estate in Leicestershire, and they got too near one of 'em new fangled mechanical threshing machines, and there was an accident and the little girl fell in.'

'Good God,' said Bunfit. 'Are you saying she's dead?'

'Might as well be. She got mangled to bits in front of her brother. By the time they put her together again, she was short a pair of legs and half an arm, not to mention her marbles. She's never spoken a word since and the only time she leaves the house is when they carry her out for a ride round the estate. So I don't think there's much chance she's been plying her wares in Brawling Alley!'

Before Bunfit could properly digest this, the door was flung open.

'What's this, Bunfit? Gossiping out here like a tea-wife when I told you to fetch the Sergeant as quickly as possible?' cried the Major.

This repetition of the Major's unaccustomed rudeness made up Bunfit's mind. He held nothing back, but with scarcely concealed relish, dumped the whole unpleasant mess into his superior's lap. Gager, mistakenly interpreting the Inspector's prolixity as an attempt to gather all the kudos unto himself, chipped in with comments and qualifications underlining his own sharpness in coming to grips with the case.

The Major listened in attentive silence but with a gloomy expression which did not prognosticate the reward of praise, and finally the detectives' flow of words faltered to a trickle.

The Major spoke.

'What do you have in writing? Statements? Notes?'

He already had Arlecdon's unsigned statement in his pocket and he sat at the Detective Department desk till Cox's report, the notes of record made in the interview room, and every jotting made by Bunfit and Gager themselves lay on the desk before him.

'This is all?' he asked.

They looked at each other and nodded.

The Major began to read, only speaking when he needed some obscurity interpreted.

'This, Sergeant, what is this?'

Gager looked and said, 'Oh yes, sir. This fellow, Eddie, the ponce. Some of the girls reckoned they'd seen him with the woman in white. Tall, good-looking fellow with wavy hair and an elegant moustache, not one of 'em soup strainers. They said as 'ow he reminded them of . . .'

'Of whom, Sergeant?' asked the Major quietly.

There was a pause. Gager's wily instincts were reasserting themselves after his earlier competitive garrulity.

'Of some chap runs a boozer in Cheapside,' he said vaguely. 'They didn't know 'is name.'

'No? But I see here they were quite certain on reflexion that the woman in white had a look of Mr Arlecdon from the Settlement.'

'Yes sir. Could be I put that idea in their minds. Very suggestible, them gals.'

'Suggestible, you say? To a policeman? How might they be to a newspaperman with a thick wallet?'

Gager didn't reply and the Major returned to his reading.

As he finished the door was thrust open and Sir Ambrose's head appeared.

'Mackintosh, a word.'

The Major went out into the corridor.

Bunfit said, 'Gager, my lad, these are deep waters. You and me had best keep a hold of each other, else we may drown.'

'Is that right, Inspector? What price without fear or favour now?'

'Listen, my boy. You want my job, you best follow my example. Show me a copper who don't know when to turn a blind eye and I'll show you a bad copper. There's bound to come times when least said, soonest mended, and no real harm done.'

'There's a young fellow lying on a slab might give you an argument there, guv,' said Gager.

Before Bunfit could reply, Major Mackintosh came back into the room and began gathering up the papers.

'Well, that seems taken care of,' he said. 'Sir Ambrose is taking his son home. He says we had no authority to bring him here in the first place and I'm afraid I must agree. However they are both willing to acknowledge honest error and let the matter drop.'

'But there's the body, sir,' protested Gager, ignoring Bunfit's warning glance.

'Ah yes. Mr Purey. A young man, I gather, of regrettably lax morals. It is sad that there are still corners of this great city which a stranger enters at his own peril after dark, but reasonable men know this and direct their steps accordingly. I regret Mr Purey should have been waylaid and robbed, and I will try to keep from his family the true nature of these dark excursions.'

'Waylaid and robbed!' exclaimed Gager.

'Your own notes suggest he was robbed,' said the Major mildly. 'Therefore it follows, or rather precedes, that he was waylaid. There are, of course, no witnesses . . .'

'No witnesses? Why, there's the . . .' Gager's voice tailed away.

'Ladies of the night, you were going to say? Yes, but in fact, what did they see? What can they say that isn't speculation? And, in their condition, both physical and moral, who would believe them?'

The questions came across as real rather than rhetorical.

Gager said, 'You're dead right, sir. Who's going to take notice of trash like that?'

He and the Major locked glances, the sergeant's defiant, his superior's doubtful.

Bunfit, suddenly eager for that retirement which earlier in the night he had anticipated with such little enthusiasm, said, 'I'll order their release then, the prostitutes, if that's all right.'

'Yes,' said the Major. 'That's all right.'

'I'll do it,' said Gager making for the door.

'We have, I suppose, a list of their names, just for the records?' said the Major. 'Only I don't see such a list here.'

Bunfit looked urgently at Gager who stood with his hand on the door handle.

'You got that list you showed me, Sergeant?' he said. 'You put it in your inside pocket, I seem to recall.'

Slowly Gager reached into his gaudy jacket and withdrew the list.

'Don't see no point in keeping it,' he said. 'Not if there's no charges.'

'That *is* the point,' said Bunfit, plucking the paper from his fingers. 'We've kept these girls here all this time without charge. Prozzies they may be, but they've got their rights, same as anybody else. So let's keep the record straight, then if any of them should put in a claim for compensation, we can make sure as how they're properly taken care of. Isn't that the way of it, sir.'

The Major took the list from him and ran his eyes down the six names.

Martha Turner
Mary Ann (Polly) Nicholls
Annie Chapman

Elizabeth (Long Liz) Stride
Catherine Eddowes
Mary Kelly

Gager at the door was standing like a man at the foot of the gallows.

'I am right, sir,' urged Bunfit. 'It's so they can be taken care of?'

'Oh yes, Inspector,' said Major Mackintosh wearily. 'You may rest assured of that. They will all be taken care of.'

Behind Gager the door slammed shut like a trap.

EDITOR'S FOOTNOTE: *Between August and November 1888, the prostitutes of Whitechapel were terrorised by the killer known as Jack the Ripper.*

His certain victims were named: Turner: Nicholls: Chapman: Stride: Eddowes: Kelly.

He was never caught.

P. D. JAMES

THE MAN WHO WAS EIGHTY

Mildred Maybrick, seated in the front left-hand seat of the Daimler, thumped her copy of *The Times* into a manageable shape and said: 'I see from the paper that Father shares his birthday with Julian Symons. They're both eighty today. That should please him. Quite a number of distinguished people have their anniversaries today but Mr Symons is the only one who is Father's age exactly. Quite a coincidence.'

Rodney Maybrick grunted. Since neither their father nor either of them personally knew the distinguished crime writer he couldn't see why Mildred regarded the felicitously shared birthday as a coincidence. He wished, too, that she wouldn't read the paper while he was driving. The perpetual rustle distracted him and, more dangerously, she was apt to turn over the pages with a flourish of disjointed leaves which momentarily obscured his vision. It was a relief when she completed her scrutiny of the court pages and the births, marriages and deaths, banged the paper into shape, although hardly the shape the publisher intended, and tossed it on the top of a wicker picnic-basket on the back seat. She was now able to give her attention to the purpose of their journey.

'I've put in a bottle of Pouilly-Fuissé as well as a thermos of coffee. If Mrs Doggett puts it in the fridge as soon as we arrive it should be drinkable before we leave.'

Rodney Maybrick's glance was fixed on the road ahead. 'Father has never liked white wine, except for champagne.'

'I dare say not, but I thought champagne was going a bit far.

Mrs Doggett would hardly like champagne corks popping all over Meadowsweet Croft. It's upsetting for the other residents.'

Her brother could have pointed out that for a mild three-person celebration it was only necessary for one cork to pop, and that this was hardly likely to provoke a Bacchanalia among the elderly residents of Meadowsweet Croft. He was, however, not disposed to argue. On the subject of their father the two were as one, their alliance, offensive and defensive, against that difficult old man, had for over twenty years given an appearance of sibling amity which, without this common and reconciling irritant, it would have been difficult for them to sustain. He said:

'This was a particularly awkward day for me to get away. I had to rearrange a number of appointments at considerable inconvenience to important patients.'

Rodney Maybrick was a consultant dermatologist with a large and highly lucrative practice which caused him little inconvenience. His patients rarely called him out at night, never died on him and, since they were as difficult to cure as they were to kill, he had them for life. Mildred could have pointed out that the day wasn't a particularly convenient one for her either. It had meant missing the Finance and General Purposes Committee of the District Council who could hardly be expected to arrive at sensible decisions without her. In addition it was she who had the trouble of preparing the picnic. Mrs Doggett, the warden of Meadowsweet Croft, had telephoned to say that a tea-party for the residents had been arranged for four o'clock complete with birthday cake and it was to avoid this gruesome celebration that Mildred had said firmly that they could be there for luncheon only and would bring a picnic to be eaten either in their father's room or in the garden. Since she, too, would be sharing it she had taken some trouble. The picnic basket contained salads, smoked salmon, tongue, cold chicken, with fruit salad and cream to follow. Enumerating these delights she said: 'I only hope he appreciates it.'

'Since he has shown no signs of appreciating either of us for the last forty years he is hardly likely to begin now, even under the stimulus of a bottle of Pouilly-Fuissé and the heady excitement of his eightieth birthday.'

'I suppose he would argue that he passed over to us Uncle Mortimer's three million and that was appreciation enough. He'd probably say that he'd been generous.'

Rodney said: 'That wasn't generosity: merely an extremely sensible and legal device for avoiding Capital Transfer Tax at death. It was family money anyway. Incidentally, he made the gift seven years ago today. He can die tomorrow and it will all be tax-free.'

Both reflected that this was, indeed, a birthday well worth celebrating. But Mildred reverted to a perennial grievance.

'He has no intention of dying, and I don't blame him. He can live another twenty years for all I care. I only wish he'd drop this obsession about moving to Maitland Lodge. He's perfectly well looked after at Meadowsweet Croft. The home is extremely well-run and Mrs Doggett is a most capable and experienced woman. The local authority have a very good reputation for their geriatric services. He's lucky to be there.'

Her brother changed gear and turned carefully into the suburban road leading to the home.

'Well, if he thinks we're going to find thirty thousand a year between us to pay for a place at Maitland Lodge, it's time he faced reality. The idea is ludicrous.'

They had had this conversation many times before. Mildred said:

'It's only because that dreadful old Brigadier is there and keeps visiting Father and telling him how wonderful the place is. I think he even took Father to spend a day there. And it's not even as if they're old friends. Father only met him on the golf course. The Brigadier is a bad influence on Father in every way. I don't know why they let him out of Maitland Lodge. He seems to be able to hire cars and travel the whole country at will. If he's so old and frail that he needs to be in a Home they should see that he stays there.'

Both Rodney and Mildred had every intention of seeing that their father, Augustus, stayed in Meadowsweet Croft. Although eighty, he was not particularly frail, but a total inability to cook for himself or, indeed, do anything which he regarded as women's work coupled with an acerbic tongue which had driven away a succession of housekeepers except those who had been alcoholic, mad or kleptomaniac had made residential care inevitable. It had taken his children considerable time and trouble to persuade him into Meadowsweet Croft. The relief for them, if not for him, had been considerable. They told him on their infrequent visits that he was a very fortunate old man. He even had a room to himself where he was able to display the results of his life-long hobby, a collection of ships in bottles.

Meadowsweet Croft was nowhere near a meadow, nor was it a croft and it could only have been described as 'sweet' by a visitor partial to the smell of lemon-scented furniture polish. It was, however, very well run, almost aggressively clean and the diet so carefully balanced in accordance with modern theories about the feeding of the elderly that it would have been perverse to expect it also to be palatable. Mrs Doggett was an SRN but preferred not to use the title or wear her uniform since, after all, Meadowsweet Croft was not meant to be a nursing-home and her old dears shouldn't be encouraged to think of themselves as invalids. She encouraged exercise, positive thinking and meaningful activity and was occasionally a little discouraged to realise that all the activity her residents wanted was to watch television in the lounge with their chair-backs placed firmly against the wall as if to guard against the possibility of anyone creeping up on them during the more enthralling moments of *Bergerac* or *Blind Date*. They had had a lifetime of exercise, positive thinking and meaningful activity. It has to be said that Mrs Doggett and the residents in general got on very well together with the exception of one central misunderstanding. She took the view that the old people hadn't come to Meadowsweet Croft in order to live a life of self-indulgent idleness, and the old people thought that they had. But they recognised that there were worse places than this Home, the grave for one, and when Mrs Doggett proclaimed, as she frequently did, that she loved her old dears, really loved them, she spoke no more than the truth. In order to love them the more effectively she made sure that they were never out of her sight.

This constant surveillance was helped by the architecture of the Home. It was a single-storey, U-shaped building built round a courtyard with a central lawn, a single tree which obstinately refused to thrive, four precisely arranged flowerbeds which were planted with bulbs in the spring, geraniums in the summer and dahlias in the autumn. The courtyard was furnished with solid wooden benches so that the residents could in summer take the sun. Each bore a plaque with the name of the person it commemorated, a memento mori which might have distressed users less tough than Mrs Doggett's old dears. They had, after all, survived sixty-five years or more of the twentieth century.

It isn't easy to manage a satisfactory picnic sitting in line on a hard bench with no table. Mildred had thoughtfully provided large paper napkins and they sat in a row with these on their laps while she passed plates of salmon and ham and distributed lettuce leaves and tomatoes. The other benches were unoccupied – the residents had no great love of fresh air – but they were watched by interested eyes while, across the courtyard, Mrs Doggett occasionally waved an encouraging hand from her office window. Augustus Maybrick ate heartily but in silence. Conversation was perfunctory until the fruit salad was finished when, as his children expected, he embarked on his old grievance.

They listened in silence, then Rodney Maybrick said: 'I'm sorry, Father, but the idea is impossible. Maitland Lodge costs thirty-five thousand a year and the fees will almost certainly rise. It would be an insupportable drain on our capital.'

'The capital which you wouldn't have had if it weren't for me.'

'You passed over to Mildred and me the greater part of Uncle Mortimer's legacy and naturally we're grateful. We can assure you that the money hasn't been wasted. You wouldn't have made over the capital if you hadn't had confidence in our financial probity and acumen.'

'I didn't see why the bloody government should get it.'

'Precisely.'

'But now I don't see why I shouldn't have a bit of comfort in my old age.'

'Father, you're perfectly comfortable here. This garden really is delightful.'

'This garden is Hell.'

Rodney said: 'In leaving the capital to you, I'm sure Uncle Mortimer thought of it as family money to be properly invested and left in turn to your children and grandchildren.'

'Mortimer never intended anything of the sort. That last Christmas, when we were all together at Pentlands, the Christmas he died, he told me that he was proposing to send for his solicitor as soon as the office opened after the holiday, and to change his will.'

Rodney said: 'A passing fancy. Old people get them. It's as well that he never got the chance.'

His father said: 'No. I saw to that. That's why I murdered him.'

Mildred felt that the only possible response to this statement was: 'What on earth are you saying, Father?' It was, however, a question which it was hardly logical to ask. Her father's voice had been embarrassingly loud and clear. While she was searching for a reasonable response, her brother said calmly:

'That's absolutely ridiculous, Father. Murdered him? How did you murder him?'

'With arsenic.'

Mildred had found her voice. She said: 'Uncle Mortimer died of a bad heart and viral pneumonia complicated by gastro-enteritis.'

'Complicated by arsenic.'

'Where did you get arsenic, Father?' Rodney's voice was studiously calm. Unlike his sister who was perched rigidly upright on the edge of her seat, he stretched back in as relaxed a pose as the hardness of the bench permitted, like a man who is prepared to waste a little time indulging his father's senile fantasy.

'I got it from Smallbone, your uncle's gardener. He used to say there was nothing like arsenic for dealing with dandelions. When Mortimer found out he pronounced that the stuff was too dangerous to have about the place and made Smallbone destroy it. But Smallbone kept a small quantity of the arsenic for himself in one of those old-fashioned blue poison bottles. He told me that having it gave him a feeling of power. I can understand that. Knowing his opinion of his employer I'm only surprised that he didn't use it on Mortimer before I did. I knew where he'd hidden it in the garden shed, so when he died I hid it even more securely. It gave me a sense of power, too. Smallbone always said that arsenic didn't deteriorate with age, and he was certainly right there.'

Rodney said sarcastically: 'And I suppose you administered it to Uncle in his medicine and, despite its well-known appalling taste, he drank it down immediately.'

His father didn't at once reply. His sideways glance at his children was one of reluctant cunning mixed with a certain self-satisfaction. He said: 'I suppose I'd better tell you the whole of it now that I've begun.'

Rodney said repressively: 'You certainly had. It's a complete fabrication, of course, but we may as well hear the whole story now that you've embarked on it.'

'You remember that one-pound box of soft-centred Belgian chocolates that you brought your uncle for Christmas? I may as well say that he regarded it as a deplorably inadequate present. That may have been one of the reasons which led to his decision to change the will.'

Mildred said: 'Uncle Mortimer was addicted to soft-centred chocolates and they were the most expensive we could buy.'

'Oh I know that. You both spoke about the cost so frequently and so openly that I've no doubt his nurse, Mrs Jennings, who is still alive, incidentally, will remember the gift. The arsenic I had was in the form of a white powder. I removed the base of the peppermint chocolate with a small sharp knife and replaced the peppermint cream with arsenic. I can't pretend the method was original but it was certainly effective.'

His son said: 'A fiddling job, surely. It can't have been easy without fear of subsequent detection.'

'It was a comparatively simple task for someone who has succeeded in building the *Cutty Sark* in a gin bottle. But your uncle wasn't after all going to examine the chocolate closely. I propped him up in bed and popped it into his mouth. He took one bite and swallowed it.'

'Without complaining about the taste?'

'Oh he complained about the taste, but I immediately popped in a raspberry cream and washed it down with a stiff dose of gin. He wasn't entirely compos mentis at the time. It was easy to convince him that he'd been mistaken about the bitterness of the first bite.'

'And what did you do with the bottle of arsenic?'

There was a second pause, a second look of sly cunning. Then their father said: 'I hid it in the blasted oak.'

No explanation was necessary. Both his children knew precisely what he meant. The large oak tree on the outskirts of the grounds of Pentlands had been their tree in childhood as it had been their father's. It had been struck by lightning in a notable storm in the early 1900s but still stood, the boughs providing a wonderful climbing-frame, its split trunk a hiding-place large enough to conceal a small child.

Rodney Maybrick said: 'All this is, of course, a fantasy, but I advise you to say nothing about it to anyone else. It may be amusing to you, and no doubt you take pleasure in its ingenuity, but other people may take a different view.'

Mildred had been thinking. Suddenly she said: 'I don't believe Uncle Mortimer seriously intended for a moment to alter his will. Why should he?'

'He disliked the thought of his money eventually coming to

either of you. You, Rodney, had particularly displeased him. You insulted the woman to whom he was deeply, indeed passionately, devoted.'

'What woman? I never even knew Aunt Maud.'

'Not Aunt Maud, Mrs Thatcher. You said you would rather dive into a tank of piranha fish than be a member of her Cabinet.'

'It was spoken in jest.'

'A jest in very poor taste. Your perverted sense of humour could have lost our side of the family a considerable fortune if I hadn't remembered the arsenic.'

Mildred said: 'What about me? What am I supposed to have done?'

'With you it was more a question of being rather than doing. Greedy, selfish, tactless and self-opinionated were some of the words he used. He said that God had given you a moustache to mark his regret at having made you a woman. Other remarks, which I'll spare you, were frankly uncomplimentary.'

Mildred was surprisingly unperturbed by this diatribe. She said:

'That proves it. Obviously he was deranged. But if Uncle Mortimer meant to change his will, did he tell you to whom he proposed to leave the money? He had a great family sense, for all his faults. I really can't see him leaving it out of the family.'

'Oh he proposed to leave it in the family all right. It was all to go to the Australian cousins.'

Mildred was outraged. 'But he hadn't seen them for forty years! And they didn't need it. They've got millions of sheep.'

'Perhaps he thought they could do with a few million more.'

Rodney's voice was quietly ominous. 'Why are you telling us all this, Father?'

'Because my conscience is troubling me. I'm an old man now coming to the end of my earthly journey. I feel I need to confess, to make my peace with the world and my Maker. You two have been for seven years in possession of money to which neither of you has any right. I had no right to inherit the three million in the first place and certainly no right to pass it on. These things weigh on an old man's mind. The air, indeed the whole atmosphere of Meadowsweet Croft is conducive, I find, to feelings of guilt and remorse. Take the Sunday visits of the Reverend Hinkley when he, and the members of his Women's Bright Hour, sing hymns for us round the piano in the lounge. Then Mrs Doggett insists on turning on Radio Four very loudly every morning for *Thought for the Day*. And of course we have the children from the local comprehensive school who come to sing carols for us at Christmas, and the local Church magazine brought round to us every month by the vicar's wife, always with a little encouraging homily. All these things have their effect. And then there's the food here, the unutterable boredom of the other residents, Mrs Doggett's voice and incipient halitosis, and the hardness of the beds; constant if petty reminders of that Hell which is supposed to await the unrepentant sinner. Not that I totally believe in eternal punishment, of course, but being required to live at Meadowsweet Croft does dispose to a certain morbidity of mind.'

There was a long silence. Then Rodney said: 'This, of course, is blackmail and blackmail of a particularly inept kind. No one will believe you. The story will be taken as the ravings of an old man well-advanced in senility.'

'Ah, but they can see I'm not, can't they?'

Rodney went on: 'And who do you expect to believe you?'

'The Australian cousins may well. I feel particularly guilty about your Australian cousins. But it won't matter whether they do or not. There will certainly be in everyone's mind a very large element of doubt. As I said, it was a pity you made such a big thing of buying your uncle those chocolates. And then there's the fact that I passed the money over to you. That might look very like blackmail. I must say I don't think the District Council will like the story, Mildred. And as far as you're concerned, Rodney, I've a feeling that your most lucrative patients will be taking their acne elsewhere.'

The silence this time was both long and profound. Then

Rodney said: 'We'll think it over. We'll let you know our decision the day after tomorrow. In the mean time, do or say nothing. Do you understand me, Father? Nothing.'

The conversation had been so upsetting to Rodney and Mildred that they left Meadowsweet Croft without retrieving the Pouilly-Fuissé from the refrigerator. Mrs Doggett felt justified in confiscating it as a raffle prize at the summer fund-raising Fête of the League of Friends. So Mr Maybrick never got his celebration drink, but he was consoled in his disappointment less by his aversion to white wine than by the knowledge that his children's birthday visit had really gone better than he could have hoped.

As soon as they had thrown off the suburbs of the town and were on a quiet country road, Rodney drove the car onto the verge and turned off the engine. There were decisions to be made to which both of them felt they could hardly give adequate thought in a moving vehicle. After a few minutes Mildred said:

'The whole thing is ridiculous, of course. The brothers never liked each other, but I don't think Father would go as far as murder. Still, it's just as well that Uncle was cremated. The doctor, apparently, never had the least suspicion.'

'Doctors who make a practice of suspecting their middle-class acquaintances of murdering their relatives usually end up without any patients. Uncle Mortimer was dying in any case. If Father did murder him' – Rodney had some difficulty in getting out the word – 'a confession can't bring him back.'

Brother and sister took some comfort from the undeniable fact that nothing could bring Uncle back. Then Mildred spoke what was in both their minds.

'It would only be a couple of miles out of our way to go to Pentlands. If Father did throw the bottle into the oak it's probably still there. Without the evidence no one will take his story seriously. There's no point in putting it off. Now is as good a time as any.'

Rodney said: 'Who was it who bought Pentlands? Do you

remember? I only know that the executors sold it below its worth.'

'I think they were called Swingleton, an elderly couple without children. They're hardly likely to go climbing oak trees.'

'I doubt that we'll find it easy now. I'm certainly too large to get into the trunk. If the bottle is there we'll have to hook it up.'

'How are we going to do that?'

'I've got my walking stick in the boot of the car.'

Mildred said: 'Of course we may have trouble in actually finding it. Even on a bright May day like this it will be very dark inside the trunk.'

Rodney spoke with some satisfaction: 'I never drive without a torch. We can use that. The problem may be getting into the grounds. If the gate is locked we'll have to get over the wall. Well, we've done that often enough in our time.'

Unfortunately the gate was locked. Although the stone wall was not more than five feet high they had considerable difficulty in getting over and only managed it in the end with the help of a folding picnic chair from the back of the car. There was also the problem of passing motorists. Twice they had to desist at the sound of an approaching car, pick up the chair and peer in the grass verge as if searching for rare plants. Rodney in particular found it difficult to hoist up his sister while keeping his eyes and ears open and Mildred's tight skirt was an embarrassing hindrance. There is something peculiarly unedifying about the sight of a stout lady of forty-five stuck on the top of a wall with her legs waving, her skirt ruffled up to expose an undignified expanse of white knickers. He trembled to think what Sir Fortescue Lackland, his most distinguished patient, would think if he could see them now, and was only fortified to continue with the expedition by the thought of what Sir Fortescue would think if Father ever carried out his threat and confessed.

Eventually, however, they were over and, folding up the chair and picking up the walking stick, crept along the inner side of the wall towards the blasted oak. With the help of the chair Rodney had no problem in reaching the necessary height and in peering down into the dark depths of the trunk. Mildred handed up the torch and he shone it down, illuminating the bed of shrivelled leaves, dried acorns, small twigs, broken pieces of bark and a twisted white plastic bag. And beside the bag he could see something a great deal more interesting: a small dark blue bottle with ridged sides.

Mildred called out quietly: 'Is it there? Is it there?'

'Yes, it's here.'

But discovering the bottle was a great deal easier than retrieving it. Rodney found it impossible to manoeuvre the walking-stick and at the same time hold the heavy torch, so both of them had to mount the chair, which creaked under their weight and, indeed, seemed in danger of collapsing. That catastrophe was averted when Mildred hooked her left arm round one of the lower boughs, thus releasing some of the weight. She shone the torch steadily into the trunk of the oak while her brother reached down with the stick. His plan was gently to edge the bottle to the side of the trunk, then hook it up. At first, to their horror, they were in danger of losing sight of it when it sank among the soft detritus of dried leaves. At the second try it became entangled with the white plastic bag. But at last Rodney managed to nudge it towards the edge and began the slow, careful, upward lift. Twice it got within reach of his left hand but twice it fell. But on the third attempt, not daring to speak in case even their breath dislodged it, the bottle came within reach of his stretched fingers and he was able to grasp it. Then, with relief, he jumped down from the chair and gave a hand to his sister.

'And what do you think you're doing?'

The voice, which literally caused them both to jump like startled cats and set their hearts pounding, was calm, authoritative, dismayingly upper-class. They turned round and saw two young men in tweed caps and jackets. Mildred's first thought was that they were game-keepers, but almost immediately she rejected this idea. The grounds of Pentlands were extensive, amounting to two or three acres, but hardly suitable for the rearing of game and the young men looked and spoke more like sons of the house than servants. One of them was actually carrying a gun. It was a moment of complete horror.

Her brother had been rendered speechless with shock and embarrassment but Mildred recovered herself with admirable speed. With an attempt at charm she said:

'I'm afraid you've caught us trespassing. We would have called at the front door and asked permission, but the gate was locked. My brother and I merely wanted to visit our uncle's old family home. We used to play here frequently as children during the holidays and this old tree is a part of our childhood memories. We were driving past and couldn't resist the temptation to visit it.'

The taller young man said coolly: 'Equipped with walking-stick and chair. What precisely were you looking for?'

He shot out his hand and took the bottle. Rodney said: 'We saw it lying there and were a little curious. It's nothing to do with us, of course.'

'In that case we'd better take charge of it. It looks like poison to me. We'll see it's safely locked up.' He turned to his companion. 'Henry, do you think it's necessary to phone the police?'

Henry was nonchalant. 'Oh, I don't think so. They look comparatively harmless. Almost respectable, indeed, although, of course, you can't tell from appearances. But we'd certainly better take charge of the bottle. And we'll take their names and addresses.'

Rodney said promptly: 'John Smith and Mary Smith. High Street, Tooting Bec.'

The younger man smiled grimly. 'Your real names and addresses, I think. Perhaps you have your driving licence on you. We need some means of identification.'

The procedure of name taking took place in an embarrassed silence. Afterwards the Maybricks were escorted to the gate which was locked after them. Dishevelled, dirty and scarlet with shame, they looked like a modern Adam and Eve summarily ejected from Paradise. Neither spoke until they were again seated in the car and Rodney had turned on the engine. Then Mildred said:

'If Father confesses now and it gets into the papers, those two men are bound to come forward. And they've got the evidence.'

Rodney wished that his sister was less liable to state the obvious. Since there was nothing helpful to be said, he said nothing. He was only grateful that Mildred was apparently too dispirited to assail him for his folly in giving a false name. After a short pause, Mildred spoke again.

'Shall you get in touch with Maitland Lodge or shall I?'

In a well-regulated and moral universe Mr Maybrick would no doubt have found Maitland Lodge a sad disappointment, the food indigestible, the wine undrinkable, the staff draconian, his fellow-residents uncongenial and the Brigadier a far less agreeable companion under the same roof than he was as an occasional visitor to Meadowsweet Croft. Regrettably for the triumph of virtue over wickedness, Maitland Lodge more than lived up to Mr Maybrick's hopes and expectations. He and the Brigadier agreed that they could certainly aim to live there for the next ten years before wondering whether it was time to shuffle off this mortal coil. Mr Maybrick was a great favourite with the staff who regarded him as a 'real character', particularly when he was at his most acerbic. He was especially matey with the buxom Nurse Bunting who occasionally ministered to the residents' aches and pains. When wearing her impeccably starched blue and white uniform and goffered cap Nurse Bunting was a model of professional rectitude. After duty hours, however, she would literally let down her hair and she and Mr Maybrick enjoyed many cosy sessions in his room over his night-cap of hot whisky.

'You are awful about your family, Gussie,' she occasionally

protested. 'No visits allowed, no letters, not even a box of chocolates.'

'Particularly not a box of chocolates,' said Mr Maybrick.

One evening in late August, three months after his admission and at the end of a perfect summer day, he and the Brigadier were sitting in their comfortable cushioned wicker chairs on the terrace looking out over the beautiful gardens of Maitland Lodge to the distant shimmer of the river. Badge the butler had just brought out their pre-dinner drinks and both were at peace with the world. The talk reverted, as it often did, to the circumstances under which this happy resolution had been achieved. The Brigadier said:

'I'm still surprised that your children actually swallowed your story.'

'I'm not. People are always ready to believe that others will act as they might have acted themselves. I had no doubt, too, they would call at Pentlands. What was more natural? Your men must have been very convincing though. Put the fear of God into them. Wish I'd been there to see it.'

'Well,' said the Brigadier easily, 'that's the advantage of being a soldier, you know. You can always find a couple of good chaps when you want a job done.'

'What was it they put in the bottle?'

'You know what it was. Bicarbonate of soda.'

There was a silence while the Brigadier sipped his gin and tonic and Mr Maybrick savoured his dry sherry. It was served at precisely the temperature he liked. He was pondering whether to try one of the delectable nuts or canapés on the drinks tray or whether that would spoil his appetite for dinner when the Brigadier said:

'Question I've always wanted to ask you. Not sure whether I should. Some questions shouldn't be asked among friends. Still, a natural curiosity, don't you know. I just wondered – don't answer if you don't want to – whether you did help your brother on his way.'

'Whether I murdered him?'

'Not to put too fine a point on it, yes. Not with arsenic, of course. Only a cad would use arsenic. That's the weapon of suburban poisoners and Victorian adulteresses. Still, there are other ways, presumably.'

Mr Maybrick appeared to consider the matter. 'Well, if I had done it I'd have used something quite simple. A plastic bag, for example. You just slip it over the head when the patient is sleeping, press it down firmly over the nose and mouth and he goes out as gently as a sleeping child. I don't see how anybody could detect that.'

The Brigadier said: 'You'd have to dispose of the bag, though. Not easy to burn, plastic. What would you do about the bag?'

'Oh,' said Mr Maybrick, taking a further sip of his sherry, 'I think I'd just throw it into the trunk of the blasted oak. Pass over the paper will you, Brigadier. What was it you said you fancied for tomorrow's two-thirty?'

H. R. F. KEATING

THE MAN WHO KILLED FOR PLEASURE

'Actually, you kill for pleasure, don't you?'

Heigh-ho. Another old chestnut, even if she's come up with one you don't get every time.

'Well, yes, I hope I do give pleasure. But you've got to remember it is fiction that I produce. Stories. Crime stories. And they do all have what you might call a moral ending.'

'You mean the one who did it being always found out? But, all the same, you show people how to get away with murder, don't you? Except for the fact that you, the author, choose in the end to have the killer caught. Isn't that so?'

Damn woman. Wants to come across like a great probing . . . I wish to hell she'd ended on *How do you commit the perfect murder?* Always do nicely with that. But, now, admit my plots aren't always perfect? Or agree I produce blueprints for murderers?

'Well, I suppose, in a way, I do invent good murder methods. But my old Mr Peduncle's pretty clever, you know, he always gets his man. Or woman.'

'Oh yes. But it's you really who's clever, isn't it? I mean, didn't a reviewer once say one of your final confrontations was, I quote, "the most jolting for years"?'

Oh God, she has done her homework. And that was the plot I pinched from an early Agatha Christie. So what now? Modestly say I'm not really very good at plotting and laughingly spill the Christie beans. Or . . .

'Well, yes, I suppose I must acknowledge I did bring that one off. But creating plots is very difficult, you know. I mean, it's a question of getting people you hope to show as being fairly real to do what in the end amount to pretty ridiculous things. I go walking all over London, actually, trying to hammer out reasons for, well, the pretty girl going into the big empty old house. That sort of thing.'

'I must keep an eye out for you whenever I'm shopping.'

Ah, thank God, off the track. Could pop in a quick little joke in response.

'Well, take care. I'm quite liable to walk straight into you when I'm in deep think.'

Laughter. If not a lot.

'Yes, but all the same, what you're doing as you walk about is devising a way for someone to kill someone else and get away with it. And you're doing it for money, aren't you?'

Blast. Ruddy woman can't leave it alone. Oh, well, here goes. Bit more coy modesty.

'Yes, of course. And the money's nice. But, you know, it's not the main object. I don't think it's the object, in fact, with all good writers.' Clever, implying I'm in the company of the greats, despite my sales. 'What we really want is readers. To get our thoughts, our ideas, into other people's heads. That's where the real satisfaction is.' Oh, God, too pompous? Better calm it down a bit. 'Not that there aren't times when I think how nice it would be to make a million. But then I suppose most of us would like that.'

'Well, let's hope your new book brings you in a million and more. And, thank you, Arnold Matters.'

'Thank *you*.'

Bitch.

*

'Arnold Matters here.'

'Ah, excellent. You won't know me, Mr Matters. My name is Mr Manoharsinh Patel. I found your number in the book, and I have a proposition for you.'

'Yes . . . ?'

'Well, you may have heard of my father, Mr Rattansinh Patel?'

'No, I don't— Oh, he's not the— the—'

'The multi-millionaire Indian playboy? That's what the Press usually call him. Yes.'

'Well, yes, then I suppose I have heard of him, to some extent.'

'Well, not to beat about the bushes, Mr Matters, what we want you to do, my elder brother, Amarsinh, and I, is to write the story of his life.'

'His life? But – Well, do you actually know anything about me? As a writer, I mean.'

'Oh, yes, Mr Matters. I had full inquiries made after I chanced to hear you on the radio.'

'But then you'll know, or should know, I write novels, crime novels. I've never done anything in the way of biography, let alone—'

'Oh, yes, I know that, Mr Matters. But nevertheless I think you're particularly suitable for this. You know, my father in his early days – it's no secret – had certain, shall we say, criminal connections. Smuggling, and so forth.'

'Yes, but all the same, my knowledge of crime is, well, purely fictional. I really don't think—'

'Mr Matters, shall we say fifty thousand pounds?'

'Fif— I suppose you had better talk to my agent, though . . .'

'Yes, of course, everything must be conducted on strictly business terms. But let me say now that we will, my brother and I, pay your full expenses as well as any fee. What we would like is for you to fly out to the yacht – it's in the Pacific just now – and spend as much time as you need talking to my father there.'

'Yes . . . I see.'

*

139

Jesus, it's a palace. A floating palace. I never imagined it would be anything like this. I swear that's an Ingres nude down in the saloon, over the fireplace – a fireplace on a boat, for God's sake – and my cabin, that sunken bath, gold bloody taps. And the crew must be large enough to man a frigate.

Manoharsinh Patel, fortyish, pencil moustached, brimming with good health, was smiling politely.

'So how do you like the *Lakshmi*, Mr Matters?'

'Fantastic. Quite fantastic. I was just thinking . . . I – I mean, how many crew are there?'

'Oh, about sixty, I think. Not counting people like our family photographer and Daddyji's chefs and his masseuse. You've seen Kamala, haven't you? A woman of great resource. As you may discover.'

Resource. I can imagine . . . Wonder if massage is all she does for the old boy? And was Manoharsinh – I suppose I'll manage to call him Mano eventually – implying that I might . . .

'Yes, she's a pretty nice craft, the *Lakshmi*. Or so our guests usually find. You know what Richard Burton is supposed to have said about the Onassis yacht? "I don't think there's a man on earth who wouldn't be seduced by the sheer narcissism." Well, Daddyji likes to think we go one better.'

'I'm sure you do. It's— It's magnificent. The only word for it.'

'Well, remember, it's at your disposal. Don't hesitate to ask for anything you want. Except—'

He came to an abrupt halt.

'Yes?'

'Well, there's Maria.'

'Maria?'

'Daddyji's mistress. Been with him a couple of years.'

So the resourceful Kamala isn't after all the old devil's playmate. So, I wonder . . .

'Mr Matters. But may I call you Arnold?'

'Please do. I'd meant to say.'

'Well, Arnold, how shall I put this? Quite simply, it's hands off. Absolutely. Same applies to myself and old Amar, actually.'

'Oh, but of course. I would never . . .'

'No, you must forgive me for issuing that sort of warning. But I think it will be necessary. When you see her.'

'Oh. Oh, well, I suppose you know best.'

It was that evening after dining alone with Mano and paunchy indolent Amarsinh – four varieties of caviare, Maine Coast lobsters, Aylesbury ducklings, Dom Perignon – that Arnold first saw Maria. At once he realised why Mano's warning had been necessary. Plump Havanas in hand, cognac swirling in heads, they were strolling the deck in the warm Pacific night when they came upon the old millionaire, dressed only in a faded pair of cotton shorts, his body lean and sleek under the lights that poured their radiance far around on the sea, looking not at all old. His arm, Arnold saw, was round a woman's waist. Or rather his hand was slowly stroking her left buttock.

She was, he realised immediately, an extraordinary physical specimen. A waft of dark hair. A face of smoothly regular features, wide eyes, rich heavy lips. A deep bosom clingingly outlined by a sarong-like garment. Long elegant legs, shaped to tautness by high-heeled shoes. She was, it was true, too plangently sensuous to be strictly beautiful, but she was nevertheless a woman to compare with everything that Ingres in the painting down below had sedulously put on canvas.

He felt a tightening through his whole body.

God, he thought, what wouldn't I give to be where that old bastard is at this moment.

It was a thought that, with variations, bloomed in his mind time and again as the *Lakshmi* proceeded through the calm Pacific towards – so he learnt – a group of Indonesian islands, the Kangeans. On one tiny uninhabited one of these there grew, apparently, orchids in varieties hitherto altogether unrecorded. There it was the pleasure in his old age of the former smuggler, and subsequent owner of a huge assortment of profit-making enterprises, to hunt down these fabulous rarities and personally to validate his finds with the paintbrush.

'We have a museum in California,' Mano told Arnold, 'where Daddyji's works are kept. He had it built some eight or nine years ago. He hopes to cover all the walls with his paintings before his death. And as that, from the look of him, is unlikely to occur for the next twenty years he stands a good chance.'

Arnold conscientiously made a note of this as soon as he got back to the sybaritic delights of his cabin – a fresh box of Charbonnel et Walker chocolates had been put beside his bed – but as he did so, he felt a twinge of shame. The existence of the museum was almost the only fact he had acquired for the account of the multi-millionaire's life he had been hired, for such a magnificent fee, to write. But, he thought as he scribbled, he had not actually been offered even one of the long interviews with his subject which Mano had implied he would get in their first negotiations. And, though he had on several occasions been promised that all the necessary newspaper cuttings would be flown out to the yacht, not a single clip had as yet arrived.

'All in good time, all in good time,' Mano said on each occasion he brought up the subject. 'In the meanwhile enjoy yourself, old boy. Enjoy yourself while you can.'

That was something Arnold found increasingly easy to do. Every pleasure, it seemed, was at his disposal. The yacht's bar was stocked with every variety of drink he had ever heard of, and some he had never heard of. So he harnessed his puritan work-ethic to sampling methodically the whole range. It might, he told himself, give him an insight into the mentality of the man who, ultimately, was supplying the luxuries.

Then to counter the effects of all the alcoholic intake, and of the huge elaborate meals cooked by the three chefs, each master of a different cuisine, he took regular long swims in the yacht's pool, kept always a computer-exact ten degrees cooler than the surrounding atmosphere.

Once even he visited the gymnasium. It was almost the last spasm of his conscientious attempts to do what he had been flown out so many miles in first-class comfort for. He had seen that Rattansinh Patel used the gym each day, a practice which no doubt accounted for that youthfully sleek body. So it occurred to him that by his side, heaving and straining on some fearful piece of apparatus, he might get one interview at least. But the idea proved totally unworkable. Maria, too, came to the gym, and the sight of her luscious body – forbidden fruit – almost bare, turning and turning in ever more provoking curves put all possibility of logical question and answer out of his power.

But his swimming – each cooling plunge helped him heed Mano's warning – improved no end. Before long he became quite proud of his skill, modestly boasting to Mano or the swanningly contented Amar about the number of lengths he had achieved. And another physical skill developed, too. Kamala, the masseuse, proved as resourceful as Mano had indicated, and he told himself that the hour he spent in her cabin every now and again also helped take his mind off what was increasingly in danger of obsessing him.

Though in his moments of self-analysis, much rarer than when he had paced the London streets – as occasionally he actually had, ostensibly to work out a plot – he had to record that, despite Kamala's ingenuities, the effect of her attentions was only to increase his desire to replace Rattansinh Patel's hand on whatever part of Maria he had last seen it resting.

It was worse when eventually they anchored off their destination. Because there, he learnt, it was the multi-millionaire's practice to have himself rowed by one or the other of his sons over to the little uninhabited island where the unrecorded orchids grew. He would stay away all the long day, locating the fantastic flowers and then painting them where they bloomed. The hobby, it seemed, took precedence even over Maria, the slide and slither of oil-paints compensating for the withdrawal of his ever-stroking hands.

Which left Maria on her own on board.

And Maria, it appeared, was not happy unless she was sharing her pleasure in the manifold delights the *Lakshmi* offered with someone. So Arnold would be patted on to the next tall, calf-covered stool at the bar as soon as she saw him. And then, torn between desire to touch, to stroke, to grasp and the remembrance of Mano's blunt warning, he would spend an hour, more than an hour, listening to her chatter and entertaining her as best he could.

Or, when at break of day Mano or Amar had rowed the old man away, easel, paints-box and safety-measure Purdey shotgun all stowed, and he would go for his first swim Maria would be already in the pool. Lazy on her back moving through the ice-blue deliciously cool water, she seemed like some swaying coloured sea-creature, at once inviting and appallingly dangerous. Then, instead of clocking up his lengths, he would find himself idling along in the water beside her, talking of nothing and wanting not to talk at all.

Where, too, in the days before they had come to anchor she and the old man – the so-young old man – had taken lunch every day, and dinner often, in his stateroom, eating from the gold service at the Louis XV table, served by four diligent stewards, now every midday she joined himself and either Mano or Amar at the long teak table in the dining-room.

And, a circumstance that was somehow additionally galling, both the idle Amar and his quicker younger brother seemed to be able without difficulty to obey that precept 'Hands off'. They seldom even looked at Maria. Whereas he himself had constantly to force his eyes to concentrate on anything else, one of the four Dutch seascapes fixed to the panelled walls, the caviare-filled eggs on his plate, the neck of the Château Grillet protruding from its nest of ice in the silver bucket.

Each evening now when Maria was back in old Rattansinh's keeping, he threw himself yet more vigorously into the delights ever on offer. His visits to Kamala's cabin became nightly affairs, and less and less satisfactory as they grew more and more varied. The cognac bottle went down at a rate that would, earlier, have caused him alarm. And as soon as it was empty another would appear. He spent hours in the plush little cinema, ordering up one after another classics he had once loved, Hollywood romps, plain pornography, and soon abruptly saying he had had enough and wanted something else.

It would have been easier, he felt, if he ever did what he had been flown half across the world to do. But now he hardly even saw the subject of the biography. Only two or three times, when he had been on deck when Amar or Mano had rowed the old man back, had he been briefly shown a painting finished that day. Then he had caught at Rattansinh Patel's muttered comments about it as if they were shreds of gold.

'Never seen anywhere in the world till today, Mr Matters. Beautiful. Marvellous. Bisexual, you know. As I am not.'

That reminder of the old lecher's rights in infinitely desirable Maria had gone like an ice-dagger into his gut as, a hand already caressing yielding flesh, she had been led away.

At last one morning, as Amar, whose turn it was to ride shotgun – Purdey shotgun – rowed off towards the orchid islet, Arnold forced himself to turn, not to the tormenting, untouchable creature standing idly by the rail, but to Mano.

'Listen, I really ought to be making a start on my research. I've been on board three weeks now—'

'Actually, nearly four, old man.'

'Well, yes. Four, I suppose. But that only makes it worse. I haven't really done a stroke on the book in all that while.'

'Yes. Yes. I think it is time we had a little chat.'

'Ah. Good.'

'How shall I put this?'

Mano paused and thought.

'The thing is,' he said eventually, 'I'm afraid you've been rather misled.'

'Misled? But how?'

'My fault entirely, I assure you. In fact, it was more or less deliberate. Or, frankly, quite deliberate.'

'Is it the money? Because, I mean, I'm quite prepared to drop the figure a bit. I've been having such a good time here, and—'

'No, no. The money doesn't come into it.'

'But— Well then, what does?'

Mano sighed and glanced this way and that.

There was no one near. All the crew were either down below or well occupied in their various tasks. Maria had wandered off in the direction of the pool on the after-deck (Arnold had not been able to stop himself noting it).

'No. Well, you see, it's like this. You're not actually here to write that biography. I've told Daddyji as a matter of fact you're just a friend of mine invited for a holiday.'

'Well, yes, I wondered rather why he never . . . But I'm afraid I don't understand.'

'My fault. I apologise once again. But, to put it absolutely bluntly, what you're here for is to devise a plot.'

'A plot?'

For a moment Arnold could not grasp what the familiar word – familiar from another existence, another way of life – even meant.

Mano was quick to enlighten him.

'You see, what I want to do is to kill my father. It's high time he went, you know. Time I took over. But he won't let me. He keeps all the reins in his own hands. And, damn it, he's good for another twenty years yet. I simply can't wait.'

Arnold felt stunned. As if, going through a doorway, he had walked into a low beam he had not known was there. But his head was filled, not with pain, but throughout every internal inch with astonishment.

This was reality. It wasn't a book. It wasn't murder for amusement that Mano was talking about. He was saying he wanted to commit a real murder. In actual life.

And – it came to Arnold like a battery of harsh lights suddenly flooding a darkened room into glaring brightness – what Mano must be wanting was a murder plot that he himself was expected to devise.

'But— But I can't invent a—'

'Oh, well, of course, you can, old man. I mean, that's what I picked you out for when I happened to hear on that radio programme you were an expert at devising ways of getting away with murder. You see, I knew what I wanted might be a bit complicated. Because, the thing is, it's not only a question of killing my father but of making sure old Amar takes the blame.'

This was impossible. The chap must be mad. He was standing there, full in the sun of a fine Pacific morning, and saying that he wanted to kill his own father and that his own brother was to be blamed. And, worse, worse, worse, he wanted that murder to be devised by himself.

'I can't do it,' he said. 'I'm sorry, but what you're asking is impossible. I mean, it's murder. Murder.'

'Well, of course it is, old boy. That's the whole point. It's why you're here, knocking back the booze, living off the fat of the land, having your little bits of fun with Kamala.'

'But— But I don't want that. I want— I just want to go home.'

'Well, it may come to that, of course. If you really won't or can't come up with what I want. Then there wouldn't be any point in your staying on here, would there? Having a nice time. A very much nicer time, if what that detective agency told me about you is right, than you've ever had a sniff of before. But if you won't, you won't. There wouldn't be any difficulty in shipping you off back in that case. We're putting in to Surabaya for twenty-four hours soon. Supplies and whatnot. So we could stick you on an aeroplane there, though not first-class I'm afraid. And in no time at all you'd be back in that poky little flat I'm told you have in dear old London. Well, cold and miserable old London at this time of year actually.'

'But— Well, what if I tell— Tell somebody, anybody, the police, Interpol, I don't know . . . What if I tell them what you've just said to me?'

'Wouldn't do that, old boy. I mean, you wouldn't want the photos of Kamala attending to you to be sent to your friends, would you? Your publishers and whatnot. All the little secretaries and receptionists bound to get to see them, you know.'

'Photos? You mean . . .'

'Well, naturally, one has had to take some precautions.'

'No. No, please. Don't . . . I mean, wait a second.'

Into Arnold's head, suffused until this moment with the riches he had wallowed in for four time-dazed weeks, there had come the picture of a particular pert little receptionist at his publisher's. She was showing his own editor's secretary a photograph, and giggling.

'Yes, well, sorry to be so brutal,' Mano said. 'But it's always as well to look facts in the face. Now, this is what I'll do. I'll give you until we dock at Surabaya – it'll be about a couple of days, depending on how Daddyji's current painting goes – to come up with a really good plan. Or plot. That's the right word, isn't it? And if you've managed that, then we'll be friends again and go on having our rather pleasant life. And, of course, I'll get your agent sent a draft for your fee, just explaining it's being paid notwithstanding Daddyji having cooled off on the idea, and that you're staying on with us. OK?'

Arnold agreed. Or at least gave a nod that indicated a sort of agreement. He told himself he needed time to think. A lot of time.

He kept to his cabin all that day. For all the rest of the morning he sat in one of its deep, leather-rich armchairs and tried to stop what Mano had said simply revolving round and round in his head. At about one o'clock there came a discreet tap on the door and a steward appeared.

'Mr Manoharsinh thought you might like to take luncheon in your cabin, sir.'

'What? Oh, yes, yes. All right.'

A laden trolley was wheeled in. A half-bottle of Dom Perignon in the ice-bucket, a hillock of tiger prawns clustering in each others' claws, crusty bread, yellow French butter, mounded many-coloured icecream on its silver refrigerated base.

After a while he began to eat, and frankly to gulp the champagne the steward had dextrously opened before leaving.

He finished everything. And cursed himself for doing so.

But he found his mind was made up. Or at least provisionally and partially so. He would see if he could not hit on some idea that would satisfy Mano. After all, merely hammering out a notion committed him to nothing. And whatever he managed to come up with probably wouldn't work in any case. He had always had a nasty idea that none of the plots of his seventeen crime novels would have been strictly practical in real life.

He went over to the pretty pearl-inlaid writing table and took a fat wodge of thickly creamy paper from its drawer.

And found his mind was blank.

Dinner was brought to him in his cabin. Blue Point oysters, roast eland, a De Latour Private Reserve Cabernet from the Napa Valley, fruits from the four corners of the world.

'Mr Manoharsinh asked me to make sure there was cognac in your locker, sir,' the steward said.

And it was with the aid of the cognac that at last an idea came to him. It was not an original idea. But, hammering away at the thought of Rattansinh Patel out on his little empty island again once they had returned from Surabaya, he had remembered a marvellously ingenious tale of Julian Symons', *A Theme for Hyacinth*. It featured, as far as he could recall, a plan to get an unwanted husband rowed out to an uninhabited island. It was the island, though in the story it had been an Adriatic one, that had brought the tale back to his mind. In it the rower, a dupe, was made to fall into a deep drugged sleep while the villain swam out to the island with a snorkel, murdered the husband and swam back arranging for the police to find body, sleeping dupe and sword-stick weapon all together.

I could pinch the notion, he thought, just like I pinched that Agatha Christie idea for my beauty-contests novel.

Then there came back to him, like a lurch of sickness, the words some hasty reviewer had used about that book, *the most jolting final confrontation for years*, and how quoted on the radio they had given Mano that disastrously false impression of his own abilities.

But the Julian Symons plot still seemed to be all there was between him and an ignominious return to a drear and chilly England and girls giggling at his publisher's. He snatched up the thick Parker from the pen-set on the table and started to write.

Next morning, as soon as Amar had set off to row his father to the island he handed over the final version.

Mano read it there and then, standing in the glittering morning sunlight, half watching Amar puffingly pulling away, with the old man, naked but for his customary sun-bleached pair of shorts, sitting in the prow, and the big paints-box and the lunch hamper bulky on one of the thwarts, the easel and the Purdey propped beside them. From the pool on the after-deck came the silky splash of Maria entering the ice-blue water.

'Yes,' Mano said eventually. 'I think that should do very nicely. I'll get hold of a wet-suit when we dock at Surabaya, and there won't be any difficulty putting some stuff into Amar's bottle of Chivas Regal. It's returned empty every time he's out there. He gets bored, you know, poor fellow.'

Arnold felt a sense of immense relief, as if up in the High Court for some appalling, nameless offence he had just heard the foreman of the jury pronounce the words 'Not Guilty'. And of course, he said to himself, when Mano starts to put it all into action, if he ever does, I shall simply tell him that, photos of Kamala or no photos, I shan't hesitate to go to the police.

But it did not quite work out as Arnold had expected. At Surabaya, to his sinking dismay, Mano did absent himself quite long enough surreptitiously to have acquired the wet-suit and possibly whatever he would need to dope Amar's bottle of Chivas Regal. However, back anchored off the orchid isle, for three days nothing more about the plan was said.

Arnold began to hope the whole business had been some sort of macabre joke, though joking was not something Mano had ever really risen to. And, true, on two of those three days it had been Mano himself rather than Amar who had been chosen for island watch duty.

Then at dinner on the third day, a meal at which for once old Rattansinh Patel had elected to be present, with of course Maria, as the old man waved away the flambéd omelette he was being offered he broke a long silence.

'Amar,' he said, 'I would like you to come to the island tomorrow.'

A few minutes later he left for his stateroom, pale brown hand resting once again on Maria's buttock. And, for the twentieth, thirtieth, fortieth time, Arnold thought *What wouldn't I give to be where the old bastard is now.*

But then in the morning, as with Mano he stood watching Amar row off to the island, he found to his thumping astonishment he was being offered, with simple directness, the gift he had been so firmly warned away from up till now.

'I see Maria's gone back to Daddyji's stateroom,' Mano had remarked with easy inconsequence. 'I expect she's waiting for you there.'

'Waiting? For . . . But I don't understand. You said once that on no account was I to— To, well, think such a thing was possible.'

Mano smiled.

'Ah, but the situation's different now,' he said. 'You see, Daddyji isn't coming back.'

Arnold found himself overwhelmed by the feeling that, dreaming what he somehow had known was only a nightmare to be blown away by daylight, he had suddenly found himself in the middle of waking reality.

'You can't—' he said. And choked.

'Oh, but I can. I told you so all along. And you were kind enough to work out for me just how it could be done.'

He stood looking down at Arnold. The faintest of breezes sent the fresh flowers that invariably decorated the *Lakshmi* fore and aft gently nodding.

'Now, shouldn't you be getting along to Maria?' he said. 'I don't think she'd appreciate being kept waiting.'

Arnold stood transfixed.

What to do? To seize that gift, that unimaginably promising gift, that had been flaunted before him for so long? Or to stand there and denounce this man for what he was? A parricide. Yes, that was the word. And probably a fratricide too.

It seemed to him that making his decision took hours. But in fact he realised later, his sudden vision of Maria's marvellous body, always evidently ready for the joys of voluptuousness, must have thundered into his mind within seconds of Mano having urged him to go to her.

It was at lunch – Maria, languid in Rattansinh Patel's huge bed, had said she would stay where she was – that he decided he ought to tackle Mano without further delay.

'Listen,' he said, 'I think you should get this straight. Despite— Well, despite anything that may have taken place this morning, I still intend to denounce you at once if you put one single detail of that plan into operation.'

Mano looked at him gravely.

'Well, this is a bit awkward, old boy,' he said. 'I mean the plan, your plot, has virtually been put into operation already. After all, we can't have Daddyji coming back to the *Lakshmi* now and finding out what you and Maria have been doing. I told you that as far as he was concerned it was absolutely hands-off, didn't I?'

'But— But— Why should he ever know?'

'Oh, come, my dear fellow, you didn't think Daddyji's personal steward didn't know all about it, did you? And Ketan's desperately loyal. To the head of the family, of course, whoever that may be.'

'But— Well . . .'

'No, old chap, we're embarked on it now, and it's just not possible to call a halt. So, if you've finished, I'll show you the wet-suit. I think I judged your size all right.'

'My size? But it's you who . . .'

'Oh, no, no, no. Whatever made you think that? No, old boy, you're the one who's got to do it. Otherwise how could I count on your loyalty? I wouldn't want, you know, to show the police from Arjasa – they're the nearest lot, I've found – that elaborate document written in your own hand. And I'd have to explain, too, what a good swimmer you are, much better than I am. And as to watching Ketan telling them about this morning's activities, well, we're far too good friends for that.'

Arnold sat, staring down at the remains of his shahi korma – it was the Indian chef today – and felt the situation permeating every part of his brain. He was trapped, totally and utterly trapped by the pleasures that had been thrust upon him. Nothing less.

'Come, old boy,' Mano said after a little, 'look on the bright side. You've enjoyed yourself on the *Lakshmi*, haven't you? A lot, even before this morning? Well, all that will be yours for ever once you've done your little job. Maria. Everything. I'm going to make you a director of, oh, anything up to a dozen of the companies. Money no problem henceforth. Everything that money can buy there for you.'

It was awful. Unthinkable. Inhuman. Vile. But he did it. And it was not actually all that difficult. The swim over to the island, just under the calm surface of the tranquil sea, proved well within his powers. Creeping up the beach, he saw almost at once Amar lying flat out beside the boat, empty bottle of Chivas Regal rolled over on the pale golden sand beside him. He picked up the Purdey, checked it in the way Mano had explained, walked slowly and carefully to the place where Mano had said he would find his father at the easel. The actual firing of the shot was as simple as if he was at a fairground booth idly enjoying himself. Then it was back to Amar, pressing the carefully wiped gun into his flaccid hands – 'I doubt if the Arjasa police will look for fingerprints,' Mano had said, 'but best be sure' – wading again into the warm sea and finally hauling himself up the rope-ladder Mano slipped over the *Lakshmi's* side for him.

'Well done,' Mano said, as he stepped on to the deserted deck. 'Knew it would work. Come down below. I've had a bottle of the Petrus opened. You deserve the very best.'

There was a small moment of shock when he saw that Mano had led him to what he still thought of as old Rattansinh's stateroom. But the magnificent wine was standing in its basket on the Louis XV table with Ketan beside it, grinning, ready to pour. And as soon as the wonderful vintage touched his lips he felt a sense of relief that blotted out everything else. All sounds, all sights from the immediate past, even all recollection.

The Arjasa police reached the island an hour or so after Mano had sent an urgent radio summons saying a shot had been heard out there. But it was only when they came over to the *Lakshmi* and began to ask their few, simple questions that every-thing seemed to go wrong.

'My brother?' Mano said. 'No, he's not with us now. He went off to Bali. He'd got a little bored with life at sea, you know.'

To Bali? What was he saying? Amar must have been found lying in an apparently drunken stupor out on the island, the only human being there, Purdey with one shot fired beside him. He had to be there. How, even if he had woken, could he have got off the island? Gone to Bali, miles away? You would need a speedboat . . .

But then a terrible thought came to him. Hadn't he heard, very faintly while he had been ensconced in Rattansinh's— In Mano's stateroom, a sound that might have been the distant throb of a powerful engine?

In his rudimentary English the officer in charge was telling Mano once more now that there had been no one on the island, except for Rattansinh Patel's dead body, shot in the head, plainly from a distance.

It was then that Mano deliberately moved away with a look

that said, clearly as a signal flag, *I have a sudden awful suspicion about this man I thought was my friend.*

'Well,' he said to the officer, 'this is all pretty unaccountable. As I told you, the custom was for either myself or my brother to row my father to the island and stay with him all day. But Amar wanted to go off to Bali, and my father said he would manage for once on his own. So I don't know how anyone could have got out there and done that. Unless—'

'Yes, please?'

'Well, unless they swam there. But you'd have to be a pretty good swimmer to manage that, wouldn't you? I mean, far better than I am for instance.'

He looked at the wide stretch of sea between the *Lakshmi* and the islet.

'Arnold,' he said, 'what do you think? You're a pretty good swimmer. Could you even do it?'

And there and then the police officer seized him by the arm.

Too stunned, as he was hustled off, to do more than dimly realise he had been comprehensively tricked, he heard Mano say, 'Poor Amar, he'll be devastated when he gets back from that hotel in Bali. I doubt if even Maria will be able to console him. Or me, come to that. At least not for a while.'

PETER LOVESEY

THE MAN WHO ATE PEOPLE

No one knew the girl. She turned up at the rec one Friday morning in the summer holiday when the hard lads from Class 5 were doing nothing except keeping the younger kids from using the swings. Gary and Clive were taking turns at smoking a cigarette. Podge Mahoney was trying to mend a faulty wheel on his skateboard. Daley Hughes and his brother Morgan were on the swings – not using them in the conventional way, which would have been soft, but twisting them so that the chains entwined. The rest of the bunch, including Mitch – by common consent the most mature – lounged on the grass talking about the bikes they wanted to possess.

None of the girls from Class 5 ventured anywhere near. This incautious miss strolled up to the unoccupied swing, backed against it to push off and started swinging, her eyes focused far ahead, excluding the lads from her vision. Thin, pale-skinned, with a straw-coloured pony-tail, she was in black jeans and a white T-shirt.

Several heads turned towards Mitch for a lead. Mitch possessed the coveted first floss of a moustache and he generally spoke for all of them if required. He leaned back on his elbows and said, 'Someone wants a swing. Give 'em some help.'

Paul, the boy Mitch had addressed, said, 'Come on,' to Clive. The pair got behind the girl on the swing, waited for it to come to them, tucked their fingers over the seat and heaved it forward. When it had soared high and swung back, they gave it another push, straining high to catch it at the peak. The rest of the lads chorused support with a rising 'Wooooo!'

Against expectations, the girl didn't scream. Indeed, as the swing soared to the high point of its arc, almost level with the crossbar, she brought her knees up to her chest to secure a footing. Then she braced and stood upright – an acrobatic feat that few, if any, of the watchers would have essayed.

The ironwork groaned. Paul and Clive stepped out of range, for the girl was imparting her own momentum to the swing, hoisting it still higher by getting leverage bending her knees and virtually kicking the seat upwards. She looked capable of going right over the top. She was fearless. The mocking chorus had already died in the throats of the watchers. The girl kept the display going for long enough to demonstrate that she was doing it from choice. When at length she signalled the end of the ride by straightening on the swing, making herself a dead weight, there was an awed silence. After the swing was still again, she remained standing on the seat, arms folded, only her left shoulder lodged against the chain to keep her balanced.

'What's your name?' Podge Mahoney asked. He'd given up fiddling with his skateboard.

'Danny.'

'That's a boy's name.'

'Danielle.' She made it sound like Daniel.

'What school?'

'Grantley.'

'Never heard of it.'

'It's a private boarding school.'

Roger, who was a good mimic, repeated the statement in the accent of the private boarding school.

The girl was undeterred. 'What are your plans for today? What are you going to do?'

'Nothing much,' said Podge.

'That's our business,' Mitch said, sensing that the girl was trying to gatecrash.

'Mind if I join in?' Danny asked.

'Course we mind,' said Mitch. 'Piss off.'

'I can get cigarettes.'

'Fags?' said Clive. 'You can get fags?'

'We wouldn't take bribes,' said Mitch, and several faces fell.

'What are you, a gang, or something?'

'No,' said Mitch, who was known, and respected, for the honesty of his statements.

'I want to join.'

'Don't be dumb.'

Clive added, 'Find some girls to play with.'

She shifted her position on the swing just a fraction and braced her legs, imparting a shudder to the structure. 'Who's going to make me?'

No one answered. Podge walked across to his skateboard and started taking an interest in the wheels again.

She was a scrap of a girl really, but her manner unsettled everyone. She said in her elegant voice, 'Anyway, you look like a gang to me. If you were a gang, what would one have to do to join?'

All eyes turned in Mitch's direction. No one else was capable of answering such a hypothetical question. Until now nobody had thought of the group as a gang. They were just the kids from Class 5 obliged to hang about the rec until they thought of something better to do. At the end of the summer they would go to secondary schools and be dispersed among a number of classes that would be called 'forms'. For these few remaining weeks they clung to the familiar.

Mitch pondered the possible entrance requirements of the hypothetical gang. He was sure it wouldn't be enough to say that girls were excluded. This one was unlikely to accept the logic that she was different.

He had to think of something she wouldn't contest. At length he said, 'If we were a gang, which we aren't, I'd make a rule that anyone who joined had to show their thing.'

The rest didn't share his seriousness. There were cackles of amusement. Morgan said, 'Girls haven't got things.'

'Shut up, toerag.'

The laughter stopped, quelled by the force of Mitch's put-down. Nobody wanted to catch his eye.

The girl Danny said, 'If I do, am I in?'

Mitch was finding it difficult to cope with her erratic reasoning. Clinging doggedly to reality, he said, 'It isn't a question of being in or out. We don't have a gang, OK?'

'Anyway,' added Clive to the girl, 'you wouldn't dare.'

Nobody anticipated that she would take them up on the dare at once, in broad daylight, in the rec, in full view of any grown-ups who happened to be passing. She unfastened the top button of her jeans and called across to Mitch, 'You won't see from over there.'

She proposed to display herself standing on the swing. For a moment everyone held back in awe. Then Podge Mahoney took a step closer. It was the signal for a general advance. Daley and Morgan disentangled themselves from the other swings. A half-circle formed in front of the girl. Mitch, on his dignity, had to decide how to react. The others had left no doubt of their commitment. If he missed this, he'd be like the kid sent early to bed the night they showed *Jaws* on TV. He was the last to his feet, but nobody noticed, or cared. The girl Danny had turned an intended humiliation into a show of power.

She gripped the front of her jeans and said, 'Ready?'

A couple of heads nodded, but no one spoke.

In a slick movement she slid jeans and knickers down a short way. Most of 5A had been initiated into *la différence* at some time in their lives; none so publicly, nor with such nonchalance.

'All right,' she said as she drew the jeans up again, 'someone else's turn.' She pointed to Mitch. 'Yours.'

The tension broke to howls of laughter, gleeful at Mitch's discomfiture and relieved that Danny hadn't pointed to anyone else.

'On the swing, Mitch!'

Mitch glared at Clive, who had made the remark. Of all the lads, Clive was the one he would have counted on to support him. How could loyalty be so brittle? 'Shut up! Shut up, the lot of you!'

They didn't shut up, so he had to continue to shout to be heard. 'This ain't a bloody game. It was to see if she could join some gang, but there ain't a gang, is there?'

Someone said, 'Chicken.'

Someone else said, 'Get 'em off.'

It only wanted someone to shout, 'Debag him!' and they would be on him like wolves.

Then Danny the girl, still aloft on the swing, spoke up. 'Mitch is right. There isn't a gang, but if there was, I'd be in. Who's going to give me another swing?'

Shouts of 'Me!' sprang up all around her.

Mitch's dignity was preserved. His authority was in tatters, and he couldn't think where he had made his mistake.

In the week that followed, Danny dispelled the summer boredom with marvellous suggestions. She knew a way into the dump where the scrapped cars were heaped high. It was her idea to cross the railway lines and build a camp on the embankment out of old sleepers and slabs of turf someone had left there. She turned the multi-storey car park into a Cresta Run, using supermarket trolleys as sledges. When they were told by the attendant to stop, she negotiated a fee of twelve pounds with the fête secretary for pushing leaflets under the wipers of cars. The experiences unified the group as never before. They actually were becoming a gang.

Yet Danny's influence was discreetly managed. She made no overt bid for the leadership; rather, she made a show of deferring to Mitch, seeking his approval. She would let him distribute the cigarettes she brought with her most mornings. Sometimes she let Mitch carry the day with his own suggestions. Unfortunately when the daily cry of 'What shall we do?' went up, Mitch could never think of anything they hadn't done before, so there were days when they played football or went fishing complaining that it was a drag.

He knew he ought to do better. His lack of originality

depressed him. He lost sleep trying to think of new challenges. In the bleakness of the night all he could see in his mind's eye were the faces of Class 5, mouths downturned, eyes glazed in boredom. It wasn't as if they lived by the sea, or in the country, where adventures were to be had. No circuses ever came through their suburban town. No pop concerts. No marathons. Not even Billy Graham.

The idea, when it came, almost escaped Mitch. Like a butterfly it fluttered within range and eluded his grasp. He captured it clumsily at the third attempt.

Over breakfast one Monday, submerged in gloom at the prospect of another meeting in the rec, he failed to hear his father the first time.

'Wake up, lad.'

'Wha'?'

'I was saying that somebody slipped a leaflet about the fête under my windscreen wiper – in my own garage.'

Mitch did his best to produce a sunny smile. 'That was me, Dad. I had a few left over. Me and some of the kids—'

'Some of my friends and I.'

'We were going round the carpark Saturday.'

Mr Mitchell's eyebrows bobbed up. 'Helping the church fête committee? Making yourselves useful for a change? Whose idea was that – yours?'

'Em, one of the others, I think.'

'Never mind. I like it. I won't be going to the fête myself, but I approve the spirit of the venture.' Mr Mitchell had long nursed an ambition to see his son as a boy scout, but Mitch, with a distaste for uniforms, had refused to join.

'Why aren't you going, Dad?'

'On principle, son. I don't approve of a certain gentleman they've invited to open it.'

'Sam Coldharbour?' Mitch was stunned. He had long been convinced that his father revered people who achieved things. Sam Coldharbour had climbed Everest and walked across America. He had boxed for Britain in the Olympics. He was the most famous person for miles around. Moreover, the Mitchells hadn't missed a fête in Mitch's lifetime. Mitch's father had twice been chairman of the committee. 'Don't you like him, Dad?'

'It isn't a question of like or dislike. I don't know the man personally. It's just that I'm unwilling to shake the hand of a man who behaves as he does.'

'Now, Frank,' said Mitch's mother in the voice she used to stop conversations that threatened to offend.

'What does he do?' asked Mitch.

'Not over breakfast,' said Mitch's mother.

'The man may be a hero to some, but he isn't to me,' Mitch's father insisted on saying, more to Mrs Mitchell than the boy. 'He isn't even discreet with his philandering.'

'What's philandering, Dad?'

'It's misconduct.'

'Frank, please!'

'But it's true. The man preys on women – ladies, I mean.'

'Prays – like in church?'

'No, you stupid boy. I used the word "prey" in the sense of hunting.'

'Hunting – like a tiger?'

'A wolf, if you ask me.'

'Frank!'

At the rec an hour or so later, Mitch related to an enthralled audience what he had learned about Sam Coldharbour, the man chosen to open the church fête. 'My dad calls him a wolf.'

'A werewolf?' said Roger, eyes popping.

'I said a wolf. He goes philandering. Any of you lot heard of philandering before? No? I thought not. Well, I'll have to tell you, won't I? It's hunting ladies. Mr Coldharbour goes around hunting ladies.'

There was a thoughtful silence.

'What does he do if he catches one?' Podge asked.

There was some coarse laughter. Class 5 knew what men and women were supposed to do together.

'You're wrong,' said Mitch with his regard for the literal truth. 'What do wolves do if they catch people?'

'Kill them?' said Clive, after a pause. Class 5 also knew a lot about horror and fantasy.

'Eat them?' said Daley.

Mitch opened his hands in a gesture that seemed to say there was no accounting for the things grown-ups got up to.

Morgan pulled a face and said, 'Ugh.'

'I don't believe it,' said Danny. 'People don't eat each other in Worcester Park.'

Mitch rose to the challenge he had anticipated ever since Danny had gatecrashed. 'Why not?' he demanded. 'He didn't always live here.'

'He'd have to be a cannibal, and you can see he isn't,' said Danny. 'How many of you lot have seen Mr Coldharbour?'

Half a dozen hands were hoisted.

'Well, then,' she said, as if the matter were settled. She walked to the swing and gave it a push.

Mitch was about to defend his assertion by claiming that anything his Dad said was the truth when he thought of a better riposte. 'He's travelled all over the world, Sam Coldharbour has. He's been up in the mountains and through jungles and on desert islands. He must have met some cannibals on one of his expeditions. If a cannibal asks you to come to a feast, you don't say no. That's how it started, I reckon.'

'You reckon?' said Podge.

'Yes,' said Mitch with decision. 'I reckon. He joined in a cannibal feast.'

Clive came to his aid. 'And then he got a taste for it. Once you've tasted human flesh, everything else tastes like old socks.'

'Podge's socks,' said Roger, and everyone laughed, including Podge. They needed to laugh.

Boys of that age are not fastidious about much, and they'll talk about anything. They argued lustily whether cannibalism could be justified for survival, but it was clear that whatever they claimed to the contrary, few, if any, cared to think of it close to home.

Danny the girl listened, contributing nothing else. She waited for the arguments to run their course and then said, 'Isn't it time we decided what to do?'

Mitch proposed cops and robbers and everyone groaned.

That evening Mitch heard his father on the phone talking about the fête. Someone from the committee was evidently trying to get him to reconsider his decision to stay away, but he was adamant. 'I don't need telling Coldharbour's fame will increase the attendance no end, but I have my principles, Reggie. I don't approve of the fellow. I don't care for the way he conducts his life . . . The women are what I'm talking about, and what he gets up to at that disagreeable house of his in Almond Avenue . . . All right, I may be behind the times, but I try to lead a decent life. I've seen Coldharbour in action. I was at the tennis club dance last autumn when he was supposed to be partnering Hettie Herzog. He got a sight of that pretty little girl who works in the cakeshop – Linda? Belinda? – something like that. She's married to the chap who runs the bar. He cut Hettie stone dead and started nuzzling Linda in front of her husband. I didn't inquire what happened later, but I've a pretty good idea. What could the husband do? Coldharbour boxed for England. He's had four different women since then, to my certain knowledge. Married or single, they're all meat and drink to Sam Coldharbour. No, I don't wish to meet him. I don't wish to go within a mile of the man.'

Mitch listened with fascination that turned to awe. If there had been any doubt before of the news he had conveyed to Class 5 – and he *had* rather overstated his confidence – such doubt had just been removed. Four women . . . all meat and drink to Sam Coldharbour.

The next morning found Mitch in Almond Avenue staring through the railings at Coldharbour's house, a modern construction with flat roofs and arched windows distinctly out of keeping with the mock-Tudor 1930s houses on either side. The grounds were spacious enough for a tennis court and a good-sized swimming pool, with diving-board. While Mitch was staring in, thinking about the owner, he had his idea.

He came straight to the point when the gang assembled at the usual place. 'You know what Clive said about eating people?' Since nobody appeared to remember, he said, 'Once you get a taste for it, you can't stop. It's like drugs. Sam Coldharbour's had five women this year.'

'*Eaten* them?' piped Roger in horror.

'My Dad says they're meat and drink to him, married or not.'

'Who said?' asked Danny the girl. It took a lot to alarm her, but there was a gratifying glint of concern in her eyes.

'I told you. My old man.'

Danny said nothing else and no one questioned the statement. After all, Mitch was always so scrupulous about the truth.

'I've thought of a brill dare,' Mitch went on. 'On Saturday, when old Coldharbour opens the fête, he isn't going to be at home for an hour or so, is he? Well, who's coming for a swim in the cannibal's pool?'

He might, perhaps, have phrased it more invitingly.

'Can't swim,' said Podge.

'Just a dip in the shallow end, then.'

'I'm going to the fête with my Mum,' said Paul.

'Chicken.'

'It's a great dare,' said Clive with more craft. 'If all of us do it, I'm in.'

'I got athlete's foot,' said Morgan. 'I'm supposed to keep it dry.'

It was Danny who swung the decision by simply saying, 'I'll be there, Mitch.'

Seven others were shamed into enlisting.

The fête organisers were rewarded with brilliant sunshine on Saturday. From behind a builder's skip in Almond Avenue at 1.55 p.m., eight of the would-be bathers watched Sam Coldharbour drive out between the stone pillars of number 11 in his BMW.

'All right, who's coming?' Mitch challenged the others.

Podge said, 'Danny ain't here yet.'

'She must have chickened out,' Clive said. He gave Mitch a supportive smile. 'What do you expect from a girl? We can't wait for her.'

Mitch led them in, sprinting full pelt up the drive and across a stretch of lawn to the green-tiled surround of the pool. Lattice patterns of sunlight made the water look specially inviting. Mitch stripped completely, ran to the diving board and took a header in. Clive followed. Some of the boys had prudently put on swimming-trunks under their clothes, but no one wanted to risk derision, so everything came off. Immersion made them feel secure. Soon they were shouting and splashing each other as if it were the town pool.

At some point Mitch came up from a dive and saw Danny standing by the edge. She was dressed as if for church, in blouse, skirt, socks and shoes. Her hair was in bunches tied with white ribbon. He grabbed Clive's arm and pointed. Clive wasn't going to miss an opening like this. He called out derisively to the others, 'Look who's finally turned up.'

'My mother made me go to the fête,' Danny explained. 'I only just got away.'

'Coming in?' Mitch called out.

'There isn't time.'

'Course there's time.'

'There isn't. He'll be back soon. When I left, he was walking round the stalls, but it won't take him long to get round. You'd better get out.'

They hesitated, each boy swivelling his head to see if one of the others was willing to climb out first. Truth to tell, the hard lads of Class 5 had turned coy. Their naked state in front of the girl – the girl with no inhibitions about her own body – was a more immediate concern than being caught and eaten by Sam Coldharbour.

She said, 'I think I can hear the car.' She turned to look along the drive.

There was turmoil in the water. Modesty abandoned, everyone struck out for the side. Lily-white bottoms were everywhere exposed, bent over the tiled edges of the pool in the scramble to get out.

'It's him!' Danny shouted.

To shrieks of alarm, the bathing party broke up. No one had time to put on clothes. They grabbed their things and scampered across the grass, dropping garments as they fled.

A squeal of brakes from Sam Coldharbour's BMW added to the panic. The car skidded and stopped, raising dust. Coldharbour leapt out and sprinted after someone. Mitch saw enough to convince himself that it would be suicidal to try and get through the gate, so he made for the railings some way down. He flung his clothes over, grabbed the top and hauled himself up. He perched up there a moment before leaping to the pavement. The sense of relief at getting out was so overwhelming that it took him a second or two to realise that he was standing naked in a suburban street. He went behind a tree and struggled into his clothes. He was a sock short, but he didn't care.

Further along Almond Avenue, Podge had made a similar escape. He'd left both shoes in the garden.

Daley and Morgan came running from the other direction. 'Anyone get caught?' Morgan asked.

'Don't know,' Mitch admitted. 'Let's go back to the rec. That's where we'll meet.'

'If he *did* catch anyone—' Podge started to say.

'Your shirt's inside out,' Mitch interposed.

Members of the bathing party arrived at the swings at intervals and told of narrow escapes and grazed flesh and missing garments. Clive insisted that he'd been thrown to the ground by old Coldharbour and only got away because he was still wet and too slippery to hold. Nobody placed much reliance on things Clive said.

Roger had gone straight home feeling sick, but all eight of the bathers were accounted for.

'What about Danny?' Mitch said. 'Did anyone see Danny get out?'

'He was chasing her,' said Podge. 'I saw the cannibal chasing her.'

'She's an ace runner,' said Clive. 'She'll turn up soon.'

His optimism wasn't justified. The shadow of the swing lengthened and faded in the dusk and Danny didn't come.

'She must have gone straight home,' Clive said eventually.

'We ought to make sure,' said Podge.

'How can we, you fat git?' Mitch rounded on him. 'We don't know where she lives.'

'We ought to tell the police or something.'

'If she doesn't come home, her Mum will report it.'

Mitch's faith in grown-ups prevailed. It was conceded that nothing could be done and they dispersed, after vowing to assemble again at the same place next day. 'And I bet she turns up as usual,' said Clive.

In reality Mitch had a horrid conviction that Clive was mistaken. Danny would not turn up, and he was responsible for the adventure that had gone so tragically wrong. In bed that night, he struggled to reassure himself that somehow his father must have been misinformed and cannibalism had not broken out in suburban Worcester Park. No one could get away with it, even if they were so ghoulish as to try. But the fears returned at intervals through the night.

In the morning everyone except Danny turned up at the rec. The optimists among them said they should wait. Clive wanted to go to the police right away.

'No,' said Podge. 'They don't believe kids like us. We'll get done for trespassing, and it'll all get in the papers, and our new schools will know about it.'

'What are we going to do, then?' said Clive. 'We can't just forget about Danny. She's in the gang.'

'It was never a gang,' said Mitch.

'Was.'

'Wasn't.'

'Was.'

'While you're arguing,' said Clive, 'Danny might still be alive. She could be killed any minute.'

Mitch may have been short of original ideas, but he was sharp enough to tell when his leadership was under threat. This was a moment for action. 'We're going back to the house.'

'What?'

'We're going to get Danny out. If we stick together, there's enough of us to take on anyone, even old Coldharbour. Strength in numbers, right?' He held a fist aloft.

'Right,' said Clive raising a fist.

'Right,' said the others with less animation.

For mutual encouragement, they marched like a platoon to Almond Avenue, swinging their arms high and trying to stay in step. At the railings of Sam Coldharbour's house they halted.

'Look,' said Morgan.

Anyone cherishing the hope that the man who ate people might have slipped out for an hour, to church, or the paper shop, or to walk the dog, must have felt a draining of enthusiasm at the sight of the prominently muscled figure reclining beside his swimming pool on a sun-lounger.

Mitch, however, was equal to the challenge. He believed that they were capable of rescuing Danny if she was still alive. And he did accept responsibility for what had happened to her. This was the right way, the man's way, to put things right. He felt like a leader now.

He explained how they would take care of Sam Coldharbour.

They climbed over the railings at the place where the foliage was thickest and crept like Indians around the perimeter, using the shrubs as cover, and staying close to the railings. The reclining figure continued to recline. No one else was in the vicinity of the pool.

A toolshed stood close to the railings near a kitchen garden, and this was where they headed first. Their luck was in. It was unlocked, and there was room for everyone inside. Better still, the shed was well equipped. The boys started arming themselves with garden tools. Roger had a large wooden mallet. Morgan and Daley started to wrestle for possession of a scythe.

'What do you think you're doing?' Mitch said in a voice that shamed them all. 'Put those things down. We don't want to get in a fight.'

'We might,' said Podge. 'We need to arm ourselves.'

'Bollocks,' said Mitch. 'We need both hands free. Our weapon is surprise.'

So it was that in a moment the Class 5 assault team emerged from the toolshed armed with nothing more lethal than several lengths of rope and a narrow-mesh net, of the sort used for keeping birds off redcurrant bushes. This was the most dangerous stage of the operation, for they had to cross an open stretch of lawn.

Mitch led the advance, his eyes fixed on the recumbent figure of Sam Coldharbour. The eight small boys moved stealthily but rapidly towards the ex-Olympian, who still didn't stir. His eyes opened only when Mitch was so close that he blotted out the sun.

This was Mitch's first close sight of the cannibal's face, and it was not so frightening as it had been in his mind's eye. The teeth were not the vampire-fangs he had pictured and the eyes weren't, after all, narrow slits edged with red. Close up, Sam Coldharbour was unremarkable, the more so when an oily rag was spread over his face and the net thrown across the entire length of his body and held down by six boys, while two others passed ropes around, to secure him to the frame of the sun-lounger. Morgan, who was strong in the arm and good at knots, drew the ends of the ropes tightly together and fastened them. Sam Coldharbour was efficiently trussed, his protests muffled by the rag. It had all been done so rapidly that Mitch doubted if any of them had been recognised.

'Leave him,' he ordered. 'We're going into the house.'

With a perceptible swagger, he led his commandos across the patio and up to the house. The patio window was slightly open. It squeaked as he pushed it aside. He had never been inside a house so modern-looking, or so large. There was steel and leather and stripped pine and huge plants in white containers. 'You three take the downstairs,' he told Clive, Daley and Roger. 'We'll try the bedrooms. And remember,' he said in an after-thought to Clive, 'to look in the freezer.'

The house was silent except for their footsteps on the spiral staircase, which was made of wrought iron, painted white. With a silent prayer that they would find Danny still alive, Mitch progressed to the landing and opened the first door. The room was some sort of office, with maps on the walls. He tried the next. A bathroom. Then discovered a bedroom with a single bed, a featureless room devoid of anything notable except what Podge noticed – a pair of blue and white trainers half hidden under the bed.

'Those are Danny's.'

'She's here, then,' said Mitch.

'She was,' said Podge in a low voice.

Mitch shuddered. 'We'll try the other rooms.'

Two more unoccupied bedrooms.

The last door on their left was ajar. Mitch pushed it open, and stood staring. The room contained a huge circular bed, out of keeping with other furnishings, which in Mitch's opinion were silly for a bedroom – a glass-fronted cocktail cabinet, a fridge, a music centre and pink-tinted mirrors the length of two of the walls. When his gaze travelled upwards, he saw that another vast, pink mirror was attached to the ceiling.

It was in the reflection on the ceiling that Mitch noticed something stir in the untidy heap of bedclothes. 'Someone's there!' he told Podge. 'Come on.'

He approached the bed, with Podge observing a judicious step behind him. For a worrying second or two Mitch wondered if he was in error. The bedclothes were quite still.

Then they were flung aside and a red-haired woman sat up and shouted, 'What in the name of Satan . . . ?'

The words didn't trouble Mitch so much as the sight of her rearing up from the bed, not unlike a ship's figurehead he had once seen in a maritime museum. She was bare-breasted and gave every appearance of being carved out of oak and painted bright pink with dabs of crimson on the points of her chest. No doubt the effect was partly due to the light from the mirrors and partly to Mitch's immaturity. Female torsos in general had yet to persuade him that they were anything but grotesque.

Without even covering herself, the woman demanded, 'Just what do you think you're doing in here?'

'Looking for someone,' answered Podge, over Mitch's shoulder.

Mitch found his voice. 'Our friend Danny.'

She said, 'Danny? You're friends of Danny? Bloody liberty – I'll have her guts for garters. Get out, the lot of you. Out!'

He heard the others act on the order. Before going after them, he stood his ground long enough to say, 'You want to watch out. It could be you next.' Far from being grateful for the advice, the woman gave signs of rolling out of bed in pursuit. That was too much for Mitch. He fled.

Downstairs, Clive was waiting with the others. 'She ain't here,' they said in chorus, and Clive added, 'We're too late.'

'Did you look in the freezer?'

'It's stacked to the top with peas and things from Sainsbury's. We couldn't move all the stuff.'

From the bedroom upstairs the woman shouted, 'I'll call the police.'

'We've got to get out,' said Podge. 'There's nothing we can do, Mitch.'

'Danny must be dead by now,' said Clive. 'If the police come, they'll find out.'

'That lady upstairs won't call them,' Mitch said, trying to calm his troops. 'She's in it. She knew about Danny. Is there anywhere we haven't looked – a cellar, or a garage?' He knew as he spoke that any gang-leader worthy of the name would have said something more positive.

Morgan said, 'I don't bloody care. I'm off.'

'Me, too,' said his brother Daley. 'Who's coming?'

172

Not everyone was so frank. One or two muttered inaudible things before they followed Morgan out.

'Wimps!' Mitch called after them.

If the slur was heard, it was not heeded. The 'gang', all of it, including Clive, deserted. Mitch stepped out to the patio and watched his friends in flight, the seven he would have claimed as his closest mates, haring along the drive towards Almond Avenue. He knew for certain that his authority, his credibility as leader, was gone for ever. They were the quitters, yet he would be blamed.

He still felt driven to find out what had happened to Danny. He was about to go around the side of the house in search of a cellar when he became conscious of something that shouldn't be. Some part of his brain was functioning independently, trying to convey information, an observation. He stared about him uncertainly.

Then he realised what was amiss: the swimming-pool was deserted. Sam Coldharbour was no longer beside it, tied to the sun-lounger. The sun-lounger itself was gone.

If Coldharbour was free, danger was imminent.

He heard a sound close by, and swung around. It wasn't Sam Coldharbour standing behind him, and it wasn't the woman from upstairs. It was Danny.

She was in shorts and a T-shirt, and was barefoot. She said solemnly, 'Thanks, Mitch.'

'We thought you were dead,' he said in a whisper. His real voice wouldn't function. 'Come on, let's run for it!'

She said in her flat, unexcited way. 'There's no need to run.'

'He'll get us.'

'He won't.'

'There's a woman as well.'

'She's my mother,' said Danny, then added, 'I know what you're thinking and you're right. Your Dad was right, too. She's another stupid woman who got tricked by Sam Coldharbour. He told her she was adorable, and stuff like that. She moved in here four weeks ago. School had broken up and I had nowhere else to go.'

'You mean you lived here all this time?'

'Stayed here.'

'Why didn't you tell us?'

'I was ashamed.'

'When you didn't come out last night, we thought you were caught. Podge saw him chasing you.'

'He did. He was in a foul temper. He grabbed my hair and pulled me inside and spanked my bum. *Him!* My mother thought it was a real joke. She locked me in my room for swearing at him. She sided with him.' Danny's lips drained of blood as she pressed her mouth shut.

Mitch said, 'We thought he was going to kill you and eat you.'

'That was dumb.' She gave a faint smile. 'But I'm glad about what you did.'

Mitch shook his head. 'We did bugger all except tie him up.'

Then Danny surprised him by catching hold of his wrist. 'I want to show you something.'

Still keeping hold of him, she led him across the patio and over a stretch of lawn to the tiled surround of the pool. She pointed to it.

A breeze was sending ripples across the surface and for a moment Mitch thought the body underneath was struggling. It was not. Sam Coldharbour, roped to the lounger, his face still covered by the oily rag, was motionless at the bottom. The water was only a metre or so in depth, but sufficient to have drowned him.

Mitch turned to look at Danny, his eyes huge with the horror of what was down there. 'We only tied him up. We didn't do that.'

'I know,' said Danny.

Mitch glanced down at the smooth surface of the tiled surround and saw how simple it must have been to push the lounger over the edge. He knew what Danny had done, and he knew why. But he stopped himself from speaking prematurely. He turned away from the pool, biting his lip. Finally he said in his usual considered way, 'It must have moved because he was wriggling. He wriggled to try and get free and it sort of moved. He couldn't see where it was going. It was an accident.'

His eyes glistened. He despised himself, even when Danny squeezed his arm.

RUTH RENDELL

THE MAN WHO WAS THE GOD OF LOVE

'Have you got *The Times* there?' Henry would say, usually at about eight, when she had cleared the dinner table and put the things in the dishwasher.

The Times was on the coffee table with the two other dailies they took, but it was part of the ritual to ask her. Fiona liked to be asked. She liked to watch Henry do the crossword puzzle, the *real* one of course, not the quick crossword, and watch him frown a little, his handsome brow clear as the answer to a clue came to him. She could not have done a crossword puzzle to save her life (as she was fond of saying), she could not even have done the simple ones in the tabloids.

While she watched him, before he carried the newspaper off into his study as he often did, Fiona told herself how lucky she was to be married to Henry. Her luck had been almost miraculous. There she was, a temp who had come into his office to work for him while his secretary had a baby, an ordinary, not particularly good-looking girl, who had no credentials but a tidy mind and a proficient way with a word processor. She had nothing but her admiration for him, which she had felt from the first and was quite unable to hide.

He was not appreciated in that company as he should have been. It had often seemed to her that only she saw him for what he was. After she had been there a week she told him he had a first-class mind.

Henry had said modestly, 'As a matter of fact, I have got rather a high IQ, but it doesn't exactly get stretched round here.'

'I suppose they haven't the brains to recognise it,' she said. 'It must be marvellous to be really intelligent. Did you win scholarships and get a double first and all that?'

He only smiled. Instead of answering he asked her to have dinner with him. One afternoon, half an hour before they were due to pack up and go, she came upon him doing *The Times* crossword.

'In the firm's time, I'm afraid, Fiona,' he said with one of his wonderful, half-rueful smiles.

He hadn't finished the puzzle but at least half of it was already filled in and when she asked him he said he had started it ten minutes before. She was lost in admiration. Henry said he would finish the puzzle later and in the meantime would she have a drink with him on the way home?

That was three years ago. The firm, which deserved bankruptcy it was so mismanaged, got into difficulties and Henry was among those made redundant. Of course he soon got another job, though the salary was pitiful for someone of his intellectual grasp. He was earning very little more than she was, as she told him indignantly. Soon afterwards he asked her to marry him. Fiona was overcome. She told him humbly that she would have gladly lived with him without marriage, there was no one else she had ever known to compare with him in intellectual terms, it would have been enough to be allowed to share his life. But he said no, marriage or nothing, it would be unfair on her not to marry her.

She kept on with her temping job, making sure she stopped in time to be home before Henry and get his dinner. It was ridiculous to waste money on a cleaner, so she cleaned the house on Sundays. Henry played golf on Saturday mornings and he liked her to go with him, though she was hopeless when she tried to learn. He said it was an inspiration to have her there and praise his swing. On Saturday afternoons they went out in the car and Henry had begun teaching her to drive.

They had quite a big garden – they had bought the house on an enormous mortgage – and she did her best to keep it trim because Henry obviously didn't have the time. He was engaged on a big project for his new company which he worked on in his study for most of the evenings. Fiona did the shopping in her lunchtime, she did all the cooking and all the washing and ironing. It was her privilege to care for someone as brilliant as Henry. Besides, his job was so much more demanding than hers, it took more out of him and by bedtime he was sometimes white with exhaustion.

But Henry was first up in the mornings. He was an early riser, getting up at six-thirty, and he always brought her a cup of tea and the morning papers in bed. Fiona had nothing to do before she went off to take first a bus and then the tube but put the breakfast things in the dishwasher and stack yesterday's newspapers in the cupboard outside the front door for recycling.

The Times would usually be on top, folded with the lower left-hand quarter of the back page uppermost. Fiona soon came to understand it was no accident that the section of the paper where the crossword was, the *completed* crossword, should be exposed in this way. It was deliberate, it was evidence of Henry's pride in his achievement, and she was deeply moved that he should want her to see it. She was touched by his need for her admiration. A sign of weakness on his part it might be, but she loved him all the more for that.

A smile, half-admiring, half-tender, came to her lips, as she looked at the neatly printed answers to all those incomprehensible clues. She could have counted on the fingers of one hand the number of times he had failed to finish the crossword. The evening before his father died, for instance. Then it was anxiety which must have been the cause. They had sent for him at four in the morning and when she looked at the paper before putting it outside with the others, she saw that poor Henry had only been able to fill in the answers to four clues. Another time he had flu and had been unable to get out of bed in the morning. It must have been coming on the night before to judge by his attempt at the crossword, abandoned after two answers feebly pencilled in.

His father left him a house that was worth a lot of money. Henry had always said that when he got promotion, she would be able to give up work and have a baby. Promotion seemed less and less likely in time of recession and the fact that the new company appreciated Henry no more than had his previous employers. The proceeds of the sale of Henry's father's house would compensate for that and Fiona was imagining paying off the mortgage and perhaps handing in her notice when Henry said he was going to spend it on having a swimming pool built. All his life he had wanted a swimming pool of his own, it had been a childhood dream and a teenage ideal and now he was going to realise it.

Fiona came nearer than she ever had to seeing a flaw in her husband's perfection.

'You only want a baby because you think he might be a genius,' he teased her.

'*She* might be,' said Fiona, greatly daring.

'He, she, it's just a manner of speaking. Suppose he had my beauty and your brains. That would be a fine turn-up for the books.'

Fiona was not hurt because she had never had any illusions about being brighter than she was. In any case, he was implying, wasn't he, that she was good-looking? She managed to laugh. She understood that Henry could not always help being rather difficult. It was the penalty someone like him paid for his gifts of brilliance. In some ways intellectual prowess was a burden to carry through life.

'We'll have a heated pool, a decent-size one with a deep end,' Henry said, 'and I'll teach you to swim.'

The driving lessons had ended in failure. If it had been anyone else but Henry instructing her, Fiona would have said he was a harsh and intolerant teacher. Of course she knew how inept she was. She could not learn how to manage the gears and she was afraid of the traffic.

'I'm afraid of the water,' she confessed.

'It's a disgrace,' he said as if she had not spoken, 'a woman of thirty being unable to swim.' And then, when she only nodded doubtfully, 'Have you got *The Times* there?'

Building the pool took all the money the sale of Henry's father's house realised. It took rather more and Henry had to borrow from the bank. The pool had a roof over it and walls round, which were what cost the money. That and the sophisticated purifying system. It was eight feet deep at the deep end with a diving board and a chute.

Happily for Fiona, her swimming lessons were indefinitely postponed. Henry enjoyed his new pool so much that he would very much have grudged taking time off from swimming his lengths or practising his dives in order to teach his wife the basics.

Fiona guessed that Henry would be a brilliant swimmer. He was the perfect all-rounder. There was an expression in Latin which he had uttered and then translated for her which might have been, she thought, a description of himself: *mens sana in corpore sano*. Only for 'sana' or 'healthy' she substituted 'wonderful'. She would have liked to sit by the pool and watch him and she was rather sorry that his preferred swimming time was six-thirty in the morning, long before she was up.

One evening, while doing the crossword puzzle, he consulted her about a clue, as he sometimes did. 'Consulted' was not perhaps the word. It was more a matter of expressing his thoughts aloud and waiting for her comment. Fiona found these remarks, full of references to unknown classical or literary personages, nearly incomprehensible. She had heard, for instance, of Psyche but only in connection with 'psychological', 'psychiatric' and so on. Cupid to her was a fat baby with wings and she did not know this was another name for Eros, which to her was the statue.

'I'm afraid I don't understand at all,' she said humbly.

Henry loved elucidating. With a rare gesture of affection, he reached out and squeezed her hand. 'Psyche was married to Cupid who was, of course, a god, the god of love. He always came to her by night and she never saw his face. Suppose her husband was a terrible monster of ugliness and deformity? Against his express wishes' – here Henry fixed a look of some severity on his wife – 'she rose up one night in the dark and, taking a lighted candle, approached the bed where Cupid lay. Scarcely had she caught a glimpse of his peerless beauty, when a drop of hot wax fell from the candle on to the god's naked skin. With a cry he sprang up and fled from the house. She never saw him again.'

'How awful for her,' said Fiona, quite taken aback.

'Yes, well, she shouldn't have disobeyed him. Still, I don't see how that quite fits in here – wait a minute, yes, I do. Of course, that second syllable is an anagram of Eros . . .'

Henry inserted the letters in his neat print. A covert glance told her he had completed nearly half the puzzle. She did her best to suppress a yawn. By this time of the evening she was always so tired she could scarcely keep awake while Henry could stay up for hours yet. People like him needed no more than four or five hours sleep.

'I think I'll go up,' she said.

'Good night.' He added a kindly, 'Darling.'

For some reason, Henry never did the crossword puzzle on a Saturday. Fiona thought this a pity because, as she said, that was the day they gave prizes for the first correct entries received. But Henry only smiled and said he did the puzzle for the pure intellectual pleasure of it, not for gain. Of course you might not know your entry was correct because the solution to Saturday's puzzle did not appear next day but not until a week later. Her saying this, perhaps naïvely, made Henry unexpectedly angry. Everyone knew that with this kind of puzzle, he said, there could only be one correct solution, even people who never did crosswords knew that.

It was still dark when Henry got up in the mornings. Sometimes she was aware of his departure and his empty half of the bed. Occasionally, half an hour later, she heard the boy come with the papers, the tap-tap of the letterbox and even the soft thump of *The Times* falling onto the mat. But most days she was aware of nothing until Henry reappeared with her tea and the papers.

Henry did nothing to make her feel guilty about lying in, yet she was ashamed of her inability to get up. It was somehow unlike him, it was out of character, this waiting on her. He never did anything of the kind at any other time of the day and it sometimes seemed to her that the unselfish effort he made must be almost intolerable to someone with his needle-sharp mind and – yes, it must be admitted – his undoubted lack of patience. That he never complained or even teased her about over-sleeping only added to her guilt.

Shopping in her lunch hour, she bought an alarm clock. They had never possessed such a thing, had never needed to, for Henry, as he often said, could direct himself to wake up at any hour he chose. Fiona put the alarm clock inside her bedside cabinet where it was invisible. It occurred to her, although she had as yet done nothing, she had not set the clock, in failing to tell Henry about her purchase of the alarm she was deceiving him. This was the first time she had ever deceived him in anything and perhaps, as she reflected on this, it was inevitable that her thoughts should revert to Cupid and Psyche and the outcome of Psyche's equally innocent stratagem.

The alarm remained inside the cabinet. Every evening she thought of setting it, though she never did so. But the effect on her of this daily speculation and doubt was to wake her without benefit of mechanical aid. Thinking about it did the trick and Henry, in swimming trunks and towelling robe, had no sooner left their bedroom than she was wide awake. On the third morning this happened, instead of dozing off again until seven-thirty, she lay there for ten minutes and then got up.

Henry would be swimming his lengths. She heard the paper boy come, the letterbox make its double tap-tap and the newspapers fall onto the mat with a soft thump. Should she put on her own swimming costume or go down fully dressed? Finally, she compromised and got into the tracksuit that had never seen a track and scarcely the light of day before.

This morning it would be she who made Henry tea and took *him* the papers. However, when she reached the foot of the stairs there was no paper on the mat, only a brown envelope with a bill in it. She must have been mistaken and it was the postman she had heard. The time was just on seven, rather too soon perhaps for the papers to have arrived.

Fiona made her way to the swimming pool. When she saw Henry she would just wave airily to him. She might call out in a cheerful way, 'Carry on swimming!' or make some other humorous remark.

The glass door to the pool was slightly ajar. Fiona was barefoot. She pushed the door and entered silently. The cold chemical smell of chlorine irritated her nostrils. It was still dark outside, though dawn was coming, and the dark purplish-blue of a pre-sunrise sky shimmered through the glass panel in the ceiling. Henry was not in the pool but sitting in one of the cane chairs at the glass-topped table not two yards from her. Light from a ceiling spotlight fell directly on to the two newspapers in front of him, both folded with their back pages uppermost.

Fiona saw at once what he was doing. That was not the difficulty. From today's *Times* he was copying into yesterday's *Times* the answers to the crossword puzzle. She could see quite clearly that he was doing this but she could not for a moment believe. It must be a joke or there must be some other purpose behind it.

When he turned round, swiftly covering both newspapers with the *Radio Times*, she knew from his face that it was neither a joke nor the consequence of some mysterious purpose. He had turned quite white. He seemed unable to speak and she flinched from the panic that leapt in his eyes.

'I'll make us a cup of tea,' she said. The wisest and kindest thing would be to forget what she had seen. She could not. In that split second she stood in the doorway of the pool watching him he had been changed for ever in her eyes. She thought about it on and off all day. It was impossible for her to concentrate on her work.

She never once thought he had deceived her, only that she had caught him out. Like Psyche, she had held the candle over him and seen his true face. His was not the brilliant intellect she had thought. He could not even finish *The Times* crossword. Now she understood why he never attempted it on a Saturday, knowing there would be no opportunity next morning or on the Monday morning to fill in the answers from that day's paper. There were a lot of other truths that she saw about Henry. No one recognised his mind as first class because it wasn't first class. He had lost that excellent well-paid job because he was not intellectually up to it.

She knew all that and she loved him the more for it. Just as she had felt an almost maternal tenderness for him when he left the newspaper with its completed puzzle exposed for her to see, now she was overwhelmed with compassion for his weakness and his childlike vulnerability. She loved him more deeply than ever and if admiration and respect had gone, what did those things matter, after all, in the tender intimacy of a good marriage?

That evening he did not touch the crossword puzzle. She had known he wouldn't and, of course, she said nothing. Neither of them had said a word about what she had seen that morning and neither of them ever would. Her feelings for him were completely changed, yet she believed her attitude could remain unaltered. But when, a few days later, he said something more about its being disgraceful that a woman of her age was unable to swim, instead of agreeing ruefully, she laughed and said, really, he shouldn't be so intolerant and censorious, no one was perfect.

He gave her a complicated explanation of some monetary question that was raised on the television news. It sounded wrong, he was confusing dollars with pounds, and she said so.

'Since when have you been an expert on the stock market?' he said.

Once she would have apologised. 'I'm no more an expert than you are, Henry,' she said, 'but I can use my eyes and that was plain to see. Don't you think we should both admit we don't know a thing about it?'

She no longer believed in the accuracy of his translations from the Latin nor the authenticity of his tales from the classics. When some friends who came for dinner were regaled with his favourite story about how she had been unable to learn to drive, she jumped up laughing and put her arm round his shoulder.

'Poor Henry gets into a rage so easily I was afraid he'd give himself a heart attack, so I stopped our lessons,' she said.

He never told that story again.

'Isn't it funny?' she said one Saturday on the golf course. 'I used to think it was wonderful you having a handicap of twenty-five. I didn't know any better.'

He made no answer.

'It's not really the best thing in a marriage for one partner to look up to the other too much, is it? Equality is best. I suppose it's natural to idolise the other one when you're first married. It just went on rather a long time for me, that's all.'

She was no longer in the least nervous about learning to swim. If he bullied her she would laugh at him. As a matter of fact, he wasn't all that good a swimmer himself. He couldn't do the crawl at all and a good many of his dives turned into belly-flops. She lay on the side of the pool, leaning on her elbows, watching him as he climbed out of the deep end up the steps.

'D'you know, Henry,' she said, 'you'll lose your marvellous

figure if you aren't careful. You've got quite a spare tyre round your waist.'

His face was such a mask of tragedy, there was so much naked misery there, the eyes full of pain, that she checked the laughter that was bubbling up in her and said quickly, 'Oh, don't look so sad, poor darling. I'd still love you if you were as fat as a pudding and weighed twenty stone.'

He took two steps backwards down the steps, put up his hands and pulled her down into the pool. It happened so quickly and unexpectedly that she didn't resist. She gasped when the water hit her. It was eight feet deep here, she couldn't swim more than two or three strokes, and she made a grab for him, clutching at his upper arms.

He prised her fingers open and pushed her under the water. She tried to scream but the water came in and filled her throat. Desperately she thrashed about in the blue-greenness, the sickeningly chlorinated water, fighting, sinking, feeling for something to catch hold of, the bar round the pool rim, his arms, his feet on the steps. A foot kicked out at her, a foot stamped on her head. She stopped holding her breath, she had to, and the water poured into her lungs until the light behind her eyes turned red and her head was black inside. A great drum beat, boom, boom, boom, in the blackness, and then it stopped.

Henry waited to see if the body would float to the surface. He waited a long time but she remained, starfish-like, face-downwards, on the blue tiles eight feet down, so he left her and, wrapping himself in his towelling robe, went into the house. Whatever happened, whatever steps if any he decided to take next, he would do *The Times* crossword that evening. Or as much of it as he could ever do.

GEORGE SIMS

THE MAN WHOSE HOLIDAY WAS A FIASCO

After the glaring sunlight on the Fornello beach the cave was pitch black, momentarily impenetrable. Steve Carroll lowered his head in an attempt to see what lay in front of his bare feet but succeeded only in giving himself a sharp crack on the forehead from a projecting rock. He swore fluently then added, 'Typical. A bloody fiasco.'

He stood where he was and started to roll down his wet swimming trunks in order to pee, saying, 'Uno bloodio fiasco.' A tendency to make up mock Italian phrases and words was becoming something of an obsession with him as the holiday in Positano proved to be more and more a lamentable waste of money.

Peeing into the unseen depths of the cave, Carroll sighed loudly as he mentally catalogued the troubles that had plagued them since the holiday began: his sharp altercation with the officious gendarme at Boulogne which had become so bad-tempered on both sides that for a while he had envisaged spending the first night of the trip in a French gaol; the unexpec-ted result of this silly argument on Jilly, leaving her in a very cold and completely silent mood so that he had to drive some two hundred miles without a word from her; Jilly's touch of food poisoning, or bug, or whatever it was that had caused her to have 'the trots', so that he was continually having to stop the car and she had completely gone off eating and drinking;

the ghastly day in Naples followed by a sleepless night; the unexpected onset of Jilly's period half-way along the twisting *corniche* to Positano, a full week before it was due, intensifying her already ominous silence; and finally his own constantly aching tooth. That had begun in an insidiously mild fashion with just a minor twinge or two as he had driven to Folkestone, followed by a vague ache in his lower right jaw while on the car ferry. The pain had intensified after the trouble in Boulogne and then he had identified the source of it with a probing tongue. 'Bit of toothache' then 'Really rotten toothache' he had said to Jilly, but by that time she was dealing uncomplainingly with her attack of 'the trots'.

Carroll sighed again and gingerly pulled up the uncomfortable wet trunks over the patch of sunburn at his waist. What a joke he thought, remembering how they had looked forward to this early holiday throughout the winter. 'Just think – a week in Positano and all the fun of getting there and back.' His own words resounded in his ears now like a bad joke. How enthusiastically they had studied road maps and pored over coloured photographs that showed Positano perched picturesquely on cliff and hill-side facing the Golfo di Salerno so that at a distance its white, cinnamon and pink buildings looked like a gigantic wedding cake.

But the real irony of the situation was that Positano had lived up to its description in the holiday firm's brochure: it did indeed consist of a giant rabbit-warren of ancient streets, colour-washed buildings, countless steps, and terraces with breathtaking views over the Tyrrhenian sea. Even the Casa Rossi had not been over-sold: it was exactly as described, a pleasant family hotel with good food and comfortable bedrooms. In fact the Carrolls had nothing to complain about – only that it was impossible to enjoy Positano and the Casa Rossi while suffering from diarrhoea or grinding toothache.

'Io non volo dentisto Italiano.' Carroll said this fudged-up phrase aloud in the privacy of the cave. After their meals in Naples at a curiously old-fashioned restaurant where the clock seemed to have stopped at about 1900, he envisaged dentistry in Naples being carried out at a primitive stage without the ameliorating contrivances to which he was accustomed: he pictured an Italian dentist as wearing a long flapping apron with pincers sticking out of the pocket. But even if this was all untrue, one was still at a great disadvantage in going to a dentist without being able to speak Italian.

Consciously frowning over his dilemma, Steve Carroll emerged into the glaring sunlight to see that a dishy blonde girl was watching him with a slightly amused expression.

'So did you find any treasure?' she asked with a hint of merriment in her voice. She had unusually clear blue eyes, a perfect tan as though she had been in the sun for weeks, and a minimal tangerine-coloured bikini which showed she had a perfect figure. 'I saw you disappear in there and when you didn't come out I thought you must have found gold or something.'

Carroll shook his head. 'Nothing to see in there,' he said, then added an afterthought to stop her peering into the cave and perhaps catching a whiff of urine. 'But I heard the sound of bats. Much flapping of tiny wings. So I retreated.'

'Then it's definitely *not* for me.' The girl's hand automatically went up to her long blonde hair, emphasising the perkiness of her breasts. She was easily able to adopt very decorative poses.

Paddling a little nearer she gave Carroll a close look, taking in his big frame which was patchily sunburnt. 'Are you enjoying it here?' She pointed at the golden honeycomb of Positano stretching up tier upon tier, towering over the two beaches.

'Yes, it's very nice . . . Well . . . Our holiday got off to a rather bad start . . . We made the fatal mistake of having a day and a night in Naples.'

'And you think that's disastrous?' Again there was the hint of amusement, the note of the experienced traveller dealing with the tyro: but if that was slightly irritating it had to be offset against her snub nose, attractive kittenish face and delightful figure. 'Did you see the Giotto frescoes in the Castel dell'Ovo?'

'No, in fact we didn't see much of anything. We'd only just started tramping round when a youth on a Vespa tried to snatch my wife's handbag.'

'Ah, yes, the *scippatori*. That's what they call those Vespa thieves, or the black knights of the alleyways. Was there much in the bag?'

'He didn't get away with anything. I clouted him round the ear and he shot off the Vespa. Hit his head on the kerb I suppose and it bled a bit. So within a minute we were surrounded by this screaming mob. A woman was shouting for the police. And my wife was upset because she thought I'd hurt the boy.'

The blonde girl nodded judiciously, re-appraising Carroll's wide shoulders and heavily muscled arms. 'Yes, I can understand that.'

'But that was rubbish. I just clipped him round the ear, that's all. Caught him off balance. But I ended up feeling like the criminal.' Carroll spoke dogmatically but in fact he was again wondering just how hard he had hit the boy. Undoubtedly his pent-up anger, pain and frustration had all surfaced then and found release in what might well have been a vicious blow.

'Did the police come?'

'No. The boy picked himself up and buzzed off without a word. Then the crowd vanished. My wife . . .'

'Which one is she?' the girl asked, looking round at the handful of people scattered over the beach.

'Jilly didn't come down after lunch. She's got an upset tummy. So she preferred to sit on the balcony. At the moment she has to stay within reach of a lavatory.'

'Poor girl! What rotten luck! What has she taken for it?'

'Not much. Nothing I think. She read somewhere that those tablets – for that kind of thing – are a bit suspect. So she's just stopped eating anything apart from bread, and she only drinks water. But she had a little soup last night and that made it worse again.'

'But there's a perfectly good chemist here. Where are you staying?'

'A small place, straight up there, more or less above us, the Casa Rossi.'

'Yes, I know it, very nice people. Well, the chemist is on the same side of the road as the Casa Rossi, walking down to the main beach – you must have passed it. Where the road bends and dips quite sharply.'

Carroll nodded. 'Yes, I saw some shops on that bend but I didn't know there was a chemist. I only walked down to the main beach once. Then a maid at the Rossi told us about the Fornello beach. It's more or less perfect here, apart from those four hundred steps down.'

'Four hundred and four I think. You see I've had lots of practice counting them. We're at the Poseidon which is even higher up than the Rossi. It's going up at lunch-time that's the real killer, with the sun right overhead. Speaking of sun . . .' She pointed at Carroll's red shoulders.

'Yes, they are beginning to feel rather sore. I always have trouble getting a tan.'

'It's your colouring, that sandy hair and light skin.'

'Sandy? Mm – well, that's a nice way to put it. I used to be called Carrots at school.'

'What about a swim then? Salt water will do it good. My name's Debbie by the way. Debbie Saunders.'

'Steve Carroll.'

'Do you fancy a dip? Have you been out towards the Saracen tower? The sea is marvellous just there. Really deep but you can see right down to the bottom.'

Carroll began to wade into the sea, smiling to himself. Strange how easily an attractive girl could change one's mind: fifteen minutes earlier he had no intention of swimming again that afternoon, he had planned to change out of his damp trunks into his shorts and lie down in the shade. But now he found himself enjoying plunging in and striking out for the tower which was perched at the tip of the headland. He swam strongly but the girl kept pace with a seemingly effortless crawl. Debbie's long hair streamed behind her in a very fetching fashion and her eyes now appeared more of a sea-green colour than blue. She opened her mouth to say something, swallowed some salt water, spat it out and laughed. 'There, isn't that better?'

Carroll mused that while Debbie seemed sympathetically concerned about Jilly her manner with him was undoubtedly flirtatious. 'Yes, it does seem to have gone off. A very soothing effect.' Saying this he realised that his toothache had also diminished to a quite bearable level and his cares had fallen away too, so that he could not remember why he had been in such a bad mood when he had descended to the Fornello beach. Then he thought, Jilly's silence – all her silent, saint-like suffering of the past few days; that had got him down even more than his blasted tooth.

'Hold on a minute. Let's have a breather.'

Debbie swam up to a large rock and held on to it with outstretched hands while she looked down between her arms into the sea's clear depths. She pointed with a slim sunburnt hand at some sea-urchins clustered on the rock about six feet beneath them. 'Watch those!'

'Too late!' Carroll twisted his leg round in an attempt to show her the black splinter-like objects in his left heel. 'I've already sampled them, thank you.'

Debbie laughed again then said, 'No. Sorry, sorry. That's mean. I say, no wonder you looked a bit disenchanted coming out of that cave. The Carrolls have certainly been rather unlucky in Positano. Tummy trouble, sunburn and now a sore heel. Has your wife got a needle? If not I have, and that's all you need to tackle sea-urchin spines. Stick it in the old soap and you're in business. I'll do it for you if you like.'

'Thanks. I may take you up on that.'

Carroll also stared down into the clear depths of the sea, realising that for the first time on his holiday he was actually enjoying himself and feeling fairly carefree. He was thirty-three and had been married for eight years. During that time he had never been out with another woman and had not wanted anyone apart from Jilly. But the Jilly of the past few days had been like a stranger, and a rather hostile, neurotic one at that.

'Have you sampled the night-life here yet?'

When Debbie said that Carroll remembered what it was like to be unmarried and fancy free and to realise that a girl finds you attractive – it was a very pleasant sensation. He said, 'No, we've had two very early nights, recovering from a couple of sleepless ones.'

'Yes, well, you'll find the Solleone club here is rather fun. Close to the main beach. Did you notice the steps up to the church?' Debbie broke off, her attention straying to the beach. She touched his arm. 'I think you're wanted elsewhere. Presumably that's for you. Not anyone I know.'

Carroll turned round to see Jilly's diminutive figure standing at the edge of the sea, beckoning him repeatedly. There was something humorous about the way she did it, silently and practically in slow motion, that made him think she must be feeling considerably better. He said, 'Yes. I'll have to go. That's my wife.'

'Her tummy trouble must be better or she wouldn't have been able to tackle the four hundred and four steps.'

'I hope so. Perhaps we'll see you down here another day?'

Debbie smiled enigmatically and paused before saying, 'Yes – perhaps you will.'

Carroll struck out for the beach, puzzled about what had brought Jilly down from the Casa Rossi's balcony. For days unspoken animosity had hung between them like a two-edged sword which neither could use without being hurt. But a blazing row would be preferable to a hostile silence that went on endlessly.

As soon as he stood up and began to wade ashore, Jilly called out, 'Who's your friend, Steve? One of your old rugby chums?' She looked much less pale, in fact she was beginning to tan in the hardly perceptible, painless way she always did. She had the colouring of a native of Southern Italy, with dark brown eyes and black hair. She looked delightful in her forget-me-not blue sundress with the white shoulder straps that kept falling down. She had thin arms and narrow shoulders but full breasts. She looked eminently bed-able. Carroll thought: still three days of her period to go. Sod it! He said, 'Just a girl.'

'Thank you, thank you very much. Yes, I did realise it was a girl. It's my tummy that's been upset, mate. Nothing much wrong with these.' Jilly used her fingers to circle her large eyes and Carroll was certain that she was feeling distinctly better. 'I don't qualify for a white stick yet.'

'Just a girl who spoke to me on the beach. Her name's Debbie. She's staying at that posh hotel, the Poseidon – where there are so many German cars.'

'Is she attractive?'

'So-so. Did you come all the way down here just to ask me that?'

Jilly did not reply but flapped a green booklet in front of his face. It was titled *All You Want In Italy* with the sub-headings, 'Hugo's Simplified System – Imitated Pronunciation Throughout'. They had found it useful, but at first sight the 'imitated pronunciation' seemed exaggerated: 'I want something', '*desidero qualche cosa*', became 'Day-zee-day-ro kwahl-kay ko-zah'.

Carroll noticed that the booklet was open at page 83 – DENTIST (*Dentista*, den-tiss-tah) – but Jilly only said, 'Oh come on, forget Debbie.' She turned on her heel and clambered up the steeply shelving shingle towards the rear of the beach, now in the shade, where Carroll had left his towel, shorts and sandals. He followed more slowly as his heel was distinctly sore when he trod on the stones.

'I don't know if you've suddenly gone deaf but I asked you why you had come down. Are you feeling better? No more trots?'

'The trots are finished.' Jilly dismissed that subject as if it was unimportant and had not been all-engrossing for four days. 'Hurry up!' She did not stop till she reached his outspread towel, then she turned and smiled at him for the first time since they had landed at Boulogne.

'Darling, I think our troubles may be coming to an end. My problem appears to be solved and I've found out there is a very good dentist much nearer than Naples. Just along the coast the other way, at Amalfi.' She raised her chin and stuck it out slightly before saying, 'A simply first class chappy. You couldn't do better in Harley Street.'

'Who told you that?'

'That Englishman we saw at dinner last night – in the white trousers and dark blue silk shirt. The one you called Colonel Blimp.'

Carroll remembered the man very clearly – he had come on the balcony to dine when Carroll had nearly finished his main course but Jilly was still toying with her bread and soup. He was tall with a very straight back, probably in his late sixties, but quite handsome and fit looking with thick silver hair. He gave the impression of someone rather wealthy to be staying at the Casa Rossi, while seeming very much at home there, joking with the Rossi boys in fluent Italian. The man's eyes had strayed over to Jilly several times before they had left the balcony, and he had made a point of saying goodnight to her in a slightly mannered English voice. Carroll had experienced an odd pang of jealousy when Jilly smiled back at 'Colonel Blimp'.

'It's funny, but he may actually have been a colonel during the war. His name is Hugh Arnold. Told me he's a doctor and that he served along this coast in the Medical Corps after the landing at Salerno. Then he asked me if I was feeling under the weather. So I said yes and told him what was wrong, and he went off and came back with a bottle of some special mixture from the chemist.'

'And it's done the trick?'

'Like magic. I took some mid-morning but didn't say anything to you in case it didn't work. Then I had another dose and now I feel fine. Hugh Arnold came on the balcony again this afternoon so I told him about your toothache. He said you should see the dentist in Amalfi, a Mr Giannini. Then he phoned Giannini and made an appointment for you.'

Jilly opened the copy of Hugo's *All You Want In Italy* and read out, 'Lay kwaht-tro ay med-dzah. In other words, at half-past four. So you must get your skates on! Under an hour to get back to the hotel, change and drive to Amalfi.'

'Arnold made the appointment? That was rather cheeky.'

'Of course it wasn't. Honestly, Steve, you are bloody hopeless! He was just trying to help – he knew I couldn't do it.' She thumbed through the green booklet till she found the page she wanted. 'Day-zee-day-ro ess-trar-ray kwess-to dent-ay impoem-bar-lo. There! And now I don't know if I asked to have the tooth extracted or drilled.'

'Jesus!' Carroll had dried himself and got his shorts on in record time but was not sure whether he was really glad about the appointment. 'I don't know . . . I don't fancy sitting in a dentist's chair unable to say anything apart from thank you, good evening and red wine please.'

'Look, just get a move on and stop grumbling! For Christ's sake Steve, you've told me your bloody tooth was aching about a hundred times. While you're changing I'll have a word with the Rossi family about what you should say to Mr Giannini.'

'Perhaps I should have something written down?'

Jilly moved away a few paces, ignoring this suggestion, and staring up at the steps that wound slowly up the cliff past a few small houses perched precariously there but also skirting a gorge. Momentarily she seemed to find the prospect daunting but then she ran to the start of the steps, called out gaily 'Race you,' and disappeared.

Carroll followed more slowly. It was impossible for him to run with a sore heel and he knew that Jilly's spurt of speed would soon peter out. Foolishly he moved his jaw which seemed to have become strangely numb and the pain made one or two preliminary screws into the tooth and then started aching again. But toothache could not completely destroy the pleasurable aspects of the walk up the steps. He liked seeing lizards scuttling out of the way, and glimpsing lemon trees and masses of bougainvillaea; he enjoyed looking into the open doorways of whitewashed houses. The pervasive odours were of orange blossom and jasmine even if they were occasionally blotted out by the rank smell of sewage. A cock crowed in the distance, and high above him Carroll could hear Italian children chattering together like sparrows. He was beginning to share Jilly's optimism that the prospects for their holiday were improving.

This feeling was strengthened when he caught sight of Jilly looking down at him from a stone balcony. She held back her hair with both hands, sucked in her cheeks to achieve a vamp-like expression and said, 'Dahleenk I haff nevair felt so tired.' Then she disappeared round another bend of the steps. Carroll plodded on steadily like the tortoise in the race with the hare, happy once more to be thinking pleasant thoughts about Jilly. He could not imagine her looks changing much nor foresee a time when he would not find her sexually attractive. He sang:

'Accustomed to her face
Her smiles, her frowns,
Her ups, her downs . . .'

When he emerged on the dusty road where the Casa Rossi was situated Carroll saw Jilly standing on the top of the short flight of very steep steps from the road up to the hotel. She was talking animatedly to one of the Rossi boys, gesticulating like an Italian. They were out of sight by the time he reached the large terrace where the proprietor grew flowers in outsize stone pots, and he entered his room to shower and change.

Steve Carroll was not remotely interested in clothes: he liked wearing a clean shirt but its colour and style did not matter to him. Towelling his hair with one hand he pulled on pants and shorts with the other, and then the first shirt that came to hand in the drawer that Jilly had assigned for his shirts and underwear. He consulted his Droopy watch on which the passing of seconds was shown by a small ball moving round the dial and saw that he had only been in the room for five minutes.

Apparently that was all he was to be allowed because he heard Jilly tooting the horn of his car as he crossed the terrace again.

His ancient Sunbeam Tiger was dusty and the dark green paint-work rather dull, but it was really a wolf in fox's clothing as he had completely rebuilt it a few months previously and installed a Mustang 5–litre engine. He drove well and the *corniche* with its scores of hairpin bends and narrow places between the cliff and precipitous drops to the sea held no terrors for him; indeed, he found driving along it an enjoyable test of his skill.

Jilly looked very young and vulnerable sitting in the Tiger, her straight black hair held back by a childish ribbon. Why should he find her sun-dress with the shoulder straps that kept falling down much more provocative than Debbie's explicit bikini? Carroll got into his car deciding that sex was a subject he would never fathom no matter how much he thought about it.

'Any good news for me?' he asked Jilly as he started the powerful engine. 'Did Mr Giannini learn his dentistry in London?'

'I have some bad news and some good news. Mr Giannini does not speak English, but the Rossis say his girl, she do. Mrs Rossi also asked me to say that she is sorry to hear you have toothache but to have no fears. For Mr Giannini he is a great man, much clever and much gentle.'

Carroll said 'I see,' as he threaded his way through the ancient narrow streets. He did not usually make a fuss about toothache but it had been a particularly painful bout, a good deal more so than anything in his previous experience and puzzling too in that it had occurred within a few weeks of a check-up with his own dentist. On that occasion, he remembered bitterly, he had been in the chair only a couple of minutes before receiving the breezy verdict that there was nothing to be done.

Steve and Jilly smiled at each other as he drove towards the area of crowded streets and deafening, tyre-screeching Italian traffic. She put her small hand on top of his as he changed down – she was wearing a red coral bracelet that made her wrist appear disconcertingly small and fragile. He looked forward to the rest of their holiday, in particular to the time in about two days when the trots, toothache and her period would all be behind them. He could visualise their bedroom at night looking out to the sea, dotted with the lanterns of fishing boats, and lit by an enormous moon.

'Claudia, pronounced Cloudia, Cossiga. That's the name of the girl who speaks English at the dentist. Mrs Rossi says you are very fortunate to have an appointment with Giannini himself. Apparently his assistant is not so hot.'

Steve Carroll sniffed. 'Funny but I don't feel very fortunate. Just wait till we get back, I'll have a bone to pick with that Gourlay bloke who told me my teeth didn't even require a polish. Bloody National Health!'

There was one particularly busy corner in Positano where the Italian drivers could indulge their naturally operatic inclinations for noise and confusion. For two minutes or so they were held up by the reluctance of a driver in a tiny car, of the type that Carroll knew was called *topolino* or mouse, to back and make way for a German coach that repeatedly sounded its musical horn.

Caught in the traffic jam, Carroll found it rather pleasant to hear a burst of song from the radio of a silver Mercedes; it was a record of Vic Damone singing 'The pleasure of her company'. Carroll sighed deeply, feeling relaxed despite his nagging tooth and the appointment for half-past four. That was what had really ruined his holiday so far, much more than the toothache: the fact that he had *not* had the pleasure of Jilly's company. Usually it was she who made his life enjoyable, usually she was the very best of company and he never wanted to stray off and find a Debbie, usually their sexual relationship was exciting; but he had not been able to contact that Jilly through the neurotic, wordless stranger who had sat beside him all the way from Boulogne to Naples.

As if she had read his thoughts, Jilly put her warm hand on his bare leg and said, 'I'm really looking forward to this evening – mm – dinner! Absolutely starving! Don't forget I haven't eaten anything for four days, so tonight to hell with slimming! I'm going to have minestrone, spaghetti, and that *piccata alla siciliana* that you had last night. Lots of vino rosso of course. And then . . .'

'Yes, and then?'

'And then, we'll see.'

At last the *topolino* backed with much angry gesturing from its aged driver, the German coach moved soundlessly forward, and the traffic jam cleared abruptly like a drain being unblocked. The Tiger accelerated round the corner and up a hill with a satisfactory throaty roar as Jilly squeezed Carroll's leg.

'Steady on, missus! I've got to concentrate.'

Once on the *corniche* to Amalfi, which was even more full of bends than the one from Naples to Positano, Carroll did concentrate completely on his driving; he found it so absorbing that he was able to forget his aching tooth. He was glad he was driving a car he knew he could rely upon, one on which he had tightened every nut himself, and fitted with the best tyres available. Nevertheless there was one very tricky corner where the road had been made treacherous by a scattering of loose stones, and for a moment they corkscrewed on the edge of nothing. He glanced at Jilly but she was looking down, absorbed in a bilingual guide book to the area.

As he drove on she made a vague gesture with her left hand, saying, 'So this is the region of Campania apparently, while Rome is in the region of Latium. I suppose region is like a county?'

'I suppose.'

'And above Amalfi, "we find Ravello on the brow of the mountains between the Valley of the Dragone and the Valley of the Reginna Minor, eleven hundred feet above the Tyrrhenian Sea . . . The Villa Cimbrone, rebuilt by Lord Grimthorpe . . . A triumphant pastiche, built in large part out of old fragments . . .

The climax of the garden is the belvedere with a row of eight-eenth-century statues, on the edge of a stupendous precipice . . ." Oh, can we go there, Steve? I mean after . . .'

'We'll see.'

'It sounds wonderful. Apparently Greta Garbo stayed there once. "The views up and down the coast are beyond descrip-tion, but a little disturbing for those with a bad head for heights." '

Carroll glanced down at his Droopy watch and drove faster – the road was comparatively free of traffic and it was exhilarat-ing to test the Tiger and his own skill. Within a few minutes they had entered the ancient town of Amalfi and Jilly had turned into a guide, armed with her book and some directions written down by one of the Rossi boys.

'Via Matteo,' she identified. 'And the Piazza Flavia Gioia.' Her accent sounded quite good and she was in a very happy mood. Carroll flicked her a glance. What a transformation from the silent girl who had shuddered at the mere suggestion of breakfast. She looked blooming again. Her legs had gone a delectable, even, pale brown colour. And the combination of her thin brown arms with the full breasts in the low-cut sun-dress made her look particularly desirable.

'And on my right – Marina Grande.'

Carroll drove along by the sea conscious of a noisy car behind them; it had a broken exhaust and it was the kind of noise that Carroll found irritating.

Jilly said, 'We want the Piazza Municipio for Mr Giannini's surgery. And that, it seems, is not very far from the Luna Hotel where we can take the road for Ravello. Yes, this is it!'

Carroll drew into the side of the square and stopped, con-scious that another car was doing the same just behind the Tiger. Carroll's eyes had been taken by a poster on a wall advertising a bank – BANCO AMBROSIANA. He pondered the matter of the poster as he pocketed the ignition key and fol-lowed Jilly. Banco Ambrosiana – why did it seem to have some special significance for him, to start a nagging worry at the back of his mind? Bank – money – lire. He visualised their room at the Casa Rossi and could see the pair of shorts he had discarded on the bed. In the back pocket of the shorts was a small wad of lire notes. The rest of his money was hidden with his traveller's cheques underneath a pile of shirts. He had come to Amalfi for this dental appointment without a single note. And Jilly did not have any Italian money. What a fool he was! He turned on his heel for no reason and saw that a swarthy Italian had parked a rather battered-looking white Alfa Romeo sports car just behind the Tiger. The Italian grinned in his direction, showing very white small teeth. For one moment Carroll had the absurd notion that a guardian angel was looking after him and that the Rossi family had despatched someone in the Alfa Romeo with cash. But the Italian simply grinned again and walked past him without a word. Carroll struck the side of his forehead with his open hand. What an idiot! As he began to climb the stone steps behind Jilly he invented a useful Italian verb: fiasco – I am a fiasco; fiascant – I have been a fiasco; fiascari – I shall be a fiasco.

He found Jilly waiting by a door bearing Giannini's name on the second floor. He said, 'Do you want to walk round the town for a while or . . .' He was going to say 'Or have a coffee' when he remembered they were without any money.

'Not till I know what's wrong. I can't remember you ever complaining about toothache before. Anyway, soon be over.' She leant forward and kissed him lingeringly. Carroll enjoyed the kiss though still trying mentally to deal with the problem of having no cash, and listening to footsteps below them.

Jilly knocked on the door and it was opened by a pale-looking girl with an abstracted expression. Jilly said, 'Signora Cossiga.' The girl shook her head and said 'Momento' as she showed them in, pointing to some brown leather chairs.

The room had a high ceiling and was pleasantly decorated, with a large window looking down to the Marina Grande. The pale girl rat-tatted on another door and then took her place behind a desk with a typewriter. The interior door opened and a cheerful looking girl with a pigtail of lustrous black hair, in white overalls, smiled first at Jilly, then at Carroll. She came over and shook their hands. She looked very friendly as well as intelligent, and Carroll's vague worry about the money receded as he felt sure she would understand that he was not out to defraud a dentist.

'Mr Carroll? I'm Claudia Cossiga. Extremely prompt! But then we always depend on the English as to time you know.' She had a very faint American accent and a warm, reassuring manner. Carroll mentally congratulated Giannini on his choice of nurse or receptionist.

'Signor Giannini will soon be ready for you but just for the moment he is on the telephone. He will not be long.'

Carroll sat down again as she left the room, and there was another knock on the front door of the office. The pale girl opened it to disclose the swarthy Italian with curly black hair who had parked the white Alfa Romeo. The man grinned and fired off a stream of Italian spoken with an unusual accent. The pale girl listened, shrugged and pointed to one of the leather chairs. The man took one facing Jilly and grinned at her, showing his unusually even small teeth; the man's eyes seemed to linger a long while on Jilly as if he was mentally photographing her bit by bit. Jilly straightened the edge of her rather short sun-dress.

The Italian grinned again at Carroll and then looked significantly at the floor, appearing very amused. Carroll began to wonder if the man was simple-minded or some kind of eccentric.

'Shoesa' – the man inclined his head to indicate the source of his amusement – 'wrong shoesa.'

Carroll looked down and saw that he had in fact got on one brown sandal and one navy-blue. He smiled rather reluctantly at the man and said, 'Yes. I was in a hurry. Too much of a rush.' He turned to Jilly. 'Not only wrong shoes, but I came here without a penny. You haven't . . . ?'

'You know I haven't. I asked you to let me have some money. Oh God, what next?'

Carroll shrugged. 'I don't suppose they'll have me shot.'

His words and thoughts on the subject of his carelessness were cut short by Claudia Cossiga opening the interior door and beckoning to him. When he went to the doorway she continued to stand there and said, 'Your toothache, it is in the lower right jaw?'

'That's right. It's been pretty bad.'

'For how long?'

'Just a few days. It started when our holiday began.'

'Have you seen your own dentist recently?'

'Six weeks ago!' Carroll exclaimed with a snort of indignation.

'Yes, well, relax. You are in good hands here. Signor Giannini's English is not perfect but mine is OK – no?'

Carroll said '*Si*' for no reason that he could think of except nerves as he followed her into another large room, bathed in sunlight, that was as clinical and modern looking as any patient could hope for. The dentist was a short man with a partly bald head and a bad case of six o'clock shadow. He gave Carroll a nod and a friendly look, then indicated the chair which was of the most up-to-date kind that inclines right back at the touch of a button.

Carroll sat in the chair and found himself staring up into Giannini's hairy nostrils. The dentist made a careful examination of Carroll's whole mouth instead of concentrating on the lower right jaw, then stepped away and spoke two or three rapid sentences to his assistant of which Carroll did not understand one word. Claudia in turn spoke rather hesitantly, 'Your teeth – those where you say the trouble is – Signor Giannini – he thinks there is nothing wrong there. So – we shall take an X-ray.'

Carroll's chair was raised and a machine wheeled round parallel with it. Claudia showed Carroll how to hold the rather sharp plate in place against his gum and cheek. When the plate had been removed he was left staring at the only wall decoration, a large coloured photograph of 'La Grotta dello Smeraldo', showing the Emerald Grotto that he knew Jilly wanted to visit, with two men in a small rowing boat suspended on unreal looking green water in a cavern hung with stalactites. Another rapid Italian conversation behind his back hardly impinged on him, and he felt unreal himself: the completely white room filled with sunlight, his relaxed position in the chair, and the unintelligible duologue all contributed to a dream-like sensation.

Claudia's pretty face reappeared. She said, 'Your dentist – he could not have known – if you did not have any pain when you saw him. The trouble – there is nothing wrong with the tooth you suspected. But behind it you have an impacted wisdom tooth. Not badly impacted. And, by good fortune, that is Signore Giannini's speciality. He is called regularly to Naples to operate on badly impacted teeth. For these one needs a general anaesthetic – and they can be difficult. But your own tooth presents no such problems. There is a doctor upstairs who can give you an injection.' She paused, obviously at a loss for words, pulling a funny face. 'Yes, pentathol. Signor Giannini – he thinks you should have it done now. Otherwise your holiday . . .' She made an inconclusive gesture.

'Please tell Signor Giannini I'm most grateful that he will do it. Do you mean right now?'

'Yes, immediately. Dr Berlinguer will come down . . .'

'If I'll be half an hour or so would you tell my wife? Perhaps she'd like to go for a walk.' Saying this Carroll visualised Jilly as the subject of the lascivious, probing gaze of the swarthy man in the waiting room.

'Yes, of course.'

Carroll felt that his luck had indeed changed. How fortunate he was to find a specialist in Amalfi! Within a minute or two he heard another step in the room, and an even smaller man than Giannini, with bushy white hair, appeared before him, also smiling but mute. He looked at Carroll's right arm and took his pulse, making some comment to Claudia.

She said, 'Dr Berlinguer thinks you must be an athlete. He says your arm – it is unusually hard and muscled. So – a difficult job for his needle.'

'No, I'm not an athlete. I run a small garage and do a lot of the work myself.'

'Ah, I see.'

Carroll's left arm was dabbed and he felt the needle being inserted. Claudia grinned down at him. 'Now please say one to twenty backwards. In Italian!'

'In Italian . . .'

The pretty face and the one with stubble trouble blurred and wavered, as did the room. Momentarily Carroll felt that he was on the verge of making some profound discovery about the world; a concept at once simple and yet of vital importance if he could only put it into words. No words came and imperceptibly he lost consciousness and then, after what seemed like only a few seconds of oblivion, regained it slowly, like a child waking from a particularly heavy sleep.

Carroll became aware that there were three unsmiling faces looking down at him silently. He wanted to say something about the profound discovery he had made but could not remember what it was. He felt light-hearted and the room about him was bathed in a rosy glow.

'Another rinse please.'

Carroll realised that he was holding a white mug containing pink liquid. He filled his mouth and spat into a white bowl. He felt pleasantly drunk; at the optimistic, friendly stage. He got up from the chair on shaky legs and was supported on both sides. He felt very grateful and it seemed important for him to shake hands with all three people. He did so, saying, 'I'm most grateful. Thank you, thank you, thank you.'

As he walked to the door his mind cleared. Claudia was holding his arm as she said, 'It was an easy extraction. Very little impacted. But do you feel all right now?'

'Fine. Really. And the pain has gone.'

'Ah, but tomorrow your jaw may be just a little sore and so

you may not feel like shaving. I'll give you some tablets. Signore Giannini will want to see you the day after tomorrow.'

'Right. Many thanks.'

Carroll's mind was functioning more normally when he entered the waiting room; the only person in it was the pale girl who turned away from her typing to glance at him.

'Did my wife go for a walk?'

'I do not know. I will ask.' Claudia turned to the typist and asked some questions which brought laconic replies. There was something about the pale girl's slightly cynical expression that Carroll found disturbing, though he could not have said why.

'It seems your friend offered your wife a lift. Back to the hotel to get some money. It was not necessary . . .'

'My friend? We don't know anyone here.'

Claudia put more questions to the pale girl, who replied effusively with gestures towards the window.

'The man in the striped shirt, the Sicilian. He said he was a friend of yours and that was why he waited there. Then, after you mentioned the money, he told your wife he could easily drive her back to Positano . . .' Claudia broke off, beset by some troubling idea, and put a further question to the typist. 'Signorina Craxi saw them go off. Not in your car but in a white Alfa Romeo.'

'Damn! Sorry! I don't like this . . .' Carroll walked to the front door of the suite of rooms feeling upset and uncertain what to do. Silently he swore more fluently, mainly cursing himself for carelessness and stupidity.

'Signor Giannini would not expect payment until you come again. But – I do not know what to say – this is difficult . . .'

'What's wrong?'

'My friend says that she watched the car and it did not go on the road to Positano. They took the road that leads up to Ravello.'

'Oh hell!' Carroll became so agitated that momentarily his mind was a jumble of fear, suspicion and doubt. Jilly did not flirt and if she did it would not be with a swarthy stranger whose eyes were too close together. But Jilly was naïve in that she always thought the best of everyone; she had even tried to find an excuse for the young villain who had snatched her bag in Naples. Normally her attitude was good – Carroll certainly did not want her to become hard and suspicious – but in these circumstances such trust in people was worrying. He opened the door, saying half to himself, 'I'll have to find her.'

'But you must not drive now. Wait a while.'

'No, I can't wait. Is there a road from Ravello to Positano, or would he have to come back this way?'

'This way.'

'Then I'll have to go.'

'Wait. Let me speak with Mr Giannini.'

'No. Sorry.' Carroll shrugged off Claudia's restraining arm and began to run down the stone steps. His legs seemed as if they were made of wood. Claudia ran too and caught up with him.

'If you must go, then drive very slowly. The road is most difficult – the one at the end of the town by the Luna Hotel. Be most careful there – it bends right back. What you call a hairpin bend.'

'Yes, OK, thanks, I'll take care, but I can't wait here.'

Seated behind the wheel of the Tiger, Carroll took a deep breath before starting the engine; he tried to think what had been in the Sicilian's mind in following them and lying about being their friend. Attracted by Jilly, he must have tagged on to see what would happen. What a cool, devious customer he must be! But just wait, he thought.

Carroll sped past the Luna Hotel rather too fast but took the hairpin bend at about the right speed. Part of his mind was still busy visualising the swarthy man with the grin that showed his unusually narrow teeth.

The sun had gone behind a cluster of clouds low in the sky and the evening air was cool; the road was empty of traffic though Carroll could hear, high above him, a coach making the same climb along the series of bends and sounding its musical horn regularly. Carroll was particularly alert for the sound of a broken exhaust or a glimpse of the white sports car, but he drove into the village of Ravello without any clue as to where Jilly might be. He stopped his car to ask a friendly looking boy where the Villa Cimbrone lay and then drove off again, swirling to a halt by the open gate which the lad had indicated.

There was a small house or lodge near the gate but Carroll, guided by instinct, walked on into the long neglected garden. He felt there was just a possibility that Jilly might have agreed to visit the garden if the man had lied by saying it could be visited on the way to Positano. Obviously the man was a reckless but plausible liar. And Jilly was just naïve enough to believe what he would tell her.

The garden was rather like that of a large English house, with an area devoted to roses growing in dry, stony ground and some sections hidden behind walls. On one wall he glimpsed an inscription in English beginning: 'Ah moon of my delight that knows no wane . . .' Carroll walked in the direction of the setting sun, sensing that this would take him towards the cliff edge and the row of statues that Jilly had mentioned in reading from the guide-book. He called her name in a voice that sounded strangely shaky and unlike his own, and the second time thought he heard a faint answering cry. He shouted 'Jilly' again and stood quite still, holding his breath. There was a groan, a pathetic sound that made him shiver.

Carroll found Jilly lying on a patch of scanty grass behind some bushes. Her blue sun-dress had been ripped at the top but she held it in place with blood-stained fingers. Her knickers had been thrown under a bush. Her face and shoulders were grubby as though she had been tussling in the earth and there was blood on her legs. He knelt down by her and held her silently cradled in his arms. She was sobbing convulsively like a child who has gone past tears and it was a very painful sound in his ears. Her face was scratched and there was a sore patch on her cheek. Carroll found it hard to speak; there seemed to be a lump high in his chest and he found it difficult to breathe properly. The combination of fear and such anger was new to him. He pointed at her cheek. 'He hit you. Did that sod hit you?'

Jilly stared at him with wet, bewildered eyes. She said nothing but nodded twice.

Carroll stood up. 'I've got to find him.'

'Don't leave me – please.'

'Ten minutes – if I can't find him right away I'll come back. But I've got to try.' He took a handkerchief from his pocket and handed it to Jilly, saying, 'Ten minutes, not more, and then I'll come back.'

'Don't go.'

Carroll's chest was heaving as he walked away and he saw things about him through a red mist, his hands tightening into fists as he broke into a run back to the Tiger.

By a church he spotted a woman dressed completely in black holding a shopping bag. He stopped the car and sprang out to ask about the Alfa Romeo. *'Automobile – blanco?'* The woman nodded, silently studying his face. He racked his brain and produced the Italian for where – *'Dove?'*

The woman in black still said nothing but gave him a curious look. He said, *'Multo importante – auto blanco? Dove?'*

The woman asked, *'Rumore? Strepito?'* and then held her hands over her ears.

'Yes – *si, si* – very noisy.'

The woman pointed silently to a small road leading out of the village and Carroll said, *'Grazie, grazie.'*

Once more seated in his car, Carroll looked to see what the time was: 5.50 p.m. He made up his mind not to pursue the Alfa Romeo for more than five minutes. He dearly wanted to hand out some punishment to the Sicilian but he could not let his desire for revenge make him forget Jilly's plight. He drove out of the village at a great lick so that the tyres screeched on a couple of bends. Would Jilly want to go to the police? – should they go to the police? – wouldn't that be nearly as much of an ordeal for her as the rape itself? Whatever happened, their holiday was absolutely ruined. Carroll was heavily built and strong – no one picked trouble with him, and he could not remember being involved in a fight since his schooldays, but he knew that if he caught the Sicilian he would remove that grin for some time to come.

The road was narrower and much bumpier than the one that led up from Amalfi. This one wound down into a dark uninhabited valley through a series of long bends with derelict lemon groves on both sides. There were a few huts and large stone water cisterns but it was apparent that the land had not been worked for years, and there was no one to be seen. After navigating half a dozen bends Carroll stopped his car with a loud sigh, glancing again at his watch. The time for pursuit had nearly run out. He climbed a stone wall, half submerged in weeds and creeper, and surveyed the desolate looking valley. Partly collapsed wooden frames that had once supported lemon trees made it difficult for him to follow the twisting road. The sun had gone down on the other side of the mountain and the air was distinctly chilly; the atmosphere was quite unlike that of Positano; he could hear a very dim murmur of distant traffic, otherwise the dismal area was silent.

Balanced precariously on the wall, on the point of jumping down, Carroll caught his breath. Only a few hundred yards below he could see a white car, and it was stationary. He jumped into the Tiger and drove at reckless speed till he turned a sharp bend to see the white Alfa Romeo with its bonnet up against a disintegrating wall – one of its tyres had burst. He drew up sharply, and saw the Sicilian emerge from some bushes. The swarthy man brandished a tyre lever. Carroll looked him up and down in silence and walked towards him, holding up clenched fists.

The Sicilian jigged about on the stony road; he called out something, then grinned and raised the tyre lever threateningly. Carroll charged at him, propelled by an unthinking desire to erase the grin. The Sicilian struck out with the lever but Carroll evaded it and took him in a low rugby tackle, the force of which carried them together over the wall. They turned head over heels, entwined like acrobats, and landed with a crash on the stony ground. Momentarily Carroll lost consciousness, and when he regained it the Sicilian was kneeling on his arms and forcing the tyre lever against his throat. The unrelenting pressure was making him choke and Carroll knew that death might only be a minute or two away: his right hand scrabbled on the hard, dusty soil and his fingers closed round a large stone. He brought the stone up and round in a terrific blow at his assailant and saw the grin vanish. The stone smashed the Sicilian's forehead with a sickening noise, as easily as breaking a cardboard box.

The pressure on Carroll's throat stopped as the Sicilian fell forward as though to kiss him. Blood flowed on to Carroll's face and he threw the inert body from him and scrambled to his feet. The massive blow had reduced part of the Sicilian's forehead to a ghastly, pulpy mass of broken bone, torn skin and blood. The dark man's mouth was open with the lips drawn back, baring his narrow teeth in a horrific grin. Carroll knelt beside him and, unbuttoning the gaily striped shirt, felt the hairy chest that was wet with sweat but strangely cold. There was no heart beat and no pulse. He not only looked dead but so dead it seemed impossible that a few minutes ago the man had been jigging about and shouting. Carroll made himself hold the Sicilian's wrist again until he was positive the man was dead.

When Carroll stood up he thought he heard a distant animal yelp and waited, as still as a statue, his ears straining to catch any other sound. But there was nothing to be heard apart from the buzzing of flies and the leaves of the lemon trees stirring in a freshening breeze. Carroll walked over to a large circular cistern and removed the rough planks on top of it. The cistern was nearly full of stagnant water with a thick covering of green slime. He returned to pick up the Sicilian and the tyre lever. When he pushed the man over the edge of the cistern a spray of green slime shot up high into the air, and the water rose to the brim of the tank. After dropping the lever into the stagnant water Carroll replaced the planks, experiencing an odd, irrational sensation: somehow he expected a protest to be made at the crime that had been so easily and carelessly committed, as though a voice from the darkening sky might condemn the act. But the desolate valley remained silent and he went back to the Tiger to fetch his driving gloves and some rag.

Wearing gloves Carroll manoeuvred the Alfa Romeo into position so that he could push it along the road to a gap in the low wall which led towards a ramshackle hut. Opening the hut door there was a stink that took his breath way – the place smelt as though some animal had been trapped and died in there. Carroll pushed the small car into the shed and closed the door with a gasp that incorporated a sigh.

Using rag and spit, Carroll cleansed his face and hands of the Sicilian's blood. He picked up a rock and used it to dent the right front mudguard of the Tiger. He could tell Jilly that he had had a minor shunt, banging into a wall, and had not been able to find the Sicilian. She would believe him, as she always did. And with any luck at all it might be a matter of months or years before the white car was discovered.

Carroll looked into the driving mirror to check that there was no blood on his face – it looked reasonably clean but appeared to him like the face of someone else, a mask of a tragic clown. He said 'A bloody . . .' but did not finish the phrase for his position was so much worse than that.

MICHAEL UNDERWOOD

THE MAN WHO SCATTERED CRUMBS

'Daddy says he's going to kill Mr Kentish.'

Peggy Stanesby looked up from the table on which she was slicing vegetables for a stew. Lucy, her ten-year-old daughter, stood in the kitchen doorway with an anxious expression. She was a nervous, serious-minded child who was apt to show symptoms of anxiety at the slightest hint of drama.

Her mother smiled indulgently. 'I wouldn't worry, darling, it's not the first time he's said it.'

'But this time he says he really means it.'

Mrs Stanesby sighed. 'What's Mr Kentish done to upset him?'

'He threw a lot of crumbs over the hedge and they landed on Daddy's seedlings.'

Mrs Stanesby sighed again. 'There are lots of places where he can scatter his bread without upsetting people.'

'Daddy's furious,' Lucy said.

'Mr Kentish seems to be a cross that the residents of Shingle Way have to bear. I suppose he might be an even more tiresome neighbour,' Mrs Stanesby added, as she tried to think how.

Arthur Kentish lived alone in the end bungalow in Shingle Way. If nothing worse, he was an eccentric. He looked scruffy and ungroomed with matted grey hair and tufts of unshaven whiskers. His teeth were an unattractive yellow. He spoke, however, with a surprisingly educated voice. Nobody had ever been invited inside his home, which had a sealed appearance, curtains and blinds being permanently closed. This gave rise to a variety of rumours, one of which was that he was a miser who had hoards of money stashed beneath the floorboards.

At all events his neighbours shunned him and he, for his part, made no effort to seek their company. If only there wasn't the matter of the scattered crumbs . . .

Twice a day he would leave his shuttered bungalow and amble down Shingle Way. In the morning he would usually visit the mini-market and buy a few groceries. In the afternoon he would walk on down to the near-deserted sea shore. Rilsby-on-Sea had never attracted visitors, save for a sprinkling at a summer's weekend.

Each time he left home he would carry a crumpled carrier bag which was full of fragments of bread. As he went on his way, a hand would dive into the bag and he would scatter crumbs right, left and centre. Frequently they were blown over hedges and landed in people's gardens. If he happened to pass a house with an inviting patch of lawn, he would aim his largesse at it and in no time at all a flock of eager birds had alighted.

It was an understatement to say that he was a thorn in his neighbours' flesh. He had become a positive obsession. They had all at one time or another remonstrated with him or let fly with an abusive shout. But nothing they did seemed to deter him. If confronted by an angry neighbour, he would simply step round him and continue on his way. Should anyone actually block his path he would wait patiently until the person moved, almost daring him to offer physical violence, which so far nobody had done.

A number of neighbours had put letters of complaint through his letter-box. These ranged in tone from the polite but reproving to the peremptory and abusive, such as that sent by Stephen Trent, the newest arrival in Shingle Way.

'I'll soon fix him,' Trent had remarked confidently when made aware of the measure of the problem.

Mr Kentish, however, remained unfixed.

Earlier that year his neighbours had banded together and had consulted a solicitor. As a result a letter full of legal huff and puff was sent. It hinted at dire consequences if Mr Kentish didn't immediately desist from his anti-social activities. It was assumed he received the letter, though he never gave any indication of having done so.

The police, to whom appeals were made, quickly showed that they knew when discretion was the better part of valour. They pointed out that feeding birds was not yet a criminal offence.

'Can't you call and put the fear of God into him?' the delegation of residents had asked when they visited Rilsby police station.

'We have to be very careful where we stick our noses these days,' a sergeant had said. 'After all, we're living in a free society.'

The residents of Shingle Way just wished they were living in a country where the KGB, or something like it, could have taken effective action.

And now Mr Kentish had actually scattered crumbs on Brian Stanesby's newly planted seedlings. If Brian hadn't been in the garden at the time and taken quick action, the birds would have been in for a real treat.

It was about ten minutes after Lucy had entered the kitchen that he appeared there, too. His face was red and he looked ready to burst.

'This time he's really gone too far,' he said angrily. 'I'll kill him.'

'Lucy's told me what happened,' his wife remarked in a mollifying tone.

'One way or another we've got to put a stop to him.'

'It's difficult to see what you can do.'

'We'll do something, all right.'

'We?'

'I'm going to call a meeting. The man's a menace. An anarchist.'

'Why don't you go and cool off? I'll bring you a cup of tea.'

'Make it a double Scotch,' her husband snorted.

It was three days later on a Thursday evening in March that the residents of Shingle Way met at the home of Stephen Trent and Wendy Wittington. Stephen was a self-assertive know-all who had set out to make himself the leader of the pack since he and Wendy had moved into their bungalow. He lost no time in telling everyone that they weren't married, but had lived together for four years. She was a pale, slim girl who seemed to live entirely in his outsize shadow. They might not have been so readily accepted by the other residents had not Mr Kentish provided a common cause to bind them together.

As soon as Stephen received Brian's call, he said, 'Meet at my place if you like. I'll get Wendy to lay on refreshments. The time has obviously come when something has to be done about Kentish.'

When they were all assembled, Brian Stanesby clapped his hands for silence.

'I suggest we begin,' he said earnestly. 'As I called the meeting, I'm taking it on myself to get things going. I'm grateful to you all for turning up. Incidentally, Peggy was sorry not to come, but she didn't want to leave Lucy alone in the bungalow.'

'I should think not with that maniac next door,' Joe King observed. Joe was a retired policeman and Helga, his wife, a strapping Serbian woman of middle years. She now nodded vigorously in agreement with her husband's comment.

'Who's going to take the chair?' asked Miss Felling, a retired schoolmistress, who was a stickler for protocol.

'If you like, I will,' Stephen said, before anyone else could speak.

Brian had been about to propose Joe King, their longest-standing resident, but now felt inhibited, particularly as they were meeting in the Trent bungalow.

At that moment there was a knock on the front door and Stephen said, 'That must be Reg Gifford. I mentioned we were having a meeting, but he wasn't sure if he could come.'

Reg was a council employee who was to be seen pushing a handcart around as he picked up litter. He was everyone's friend. Everyone's, that is, save Mr Kentish's for the birds created a mess of their own. He had been one of the first to remonstrate with the old man, who had responded with a watery stare before going on his way.

Thereafter he had resorted to angry shouts that seemingly fell on deaf ears.

'You all know Reg,' Stephen said heartily when he came into the room.

Nods and smiles were exchanged and Wendy handed round cups of coffee and a plate of sweet biscuits.

'Hope you've all got some ideas for ridding the neighbourhood of a pest,' Reg said, as he sat down beside Joyce Felling.

'Well, we all know why we're here,' Stephen said, 'but I'll ask Brian to tell us the latest outrage.' Brian cleared his throat, but Stephen went on, 'It seems that Kentish deliberately threw crumbs on to Brian's newly planted seedlings. If that isn't criminal conduct, I don't know what is.'

'I would have thought it was certainly a tort,' Miss Felling remarked judiciously.

'The thing is, what are we going to do about it?' Stephen said in a challenging tone. 'If the authorities are not prepared to take action, then it's up to us to protect ourselves.'

A silence followed, broken by Miss Felling who said, 'It's difficult to know what we can do and still remain within the law.'

'Ah! Now we're getting somewhere,' Stephen broke in. 'I've always held the view that if the law can't help us, we're entitled to help ourselves.'

'What exactly do you mean by that?' Joyce Felling asked.

'That there are times when one is driven to act outside the law.'

'I'd like to hear what Joe has to say about that?' Brian said, turning to the ex-policeman.

'It rather depends on what Stephen has in mind,' Joe said

cautiously. 'Like Joyce, I feel it's hard to see what legal action remains open to us. In those circumstances, we may have to operate outside the law.'

'I can't think of anything we could do which would force him to leave,' Joyce Felling observed. She let out a hollow laugh. 'In fact, he'd probably still be in Shingle Way after we'd all departed.'

'Supposing he had an accident? A really nasty accident.' It was Reg Gifford's blunt contribution.

Stephen nodded. 'Just what I had in mind. I've always believed that if you want to get away with murder, you should make it look like an accident. That's right, isn't it Joe?'

'I reckon so,' Joe agreed.

His wife leaned forward. 'This is not a time to be squeamish,' she said in her accented English. 'He is not an animal and the British only get sentimental over animals. After all, in some countries he would already have been put away.'

'So what exactly is being proposed?' Joyce Felling inquired, looking about her as she might at a class of children. 'Who is going to arrange for Mr Kentish to have an accident? Incidentally, not a fatal one, I hope?'

'You mean, just break his arms and legs?' Stephen said with a grin.

'There's no need to be facetious, Mr Trent. But Mr Kentish is an old man and not particularly robust and I don't see any need to do more than the minimum to defeat his anti-social behaviour.'

Brian, who had been looking thoughtful for a while, now spoke. 'It was I who called this meeting and I feel a certain responsibility for its outcome. If I'd been able to set my hands on Kentish when he threw his wretched crumbs into my garden, I truly believe I might have killed him. Perhaps it's a pity for all of you that it didn't work out that way, but it didn't. As far as I'm concerned he's no better than vermin and if he can have a sudden, quick accident, I'm sure none of us will be found weeping at his graveside.'

'As far as I know he has no family,' Joe remarked. 'His mother who lived with him died six years ago. She was scatty, too. And he certainly has no friends.'

A fly on the wall might at this point have concluded that they were discussing how best to put a stricken creature out of its misery.

'Well then! Accidents!' Stephen said eagerly. 'Anyone got any ideas? And who's going to arrange it? Personally I suggest we draw lots. Whoever gets the short straw must obviously have the final say as to method, but the rest of us will be ready to back him up as required. Everyone agree?'

'I think it should be a secret ballot,' Brian said, 'the person drawing the short straw can then remain anonymous.'

'Is that being realistic, Brian?' Stephen inquired in an indulgent tone. 'After all, there are only seven of us in the room and we're all friends, so it's not going to remain a secret for long.'

'Six, if you leave me out,' Joyce Felling said. 'I may be hale and hearty, but I don't indulge in criminal violence.' Her tone was firm and uncompromising.

'As a matter of fact, I think there's a case for excluding women from the ballot,' Stephen remarked. He glanced at Wendy, who gave him a look of relief.

'If it's Joe, I'll certainly help him,' Helga said robustly. 'I'm not afraid.'

'There are only four of us men,' Brian observed, 'and a ballot seems a bit silly.'

'Somebody has to devise a plan,' Stephen said. 'Surely a ballot is the best way of settling who.'

His tone was patronising and Brian reacted immediately.

'Seeing that I'm responsible for getting you here, I'm prepared to do the necessary.' He spoke with an air of resigned heroism.

'That'll certainly save a ballot,' Stephen said quickly. Rather too quickly, Brian felt. Stephen went on, 'And as you live next door to Kentish, you're the best equipped. The rest of us will, of course, be ready to back you up. Why don't you give yourself a week to come up with something and then we'll have another meeting?' Brian gave a sulky nod and Stephen added encouragingly, 'Don't forget, we're your co-conspirators, Brian.'

It was on this note of dubious solidarity that the meeting broke up.

'How did it go?' Peggy asked when her husband arrived home. 'Was anything decided?'

He gave her a grim look. 'I've opened a can of worms,' he said and went out to the kitchen.

Arthur Kentish was strangely unaware of his neighbours' dislike. At least, not so much unaware as insensitive to it. He didn't scatter crumbs to annoy *them*, but to benefit the birds. He had no wish to tell them how to live their lives and, by the same token, rejected their efforts to restrain his own activities.

After all, the birds were his friends. His only friends. And he much preferred their company to that of any human being. After his mother's death he had decided to stay on in Shingle Way. If people didn't like him, let them do the moving. He was totally incurious about his neighbours and if he had been told there had actually been a meeting to discuss his demise, he would have been neither frightened nor flattered. Apart from the fact that he was now somewhat scattier, he had been the same all his life. His colleagues in the department where he had spent his working life had grown used to his reclusive ways and had accepted him as he was. He was almost entirely self-educated and had always taken much more care of his mind than of his body. The walls of his bungalow were lined with higgledy-piggledy piles of dust-laden books.

Who needed people when they had birds and books as companions?

It so happened that Brian Stanesby was not going to work the next four days, but was proposing to do various jobs in the bungalow, of which redecorating the bathroom was number one on the list.

He usually kept a few days' holiday up his sleeve and his wife was always reminding him of things that required attention. Washers on taps, cupboard doors with broken hinges, lopsided blinds, these were just a few of the minor tasks; redecorating was a major undertaking.

Ever since the meeting he had been heavily preoccupied with thoughts about despatching his neighbour. He had not told his wife what he had volunteered to do and hoped she wouldn't get to hear of it. Those who had attended the meeting had sworn not to breathe a word of their discussion outside the room.

'Of course it's up to you, old boy, whether you tell Peggy what we've decided,' Stephen had remarked when they broke up. 'Maybe you'll want to co-opt her.'

But that was the last thing Brian intended doing. He was grateful he'd be spending a few days at home, for redecorating the bathroom would give him the opportunity of observing Arthur Kentish's comings and goings from a window that looked on to his bungalow; in particular, the side door which was his usual means of egress and entry. He hoped his observation would help him concoct a foolproof plan.

As he watched the old man come out of his bungalow on the first morning he was at work in the bathroom, he noticed that Arthur Kentish slipped on the brick path and almost fell, but managed to right his balance and set off, his bag of crumbs in hand. Had he fallen, however, a fractured skull might well have resulted. A tragic accident, indeed! Brian had already been won over to the idea of an 'accident'. For a reason he had not yet fathomed, it was an idea that didn't disturb his conscience as much as the thought of bullet or bludgeon, knife or ligature round a scrawny neck.

Two days later he decided to follow Arthur Kentish on his afternoon perambulation. His wife had gone up to London and Lucy was going straight from school to a friend's house where he was due to collect her at six o'clock. He waited by his front door until he saw Kentish leave his bungalow and set off down

Shingle Way. Almost immediately the old man began distributing crumbs left and right. Brian wasn't displeased when one handful sailed over the hedge and landed on Stephen's lawn. Ever since the residents' meeting he had felt resentful toward his young neighbour, who, he felt, had manipulated him. He was far too uppity and pleased with himself.

'Afternoon, Brian,' Joe King called out as Brian went by. 'How are things going?'

'Getting on well, I've almost finished the bathroom.'

Joe frowned. He couldn't have been less interested in Brian's bathroom. What he hoped to hear was how Brian's plans for eliminating Arthur Kentish were proceeding. All he could do, however, was shrug when Brian passed on his way with a brisk wave.

Meanwhile, Arthur Kentish had reached the junction of Shingle Way with the road that led into Rilsby. Without looking in either direction he walked straight across and took a path through the sand dunes that separated the road from the shoreline. From time to time he paused to throw pieces of bread into the air for the gulls which wheeled overhead and swooped to catch his offerings.

The old man lurched and wove without ever actually losing his footing, but it occurred to Brian for the second time that day how easily he could succumb to an accident.

'You're not really going to kill Mr Kentish, are you, Daddy?' Lucy inquired earnestly as he drove her home later that afternoon.

He was so shocked by the unexpectedness of her question that he had to make a conscious effort to control the car. He gave her a sidelong glance and found her eyes focused on his face.

'What on earth makes you say that?' he asked in a voice that sounded unnatural to his own ears.

'You said you were going to that time he threw crumbs on to your seedlings. And you said you really meant it.'

He gave a forced laugh. 'Oh that! I admit I was angry, but one doesn't actually kill people for such trivial reasons.' He was aware that she was still staring at him and he wished she wouldn't. 'You didn't really take me seriously, did you?'

'I know you all had a meeting about Mr Kentish. You might have decided to kill him,' Lucy remarked. 'Nobody likes him and he is rather dirty and smelly.'

'You've been watching too many crime films on TV.'

'No, I haven't. I don't like them.'

'You've not been dwelling on this, have you, Lucy?'

She turned her head away and stared out of the window.

'Not exactly,' she said slowly, 'just thinking.'

'Have you spoken to Mummy about it?'

'No. Though I did tell her what you'd said immediately afterwards. She said you didn't mean it.'

Brian let out a silent sigh. 'Grown-ups often let off steam and say silly things they don't mean.' He gave her another sidelong glance. 'Satisfied?'

But she didn't say anything and continued staring out of the window.

He was in an unusually sombre mood by the time they arrived home. He locked the car and followed his daughter up the path to the front door.

It was the next evening that Stephen Trent phoned and suggested a meeting at his bungalow two days hence.

'I'm calling you first, Brian,' he said cheerfully, 'because you're the most important person to be present. I don't suppose you want to talk over the phone, but we'll look forward to hearing your report. Got something to tell us?'

'Maybe.'

'Good. We'll look forward to hearing it.'

Two evenings later the residents of Shingle Way once more assembled at the Trent bungalow. Wendy Wittington again played the nervous hostess, handing round cups of coffee and a plate of sweet biscuits.

'We all seem to be here, save Brian,' Stephen remarked, looking round the room.

'We can't start without him,' Helga King observed.

'We'll give him a few more minutes,' Stephen said.

'And then?' Joyce Felling inquired.

'I'll phone his home.'

'Anyone know what he has in mind?' Reg Gifford asked.

It turned out, however, that none of them had spoken to Brian since their previous meeting. At least, not to have a proper conversation.

'I'll call him,' Stephen said. 'Maybe he's forgotten the time. Meanwhile, why doesn't everyone have another cup of coffee? Wendy, go and make some more.'

He left the room and returned a couple of minutes later.

'There doesn't seem to be any answer,' he said. 'I'll nip along to his bungalow and see what's happened. There must be somebody there. I won't be gone more than a few minutes.'

He was away nearly fifteen minutes and had a puzzled expression when he got back. His normal aggressive self-confidence seemed to have deserted him.

'We were about to send out a search party,' Joe observed.

'I wanted to make absolutely sure,' Stephen said in a somewhat breathless voice.

'Sure of what?' Joyce Felling inquired.

'That there was nobody at home at the Stanesbys'. There isn't. The whole place is in darkness. I walked right round it.'

'He obviously had no intention of coming,' Helga said bluntly. 'Was there any light in Kentish's bungalow?'

'I don't think so . . . I didn't really look . . .'

'He goes to bed as soon as it's dark,' Reg observed. 'Like his ruddy birds.'

Joyce Felling rose from her chair. 'There's no point in hanging about here. We'd best go home and await events.'

In her own mind she thought it probable that Brian had lacked the courage to face his co-conspirators and admit failure. She didn't really blame him, though a phone call would have saved them all turning out on a wretched evening of mist and drizzle.

Anyone who was still awake would have heard a car driving up Shingle Way around midnight and turning into the Stanesbys'.

It was just after seven o'clock the next morning when another car came up the road and parked outside Arthur Kentish's bungalow.

It was a police car.

Brian watched mesmerised as two officers bent over the crumpled body lying outside the side door. He ducked quickly when one of them looked across at the bathroom window from which he was observing their activity. When, about five minutes later, his front door bell rang, he knew whom to expect.

'Good morning, sir,' a police officer said. 'Sorry to disturb you at this hour, though I see you're up and dressed.'

'I was just about to make a cup of tea.'

'The first is always the best,' the officer remarked with a reassuring smile. 'How well did you know your neighbour, Mr Kentish?'

'Not well at all. I don't think anyone did, he was a bit of a recluse.'

'When did you last see him?'

'I . . . I don't rightly remember. Yes, I do, it must have been yesterday afternoon.'

'What time?'

'Around three o'clock. He was just going out.'

'Did you see him return?'

'No.'

'I believe you were watching us from one of your windows just now, so you probably realise something's happened . . .' He stared at Brian waiting for a reaction.

'Well . . . yes . . . I did wonder what you were doing?'

'I'm afraid Mr Kentish is dead.'

'Dead?' Brian echoed feebly.

'That's right. The milkman found his body lying outside the side door when he made his delivery this morning.'

Brian blinked stupidly and had difficulty finding his voice. 'How did he die?' he managed to say.

'We shan't know until there's been a post-mortem.' He turned as a plain van came lurching up Shingle Way and drew up outside the next-door bungalow. 'There's his transport arriving now,' he remarked. 'Well, I'll leave you to do what you usually do at this hour of the day. Don't take any notice of us, we'll be coming and going for the next hour or so. We'll be making a thorough examination of the scene.' He fixed Brian with a hard stare. 'Have to make sure there's not been foul play.'

'Best not to say anything to Lucy, it'll only upset her,' Brian said to his wife shortly after the officer had departed and he had told her the reason for the visit.

'What do they think Mr Kentish died of?' she asked in a worried voice.

'Probably a heart attack,' her husband replied.

Fortunately Lucy's room faced the other way and she was unaware of events next door. And when she left to be driven to school by her mother, she was too anxious about a French test to notice anything untoward. It was while they were away that Brian was again called to the front door. He found Stephen and Joe standing there.

'Thought we'd come round and see if everything was all right?' Stephen said affably. 'Couldn't help noticing a police car outside.'

'Why shouldn't everything be all right?' Brian asked in a bristling tone.

'No need to take offence,' Stephen said. 'We had every reason to wonder what had happened after you failed to turn up at our meeting last night.'

To be truthful the morning's events had driven all thoughts of the meeting from Brian's mind.

'Yes, I'm sorry about that,' he said after a pause. 'I'm afraid I wasn't feeling terribly well. I should have phoned.'

'We thought you'd gone out and forgotten,' Stephen said. 'That's right, isn't it, Joe?'

Joe nodded. 'Has something happened to Kentish?' he asked abruptly.

'Yes, he's dead,' Brian said awkwardly. 'The milkman found him lying outside the kitchen door.'

'Want to tell us about it, Brian?' Stephen said with a knowing smile.

'There's nothing more to tell.'

'Well, don't forget that we're all on your side, Brian. That's right, isn't it, Joe?' Joe gave a wooden nod and Stephen went on, 'So it's mission accomplished.' Placing a finger alongside his nose, he added, 'Don't worry, Brian, your secret's safe with us.'

As Brian watched them depart, he knew one thing for sure. As soon as the dust settled, he, Peggy and Lucy would leave the district. He couldn't possibly go on living in Shingle Way. For the time being, however, he must sit tight.

He stayed at home the whole of that day, observing the comings and goings next door where forensic scientists pored over the scene of Mr Kentish's demise and removed specimens for examination.

He didn't know whether it was a relief or not that he received no further visits from the police.

In the days that followed the residents of Shingle Way seemed, as if by agreement, to keep their distance from one another. They exchanged neighbourly greetings, when these couldn't be avoided, but refrained from discussing what lay on all their minds. Even Stephen Trent seemed willing to adopt a lower than normal profile.

Brian, for his part, accepted this state of affairs with relief. He had become withdrawn, however, and his wife worried about him. Lucy was told that Mr Kentish had died suddenly, without pain or suffering. Her only reaction had been to ask what would happen to all the birds which had depended on him for food and to answer her own question by saying *she* would scatter crumbs for them, but not in other people's gardens.

One evening about five days later Brian received a call from a Detective Inspector Richards who said he would like to visit him about his neighbour's recent death.

Trying to sound calm, Brian said, 'Yes, of course,' and it was agreed that the officer should come round at eight thirty that evening. By then Lucy would be in bed and his neighbours would be in front of their television sets with curtains drawn. He found it ominous that an officer of such senior rank should have become involved and he spent the intervening hours trying to rationalise the fact.

'I thought I'd better have a word with you before the inquest,' Richards said when they were seated in the front room and Peggy Stanesby had withdrawn to the kitchen. 'You'll be required to give evidence and I'll take a statement from you before I leave.'

'A statement?' Brian said tightly.

'Yes, a witness statement. We can keep it quite short.'

'Have you established how Mr Kentish died?'

'The pathologist found he had suffered a fractured skull. He obviously slipped and fell and caught his head on the sharp edge of the doorstep. He also had a heart condition and the two things combined were enough to kill him.' He gave Brian a thoughtful look. 'We suspected at first there might be a criminal angle, that he'd been assaulted by some would-be intruder – something of that sort – especially when we found over thirty thousand pounds in cash in the bungalow. But we're now satisfied he slipped and cracked his head, like I said.' He paused and went on, 'It seems he'd thrown out some bread for the birds. As you'll recall there was a fine rain the previous evening and some of the bread must have landed on the step itself where the rain made it as slippery as ice. We found traces adhering to the soles of his shoes. Our guess is that he opened the door to go out an hour or so before the milkman came and had his fatal fall.'

Brian let out a long, silent sigh. 'So nobody else was involved?' he said, with obvious relief.

'Nobody. I gather the old boy spent his time feeding the birds. Finally, it appears to have been his undoing.'

After the officer had gone, Brian sank down into a chair. He felt completely exhausted. He had just experienced the worst two weeks of his life. Moreover, he had nobody to blame but himself. How could he ever have seriously undertaken to kill another human being! Even one in the shape of Arthur Kentish! It was terrifying to think back to that meeting when the decision was reached and stupid bravado had made him volunteer.

Long before the second meeting which he had funked attending, he knew that, far from mission accomplished, it was going to be mission abandoned.

Admittedly, he had once contemplated throwing bread into Mr Kentish's backyard, as a tit for tat. But that had seemed petty and futile – and, in the event, unnecessary.

As for the situation vis à vis his neighbours, it was obviously irremediable and they would just have to believe what they liked.